H . A . Nicola

WHARF KNIGHT

D

This work is dedicated to the collective mission of finding your soul's purpose and serving it to the world.

ISBN: 9798440508804 (Paperback)

3

A CIP catalogue record for this title is available from the British Library.

To Peach Ri and Pepa

WHARF KNIGHT

She knew the moment the elevator door closed that an attack was imminent. She could have cut the tension with a knife.

They had managed to conceal any hint of dissension from the restaurant staff and the other patrons dotted around as they made their way across the floor.

She held her breath knowing he would not want others to be alerted to the fact that the woman he secretly held under arrest, was in grave danger and if she dared give away any sign of apprehension, she would surely pay the price.

The last sound she heard before her incarceration was sealed, was the sound of clanging steel from the knives being shunted and sharpened, ready for execution as clatters and loud banging erupted from the nearby kitchen as the staff readied themselves to meet the demands of the Michelin Star clientele.

Once behind closed doors, as the elevator signalled it's ascent, so his tongue thrusted hurriedly under her skirt, mindful time was of the essence and that his search must be complete before the doors re-opened.

Luckily, he now had a willing participant who observed the urgency with discerning rapidity and expertly lowered herself towards his mouth, with her hands still clasped behind her back, steadying herself on the shiny handle bars. She straddled him, widening her legs as far as possible, tilting her pelvis backwards and forwards over his kneeling form, basking in the delight of his velvet tongue flushing her genitalia as he ensured her own swift euphoric climb to a higher level of ecstasy.

As the lights on the wall panel flashed upwards with each passing floor, in haste she pulled his head towards her in order to propel the full force of cock simulation.

Her feminine spurt was as soft as Bombyx Mori silk, woven from Mulberry Larvae, spraying celestial graffiti over his face creating the most delicate chiffon. White upon white, which he hurriedly swept onto his palate to form a tantalising canapé.

He just managed to guzzle the remnants dripping from her coochie as the fourteenth floor announced it's approach.

Their poised meander to their table belied the feasting frenzy that had just taken place within the elevator walls.

He sat silently, his face a mask of delirium, leaving her to deal with the waiter who was standing with pen and paper at the ready, to take their order.

Cayenne was so hungry that her stomach rumbled as she listed her preference for smoked mackerel paté and grilled swordfish.

Glancing discreetly at the stranger who still had his head bowed over his menu, she decided to choose for him ordering Seared Yellowfin Tuna Loin and Beef T-bone.

As the waiter disappeared to the noisy kitchen, he sighed with relief that she had taken the initiative to order his meal whilst he savoured her very own after taste which now coated his taste buds gloriously. Not only had her intimate fragrance fucked with his senses, but the last thing he would have wanted to do was contemplate a replacement for the tang of her sumptuous pussy manna.

THE MIDDLE

CHAPTER 1

The audience erupted in thunderous applause and it was several moments before they reluctantly quieted, sufficiently for the play to resume.

…

Julia

And wouldst thou have me cast my love on him?

Lucetta

Ay if you thought your love not cast away

Julia

his little speaking shows his love but small

Lucetta

Fire that's closest kept burns most of all

Julia

they do not love that do not show their love....

Cayenne glanced down at the program in her lap, but the room was too dark for her to make out the tiny printed words. She tilted the iconic image of William Shakespeare on the front page towards the illuminated stage and squinted at the fine print.

She wanted to see which of Diego's classmates was playing the part of Julia.

Aaaah,Just as she thought. Brenda Baker. The name that seemed to be constantly on the tip of Diego's tongue.

"Is she a close friend of yours then, Brenda Baker?", she had asked when he had mentioned her name for the 20th time that day.

He had screwed up his face vehemently at the perceived implication.

"Mom she's just someone in my class", he had insisted.

She had smirked in response, in way that let him know that she wasn't sure whether she believed that.

Before she could remark further, she could sense him rushing towards her as he always did when he felt she was about to mock him. Throwing his full weight on her, with no regard for the fact that he was now almost twice her size. Then she would feel his fingers digging into her ribs in his warped interpretation of a tickle, but which felt much more like a torturous pinch. Such was his enjoyment of this momentary domination, she knew she only had seconds to nip his delusion in the bud. The moment he sensed prolonged victory, she would have no hope of escaping. She would think nothing of resorting to skin twisting or grabbing for any vulnerable, sensitive area of his body which would force him to release his hold. His low pain threshold made short work of this objective.

"aaawww mom, get off", he would yelp, allowing her just enough leeway to overturn him and attempt to pin him down.

Amidst fits of laughter, he would mock her attempts to overpower him by saying in his best superhero voice whilst holding her wrists, "Mother, I don't want to hurt you".

Cayenne was glad of the darkness in the auditorium, as should anyone catch sight of her laughing to herself, they would surely have looked at her curiously.

Yes indeed, that must be the lovely Brenda, she concluded as she admired the mixed race girl on the stage. Diego hadn't expressed any particular interest in having a serious girlfriend which she was pleased about. He was focused on his career and seemed to have developed the notion that girls brought nothing but trouble. At least that's what he told her.

Diego was cast as Valentine in Shakespeare's comedy Two Gentlemen of Verona and his mother was genuinely enthralled with his performance. This was only the second time she had seen him perform professionally and she hadn't been disappointed. He knew that she would have high expectations of him and the very fact that she was invited was testament to the obvious confidence he must have felt in his portrayal of the character. He was poised, self assured and engaging. It was magical for her to see her son transformed into an ancient man, seeking romance, and speaking effusive words of love fourteenth century Olde English. It was clear that the whole cast had all worked incredibly hard. She glanced over to the left of the small theatre where Oliver the class tutor stood watching his protegees in action.

What a wonderful feeling it must be to see months of hard work come together. To witness a project unfold and come to fruition. To have everyone show up and know their lines and give their best. She felt proud of them all.

She sat upright in her chair as Diego as Valentine performed the closing line. He walked confidently to centre stage, his ownership of the character, completely filling the room. Cayenne thought she might burst with pride.

Valentine puts his arm around his friend Proteus as they stroll towards the audience.

"Come Proteus, 'tis your penance but to hear

The story of your loves discovered

That done, our day of marriage shall be yours,

One feast, one house, one mutual happiness".

Just as the audience, made up of parents and siblings of the cast, began to lightly applaud, not being fully certain that this was in fact the end, the cast seemingly oblivious to the crowd's response were holding hands jubilantly, jumping up and down in victorious celebration of another fine performance. Diego's warmth and exuberance was infectious and she could tell that he was an integral part of the team. The sincerity of his personality was palpable which manifested in his obvious desire for everyone to do well.

CHAPTER 2

Cayenne swiped downwards as she perused the online booking page for the gym. The early morning yoga class, run by the gym director Josephine Parker, usually filled up to capacity within minutes and she could see that this morning was no different. She pressed the option to be added to the waiting list and was surprised to see that she was only second in line. It was almost certain that at least a few people would wake up and decide that they would prefer a lie in or discover that they had conflicting appointments or be running late which would create some cancellations. The system would automatically move the waiting list in place and alert by email, the people that had now been inducted into the class.

After coming out of the shower, she checked the status again and was pleased to see that an email awaited, confirming her place in the holistic line up.

She pulled on her favourite yoga pants with the shiny waist cinching panel which held her tummy in, covering up evidence of child bearing whilst exposing the upper abs that she was proud of. The less resistant part that showed off all the hard work she had done on her abdominals and that respected the extra effort she had applied to her core and rewarded her with muscle definition and toning.

She deliberately selected her red halter neck top that exposed the carvings that had started to develop across the top of her back and shoulders.

Being able to visibly see the progress in the mirror and in her clothes, was a great source of accomplishment for her after many months of frustration where she felt she was pushing herself very hard at the gym but not seeing the desired results.

She prided herself on her level of commitment and her determination to challenge herself. To resist apathy and complacency, set an intention and push towards it with single minded focus.

Josephine was an interesting character. Average height, very slim with the perfect yoga physique. At first glance she came across as relatively warm and friendly, ordered and professional. Her speaking voice was a bewildering mixture of university eloquence and east end street dialect. Almost as though she had been shaped by both but hadn't quite decided which would attain her allegiance. Similarly, her hair was a discreet mixture of both blonde and brunette. If Cayenne were asked the colour of Josephine's hair, she would most certainly pause, scouring her mind for a memory or an image. It wasn't one or the other and in the most undeliberate way, she was a complete juxtaposition. Her warm, easy-going, demeanour, would momentarily disappear at any perceived slight. A couple chatting under their breath whilst Josephine was attempting to demonstrate the next pose, or her perception of a yoga mat being casually thrown onto the shelf instead of being carefully rolled up and gently replaced, would result in a fiercely penetrating glare.

"You can just liiiiiie back in Savasana for a few moments while the others are comin' in". Her voice almost always sounded nasally as though she was battling a permanently blocked nose.

The room was already half full and late arrivals were bustling hurriedly through the huge fire door, which intermittently banged shut abruptly, accompanying every entry with a loud thud, temporarily piercing the zen stillness.

Josephine was silently fiddling with the sound system until a hauntingly whimsical melody began to drift across the room, dispensing it's calming essence on the prostrated gathering.

"Just begin to sloooow down your breavin'. Taking deeeep, intakes of bref. Makin' sure you are breavin' out for longer than you are breavin' in". Josephine's clipped half cockney, half Etonian tones pierced the solemn ambience.

"See how much of your spine that you can lay on the mat, fooooold your chin inwards to eeeeelongate your spine on the mat".

Cayenne couldn't help but notice that whenever Josephine used the word 'mat', which was frequently in this context, the sound of the letter 't' seemed to be suspended in mid air.

"Spread your aaaaarms and legs out awaaaaay from your body with the paaaalms of your hands facin' the ceilin' and the back of your fingers touchin' the floor.

We're going to stay here for five more brefs. Niiiice and slowly. Clasp your knees into your chest and roll from side to side masaaaaaaagin' the lower back".

Cayenne always found herself stifling a smirk as she listened to Josephine speak. Not only because of the clipping of the words and the discarding of offending consonants at every opportunity, but the way in which she dramatically stretched out the vowels whilst simultaneously pulling her hands apart for emphasis, no doubt the legacy of her yoga school training.

"When you're ready, roooooll backwards and forwards and come into a comfortable sittin' position".

Cayenne rocked backwards and forwards as gracefully as she could and rigidly manoeuvred herself into a cross legged position, which didn't come as naturally to her as it did for most of her fellow yoga devotees. Something to do with stiff hips apparently, which for her had improved only minimally in all the months that she had been practising. She glanced admirably at Josephine and some of the other women in her eye line as they effortlessly rolled their knees towards the ground. Much like the way one did when one was a little child sitting in assembly. No-one ever complained in primary school that they couldn't cross their legs properly.

Somewhere along the line, unless one kept oneself active, which Cayenne rather thought she had, the flexibility seemed to diminish with age.

Josephine was poised on her mat with her knees almost touching the floor. She was smiling her welcome to the class.

"Rest the palms of your hands on your knees, sit up as straight as you can, lengthenin' your spine, reeeeachin' the crown of your head towards the ceilin' and then just sloooooowly tuuuuuurrrn your head from side to side to loosen up the neck. Then touch your shoulders with your ears, from left to right, and then right to left, slooooowly openin the neck. Stretch your hands out wide and circle your wrists one way then the other. Clasp your hands togever in front of you, elbows touchin' and circle your wrists again in bofe directions.

Now come into table top position and we're goin' to cat stretch for a few moments. Aaaarchin' your back as you breave in and rollin' forwards as you breave out, openin' your neck towards the back of the room. Now we are going to come into our first downward facin' dog".

Cayenne watched out of the corner of her eye as Josephine lifted her hips with effortless fluidity into the downward dog position.

Cayenne had to steel herself at this point, garnering as much strength and fortitude that she could muster for this supposedly restorative position, which seemed to have the opposite effect on her. She found she tired quickly as she tried to balance her weight between her legs and her arms equally which she never quite managed to attain.

"Lift your right leg to the sky with your toes pointin' towards your face in free legged dog, then bring your right knee forward to touch your right elbow….. then lift your right leg back to the sky, flexin' the foot…. then bring your right knee forward to your chest…. Then back into free legged dog then forward, this time touching the opposite elbow wiv your knee, then for the last time bring your leg back to the sky, then let's come back to downward facin' dog".

Cayenne was about to collapse into a heap, thankful that she had willed her mind to follow Josephine's instructions as though it were painless. Josephine surely detected the fatigue.

"At any poin' in the practice, if you feew tired, you can come into child's pose".

Cayenne obliged immediately and propelled herself into the recommended recovery pose resisting the temptation to fold into a complete foetal position. All too soon the rest was over.

"Now we are goin' to do the same on the other side… raise your left leg………."

After balancing out the sequence, soon the class were invited to stand at the top of the mat bringing their hands to prayer with their toes pointed slightly inwards.

"Now come into tree pose, bein' aware of the liftin' in your hips and the top of the knees, then liftin' your right leg behind you and reach forward wiv bofe hands. Try and put your hands in line wiv your ears. Reach your leg out behind you and stretch your arms out in front".

The standing poses were easier for Cayenne than the flexibility and agility aspects of the practice that she found more challenging.

She eyed the clock in the left hand corner of the room discreetly, not wanting eagle eyed Josephine to think she wasn't enjoying the class. It was almost relaxation time and if she hurried, she would get back home in time to grab a quick cup of tea before having to rush Ocean to his pick up stop outside of the dry cleaners on the corner of Glengall Grove and East ferry road.

Unsurprisingly the relaxation part was her favourite. "Let's liiiiiie back in Savasana and begin to breave deeply allowin' the body to absoooooooorrrrrb the practice". It was a time when the lights were dimmed completely and the music softened, strategically designed to help the class drift into deep restorative relaxation for a few minutes. Sometimes Josephine would talk them through it, taking their minds on a journey following the course of their breath. Just as sleep threatened to engulf them, Josephine's softened tones would gently nudge them back to full awareness.

"Start to take some deeeeper breafs, slooooowwwwwwly begin to bring the awarenisss back to your body. Mooooooovin' your hands and your feet, geeeeeeently circlin' them in bofe directions. Turn you head geeently siiiide to siiide to awaaaaaaken your neck. Stretch out your body reeeeeachin' in bofe directions into a compleeeeeete stretch. Then roll onto your right side and rest there for a moment, then use your left hand, pressed into the floor to push yourself up into a comfortable sittin' position. Bring your hands to prayer at your heart's centre and gently bow your heads towards your heart space and cloooose your eyes and fank your lovely able self for takin' the time to practise today. Namaste".

CHAPTER 3

Cayenne needed every ounce of the tranquillity that the early yoga practice had created in her mind and body, for the hectic school routine with Ocean and Sugar. Ocean loved school, so it wasn't difficult to motivate him to speed up. In fact, he became so excited that his giggling and hysterics, which belied his fourteen years, seemed to make a simple sequence of actions, turn into a chaotic amalgam of activity, resulting inevitably in a desperate sprint to the designated pick up stop, whilst simultaneously steering an over excited lanky teenager through the morning stream of pedestrian traffic. Ocean would attract strange and curious glances from people that could sense an unusual energy about this exceptionally tall young man, who was dressed in school uniform and carrying a school satchel, and who was seemingly unaware of the

20

impact his elongated body would cause, if it just so happened to collide with theirs.

"Ocean, look where you're going... mind the lady", she would chastise as he giggled and continued his kangaroo jaunt towards the main road.

The bus had arrived early and the sight of the white twenty-seater on the opposite side of the road only served to speed Ocean up even more. If only she could get him to realise his potential, Usain Bolt would be glad to have retired from the International circuit just so as not to have to compete with the likes of Ocean Richards. How to train the autistic mind towards a national purpose. How to channel his misdirected energy towards an objective or worthy ideal, she often found herself wondering as she watched him speeding ahead, thoroughly enjoying the fact that he could scarcely be caught.

Cayenne winced apologetically as Ocean charged up the steps of the school bus, barging unceremoniously past the two female guides in his bid to dash towards his seat near the back, chortling as he clicked his seat belt into it's socket. Cayenne secretly thought Ocean and his naturally mischievous nature, was glad to escape the constraints of her dictatorship and relished spending eight hours within the more sympathetic environment of a special needs school, which scarcely took into account the progress he had made at home and so in her assessment, were doing him a disservice by allowing him the luxury of behavioural underachievement.

"Ocean!. Say excuse me. Walk to your seat Ocee". The assistants would lift their hands as if to say 'don't worry, it's ok'. She was used to this response and it often made her feel as though she was expecting too much of her own son. That it was unrealistic to have expectations for him to execute a certain level of behaviour. It was disheartening for her and for Diego as they had decided long ago that they would continue to challenge him to reach his full potential and not minimise their expectations of what he could achieve. She often felt trapped in a system that seemed to depend upon a lack of progress, as though encouraging children with special needs to challenge their disabilities would threaten its very existence.

Cayenne sighed these thoughts out into a deep exhale as she waved the school bus on it's way before turning on her heels and jogging back to get Sugar ready, stopping briefly to do a double take, as she could have sworn she was witnessing a perfectly able bodied lanky rascally teenager, almost visibly regressing into a needy, attention seeking challenged little boy before her very eyes.

Sugar by contrast, resolutely refused to be cajoled into any sense of urgency that didn't align with her own unruffled inbuilt timetable. She moved no faster, no matter that the clock suggested that she really ought to. If anything, any detection of an attempt to apply pressure seemed to have the opposite effect on her daughter.

"Suguuuuugaaaaaaaar. Have you even brushed your teeth yet?". Cayenne already knew the answer. In spite of the dentist's careful admonishment, toothbrushing, even once a day, was low on this ten year old's list of priorities. Feeding the cat, when she felt like it, rearranging her ladder desk, taking inventory of her school bag and even cleaning and re blackening her Nike trainers were all deemed more important than removing hot chocolate and canned cream fragments that had accumulated in between her remaining molars since the last brutal Sodium Fluoride attack. Diego often teased his mother as he navigated the mother daughter tirade in the mornings. "What do you expect if you name her after your favourite childhood snack".

Cayenne often regretted that particular revelation after sharing the childhood tales of summer holidays spent in the countryside in Jamaica with her brothers, climbing trees, wading through brooks and chewing on endless barks of sugar cane on the veranda of their maternal grandparent's house. Her grandmother would scold them to brush their teeth with vigilance afterwards, even though, or perhaps owing to the fact that she could count her own stained remaining teeth on one hand. Grandmother would happily point out several senior citizen neighbours, who if they had any teeth left at all, were in varying states of decay.

Even when they were hurrying along Pepper street, weaving amongst the other families meandering casually towards the school, Cayenne would find herself running at speed as though it was her name on the class register. Then upon noticing that she was alone in her efforts, she would slow down and glance behind her, only to see Sugar strolling in her own distinct casual manner with an inherited fierce look on her face, silently warning her mother to not even think about embarrassing her in front of all these people.

She would stand on the designated spot, the spot where parents stood when their children were clearly too grown to have be escorted right up to the school entrance and wait for Sugar to catch up, catapulting a stolen kiss onto her daughter's forehead before the girl could dodge it and watching as she continued apace, disappearing through the iron gates. Cayenne would then defy her daughter's strict orders to 'to go straight home' and wait to catch a glimpse of her as she passed the small window, midway up the stairs to her first floor classroom. If she was lucky, she would receive a reluctant hand in the guise of a wave, but mostly she would simply wait to see a flash of the bright pink of her daughter's rucksack, the official school bag having been discarded promptly at the beginning of term, and then go about her day.

That particular day, consisting of an interview at Province Primary School, having been informed that her application had been approved and that she was cordially being invited to visit the school at 9.45am for an interview.

The stint at E-Quip, supervising children during the school holidays, had been somewhat of an interesting, yet short lived experiment, but the long hours were exhausting and the pay unenticing. Clive, the would be university graduate turned manager, had said that few people return after the first inaugural spell, so she hadn't felt too guilty about informing them that she had decided to follow the exodus.

At least the position of lunch time supervisor, should she be successful, ought to be exactly what it said on the tin. A couple of hours work, which was about her limit with small children, ensuring that the six hundred plus pupils in attendance, were swiftly cajoled through the dinner line and back out onto the playground during the relatively short window of 1 hour and 45 minutes every weekday afternoon.

This was a particularly large school compared to most Primary establishments within the Tower Hamlets Borough which typically tended to inhabit somewhere in the region of three to four hundred pupils.

The new structure of the school was impressive allowing for a further intake of children in recent years, bringing it to it's current capacity. It's imposing colourful façade was visible from a mile away, towards the end of Pepper street to be exact and Cayenne wondered what challenges awaited as she headed towards the recently completed remodelled construction. The large glass door opened and she stepped into the double storeyed reception area which had huge windows half way up and a sky light that flooded the space with a natural radiance. Complementing the brightly painted walls was an unusual installation made up of pieces of dented, stained metal, suspended in mid-air, reminding her of the foyer of some of central London's top hotels. The reception staff were encased into a huge glass box in what looked to her like a deliberate statement of separation.

After eyeing her up curiously, the lady behind the glass asked her to take a seat next to the double doors.

A middle-aged white lady came through the door and greeted her warmly. Cayenne was about to introduce herself. "Oh are you here for the interview?".

"Yes".

"Yvonne will be with your shortly ok".

A few moments later a mixed-race lady let herself through the security door using her ID. Cayenne would guess that she was what they used to call quarter cast. That perhaps one of her parents was mixed race and the other white. Statistics would confirm that her children, supposing her partner was also white, could be easily mistaken for olive skinned white people and that their children, if the procreative tradition continued, would barely be aware that they had any black blood in their dna at all, let alone be fully exposed to the culture or traditions of their heritage. Yvonne herself was very pale in her complexion, but there was just enough kink in her hair and colour to her skin tone to suggest that there was a mix somewhere. Not that it was evident in any other way. She possessed a strong cockney accent that would place her in direct competition with Jill Hopley, Sugar's school coordinator.

 She would also guess that Yvonne had to be in her fifties, judging by the fine lines crowding her small eyes, but for some reason her peppered brunette spirals were scraped up into a high pony tail, secured with a bright red silk ribbon and her clothes looked like something one might wear to a 1950's themed party. A cute little blouse with a pussy bow and a flared 50's style skater skirt which looked like it may have been bolstered with underlay causing it to stick out slightly more irreverently than it should. It was red with white polka dots. The kind of style that Sugar would turn her nose up at. Growing up with two brothers had drained every last bit of girlyness from her where clothes were concerned. To finish off, she wore a bright red belt that cinched in the would-be waist and red shoes that wouldn't have looked out of place clicking their way along the yellow brick road. Cayenne was sure she herself had had a pair of similar tap shoes, complete with ribbon fasteners, during her tap dancing days as a child. She observed that Yvonne was clearly one of those people that believed that if they dressed youthfully, then surely their youth remained, though by Cayenne's close observation, the diluted Melanin in her skin begged to differ.

Yvonne Frazer introduced herself with a firm handshake and a bright, albeit stiff smile and invited Cayenne to follow her across the reception foyer and up the two storeyed glass panelled staircase. They walked along a brightly painted corridor adorned with mosaic prints in colourful frames and into the room at the very end which turned out to be one of the staffrooms complete with comfortable seating, a large table with several chairs and a kitchenette with an under the counter fridge.

"Take a seat there my love". Yvonne waved her hand towards the row of white chairs around the long wooden table

"Thankyou". Cayenne sat upright in her chair and attempted to adopt as positive a demeanour as possible. She rather enjoyed interviews. She liked the fact that it was an opportunity to sell herself and present whoever she chose to be that day and fortunately, that particular day, it just so happened that she chose to be a dependable, reliable, hardworking individual who thrived working as part of a team, but who could also use her initiative and work independently when necessary and who absolutely loved working with children, as she determined her winning smile would confirm.

It didn't take long for her to get the distinct impression that her interviewer had little interest in the surplus of what Cayenne had prepared herself to convey. It was as though she had a check list and as long as Cayenne hit certain words, then that would suffice. When it seemed that she wasn't answering the questions as expected, she would feel the definite and strategic prompting from Yvonne, stopping short of spoon feeding her the words she wanted to hear. It seemed things had certainly changed since the last time she had been interviewed, during the years before Ocean's challenges had commanded her attention.

By the time Cayenne was heading back towards home, she realised that the hectic morning had distracted her from having breakfast.

Taking a diversion from Pepper street, she wandered along the embankment, past the floating Chinese restaurant where some of the workers were cleaning up inside in preparation for the lunchtime rush. Past the gym where she gave a cheery wave to Casey on reception who had the phone to her ear and had looked up just as Cayenne was passing. She saw a few people running on the treadmill. People that she used to laugh at before she became a gym bunny herself. She still wondered whether those people that came simply to run on the treadmill, the same people who she scarcely remembered seeing in classes or using the equipment, were actually seeing results. Perhaps it simply made them feel better that they were making some kind of effort.

Canary Café, or Chanel, as Cayenne had affectionately christened it, owing to the interlinked C's imprinted on the glass door as an abbreviation of the shop sign, was an enchanting and rustic coffee shop set on a terrace, positioned just off Harbour Exchange Square. It was relatively quiet as the early morning rush had subsided. She scoured the cooling shelf and read the labels on the neatly packaged items, to identify exactly what she would be eating should she purchase the unusual looking delicacies. Undecided, she moved along to the fruit section. The Greek yoghurt and granola always looked tempting, until she became aware of the amount of calories it contained, especially after she had taken one of those miniature tubs of honey that were reserved for tea and coffee and drizzled that over the top as well.

The cakes in the display cabinet beneath the serving counter were especially hard to resist on an empty stomach.

She could see that the only available assistant was eyeing her up impatiently, waiting for her to make a decision. Cayenne was beginning

22

to get impatient with herself. She smiled and raised her hand and pointed back to the cooling cabinet as if to say 'I think I've decided now'. She handed the assistant the Greek yoghurt and granola and ordered a pot of earl grey tea. She would take advantage of the quiet mid-morning ambience and read her magazine before heading home.

"I'll have one of those little pots of honey as well please".

She was relieved to see that the sofa chairs towards the rear of the shop overlooking the quay were mostly vacant as well, though a few of the booths were occupied with people in business suits tapping away into their lap top computers.

She positioned herself in a seat facing the window, even though it was overcast and cloudy outside and the lustre of the iconic Canary Wharf skyscrapers was dulled slightly in the grey mist.

She looked up at the apartments directly overlooking the opposite side of the quay, whilst pouring some fully brewed Earl Grey into the porcelain cup and saucer at the same time. The lower half of the building looked fairly standard and almost blended with the Turkish restaurant on the ground level. But as she cast her eyes upwards, the apartments seemed to get bigger and more extravagant and she noticed that the last few levels had balconies that seemed to be half the size of the apartments themselves. Even though she couldn't see much from her low vantage point, she could tell that some of the balconies had exotic looking plants and miniature trees set back from the balcony's edge and she could just imagine the opulent seating and ornaments that would be arranged in and around the space as the occupants welcomed friends and family over to enjoy the wonderful views of South Quay.

"A penny for your thoughts". A familiar voice interrupted her thought journey. Without looking she knew exactly who it was. Her breathing pattern threatened to betray the cool calm collected demeanour that she really wanted to display. She desperately hoped that she was managing to conceal the dramatic rise and fall of her chest or the stiffening of her frame as a result of holding her breath. She replaced her cup in the saucer, losing trust in her own ability to regulate her nervous system.

The face, the face of the stranger was staring at her. He had dropped into the seat next to hers, forming a barrier between her eyeline and the window. His shoulders relaxed as he rested his elbows on the top of his thighs. Even though he wasn't smiling, he was looking intently and searchingly at her, scouring her face, desperate to read something that would inform him of where she was… inside. She could somehow tell that he was flooded with relief. She could literally feel that she was the perfect sight for his sore yearning eyes. She just knew it without him having to say a word.

She looked at him, directly, inwardly hunting for the anger and disappointment that she was certain she had felt. Urging those emotions to resurface and fuel the barrage of resentment that she had rehearsed in her mind, but she simply couldn't find them, as though they had somehow evaporated.

Her hand suddenly felt warm. She became aware of a stroking sensation across the palm of her hand. Dropping her eyes from his, she saw his hand in hers. His mouth fell open, fully expecting words to emerge. Some form of explanation. An offering that this canny, intuitive woman would understand and tolerate without giving away his total sense of helplessness. His lower lip fluttered and then closed, resigning itself to defeat.

He let go of her hand and sighed intensely as he turned his head toward the window. She watched him eyeing up the harboured boats and glancing at the small figures passing on the other side of the quay. A distant bird carried his vision upward until he rested them on the apartments above, gradually climbing higher towards the penthouses, as though tracing her very own thoughts just moments earlier.

Eventually his head dropped, suspended over his body, held in place by his stiff shoulders, anchored by rigid elbows still resting on his legs.

"I'm…. so sorry".

She still couldn't speak though she was sure she was supposed to. That she really ought to respond in some way. Instead she stared straight ahead and through the window, lifting her chin slightly to capture the movement in one of the harboured boats that had caught her eye. Someone was emerging from the lower quarters of the boat and had begun pottering around in their prized floating front deck.

She returned her gaze to the tray on the table in front of her in response to the sound of him stirring her tea which now had a thick layer of lactoderm forming on the top due to the lack of sipping activity. She was sure it must be cold by now. He topped up her cup with the remainder of the tea left in the pot.

She watched silently as he opened up the lids of both the Greek yoghurt and the honey pot, unravelling the black plastic spoon from it's serviette wrapping, he drizzled the honey over the top layer of granola. When it was half way poured, he glanced up at her, she nodded affirmatively and he continued to pour out the remaining honey until only a thick resistant gloop lay on it's tilted side which he scooped out with the spoon. Picking up the yoghurt pot, he gently began to mix the honey and granola into the plain Greek yoghurt beneath until there was a harmonious blend of texture and colour.

He tenderly unfolded the serviette and placed it on her lap, covering the smart black pencil skirt to protect it from any loose fragments that might escape. Dipping the spoon into the mixture, scooping out a generous mouthful, being careful to wipe the bottom of the spoon on the rim of the container, he positioned himself to feed her.

She intuitively leaned towards him. It was barely visible. A very slight readjustment to her position in her seat. He lifted the spoon towards her mouth, trusting his hand to make the right manoeuvre which freed him to gaze directly into her eyes again.

She trusted her mouth would automatically capture the sweetened substance with accuracy, freeing her to look directly into his eyes........ again.

CHAPTER 4

"Happy Easter…. I need a chocolate feed.

I bet you know I've been a dribbling wreck… withdrawal symptoms are horrendous as I head to white suburbia – so desperate for a feed from your tight juicy black pussy.

It's the only chocolate I want this Easter

Bitch :) I need blacking. Kindly confirm availability".

"The Queen is otherwise engaged on Friday … so on this isolated occasion would consider Wednesday late afternoon followed by a return on Thursday".

"I'm glad the Queen is back… her white whore's cock rose immediately on her responses and the news he might get blacked again.

Have you decided where I can make it up to my Queen?".

"Who knew that there was a suite especially designed for me at the Savoy. Does that make you hard?".

"Mmmmmm nice, yes the thought of you spread on all fours in the decadent Queen suite would certainly make me hard".

"I am daring to suppose there will at least be an attempt to locate my vaginal pressure valve".

"Mayfair, Park Lane, Bond Street… bad cheeky greedy naughty black milf".

"You do realise that all the options that you mentioned are synonymous with designer shopping. Handbags, shoes, jewellery and the like. Platinum executives with high regard for their Queens would be prudent to bear this in mind".

"Chanel tomorrow before you start your new job?. The coffee shop Chanel I mean".

"What a perfectly poor excuse for a whore".

"That's better messaging".

"Oh I'm sorry, perhaps I should disguise my pussy hunger as an executive financial crisis...

Yeeeeesss... that way, you will undoubtedly put all else on hold... work into the early hours if needs be and stop at nothing to rectify my sexual starvation crisis.

No more leaving in the early evening, but just as in your corporate world, you will gladly burn the midnight oil to be of service and get one of those chauffer driven car thingies to take you home.

I'll not have any more of this part time bull shit.

You stick to numbers... leave the imagination and initiative to me".

"Well you do have such a wicked imagination".

"Speaking of, have you had any further thoughts on pursuing a career elsewhere. Germany, Hong Kong, New York?

I bet those Mandarin Executives are bloody thorough.

They'd never see a damsel in vaginal distress. Bet they know how to start and finish.

I really don't think you should pursue opportunities in Germany either. No No. Noooooo. You stay put in England. Preferably the suburbs…

Strive to start at 9am and finish at 5pm. Don't even think about living on the edge.

Pick up a safe Sally, who'll no doubt be plain and agreeable, with marginal affinity for style and charisma. She will naturally wrinkle prematurely as is the norm for your cultural heritage and undoubtedly develop a generational turkey neck just like mother. Whose illuminous pussy curtains will make her vagina unsightly after the first or second pregnancy and the third executive sprog will surely drop out unaided.

Sex will last 2 minutes precisely, provided your technique has improved and foreplay will be a quick snog in a lift, pardon me, stairwell.

Any extreme fantasies about hot exotic fucking in elegant hotels with a body that maintains it's form, must be kept well hidden.

Stroll through Waterstones on occasion in search of exotic fruit, but do not follow… do not approach… leave well alone Suburban Sam… you can't possibly stand the heat".

"Any good things to say tonight cheeky?".

"I'm such a cruel black greedy bitch".

"Yes you are... you need a fucking hard spanking.

Nasty Bethany...". He was resurrecting her pet name. "I really do need to shut her up by putting my hardened white cock in her mouth".

"Yes. God forbid you silence her with a fucking orgasm".

"Let's not forget it was your seductive fucking stroking that ruined my hold.... As I get more blacked, I'm sure my tolerance will improve.

Check out this video: https://www.redtube.com/6712"

"Why are you sending me videos which portray foreplay, no rubber and extensive satisfying fucking?...

This must surely be from the Disney Channel, as the likelihood that my White Suburban Fuck could perform like the Zeus in the video, has thus far proven doubtful".

"I need a black pussy feeding. I need my cock blacking. I need using by the Black Queen.

I need the taste of black berry juice,

I need to release my white cream,

I need to be treated like a naughty white whore".

"All will be granted generously… provided the terms of the agreement are honoured and executed to high end specifications".

"Happy Easter gorgeous Black Chocolate Caramel Mocha Queen".

"The Black Queen is honing her black exoticism in the gym, safe in the knowledge that every chiselled curve is going to be adored and worshipped".

"Mmmm nice…. I love those black toned arms of yours around me… bet you have a number of guys creaming themselves over you".

"Many are secretly drooling… seemingly scared to brave the Queen's mordant demeanour. Pitiful".

"Plebs :)

I need my hands on your firm chocolate ass".

"The firmness is increasing rapidly... it must be appreciated and scrutinised at close quarters".

"You must indulge in some face sitting".

"You must indulge in some pussy foraging".

"I want to see that fucking tight firm black ass bouncing. It needs fucking worshipping.

Make me suck it

Suffocate me with it

Drench me in your black cunt cum juice.

Your whore has gone NOWHERE".

"The SWF is pleasing the Queen with this devotion to the chocolate cause...

He will be duly awarded with pussy and ass smothering, full face moisturising with cunt juice au noir".

"The only chocolate this SWF wants to eat this holiday is yours, you seductive black chocolate goddess :)

White Suburbia has no idea what a whore I am for chocolate cunt now:)".

"I can sense the suburban hum drum… the lack of exoticism…. Sheer atmospheric dryness… the bland horizon… all flat droopy bottoms, devoid of curvature, pasty skin and ultra thin lips.

By contrast, my juicy thick lips will envelope your cock with my big black rounded booty in the air.

Get your fill of anomalous sensuality this week before white suburbia absorbs any hint of sexual excitement. Enjoy exotic cunt juice aplenty.

I am always bemused by my Caucasian compatriots in the gym and their delusion that squats and lunges are going to have even a remote effect on their white flat iron board bottoms and elusive hips.

I am suddenly overcome with a sense of foreboding.

Could it be that you are experiencing delusion as to the purpose of our next encounter?

You mentioned YOUR NEEDS as though there was a modicum of significance.

Avoid an immediate cancellation of the proposed black cunt feast…

Raise your right hand now and state with absolute conviction, that the onus of the encounter is to locate and utterly satisfy MY release valve.

Once located, pursue it, study with fervour what makes it tick… what excites it and equally what makes it go cold, though you may find the latter, wholly ingrained and your susceptibility to it irreversible.

Become a scholar of my black clit until any other suitor is catapulted out of the running, such is your understanding of my vaginal mechanics.

Master with precision, how to release the pressure from my daily existence and the weight of my monarchical responsibilities to enable me to relax and be at your temporary mercy and ultimately serve my famished body.

Commit now to this pussy cause or stand aside oh White man of Suburbia and let your mounting contemporaries show their own vigour for the crown".

"Absolutely no need for that sense of foreboding to develop…. I am your whore. Your needs are paramount… full subservience to the black mistress will be adhered to".

"Then the appointment remains intact according to the aforementioned itinerary.

Any ill-fated omissions or perceived breaches of the indenture, will result in your immediate discharge".

"I will confirm itinerary in the week".

"Excellent… Meanwhile the Queen will entertain herself daily, contemplating what luxurious gifts her charge will bestow upon her. The mood rather hankers for a weekend country retreat. Temporary contrast to the thriving city. Summer thoughts of Seaside Ice-cream…Rural forest fucking, fish and chips and country air pussy eating".

"Greedy Queen".

She corrected him immediately. "Your Royal Highness".

CHAPTER 5

Skipping down the last tier of the metal stairs, descending into the basement of the gym, Cayenne could sense that the place was almost full to capacity this evening.

Fenton, today's boxing instructor was leaning against the curtain covered frame of the boxing ring, chatting to one of the other ladies.

For some reason, it was mostly women in the boxing classes, possibly because the new Liston ABC program, promised to be a relatively fool proof basic introduction to this particular discipline, which eradicated any concern that it may be too masculine or male dominated.

Cayenne wondered whether a change of name would attract more males. She was quite certain that if the class was retitled MWA warrior class, that hoards of testosterone fuelled, self proclaimed, boxing champions would suddenly emerge like purpose driven ants.

This wasn't her favourite class by any means. Not because she didn't enjoy the actual boxing, and she knew Fenton always made the classes really enjoyable and informative, but rather because her enjoyment of it seemed to be fully dependent upon whoever she happened to be partnered with.

Cayenne considered herself a fast learner, but when partnered with some ultra ardent souls who perhaps took the exercise a little too seriously for her liking or girls that seemed more interested in batting their eyes and hanging off the instructor's every word, it somehow seemed to put a

37

dampener on the experience. There was nothing to be done about that, it was the luck of draw, she supposed. Fortunately, she hadn't had a repeat of one particularly unfortunate experience she'd had the previous year, when she found herself at the mercy of an overzealous ego maniac who thought nothing of pummelling her into near oblivion just to prove a point to a spectating rival.

The class were facing the mirror for the warm up period as Fenton insisted it was important to face themselves to provide something to aim for in their reflection, but also to correct any posture issues or technical errors in their execution.

Fenton was at the helm demonstrating the jabs, crosses, hooks and uppercuts they would be utilising in the class.

"I don't wanna see any a' this", he was stating in his Essex tinged accent, showing exactly how they shouldn't be doing the uppercut, in a way that would carry little or no power with it. "I wanna see this", he dipped down and powerfully arose hooking his right arm as though punching under an opponent's chin.

"…and don't stand still, I want you movin' around".

After a few minutes had passed, the group were partnered into pairs and told to don their gloves and pads.

Fenton partnered Cayenne with Ella which she was pleased about. She had been discreetly holding her breath, hoping that Fenton wasn't going to pair her with Doreen, even though just months before, they seemed to be getting on well. Cayenne had even considered lifting her unofficial friendship ban for Doreen. It had all started so well. A drink after the gym occasionally and meeting midweek to go running. Cayenne had reasoned that an additional five or six mile run per week on top of all her classes wouldn't hurt her regenerated fitness goals. Doreen was especially keen to do it, though Cayenne suspected that this was in part due to her considering herself quite a proficient runner who tended to partner with people that were not, at least in her own estimation, which no doubt boosted the diminutive woman's ego. Though Cayenne hadn't run for some time, she knew that it wouldn't take her long to get up to speed again. As the weeks went by and Cayenne found she became less out of breath and was able to barely need a rest break, she couldn't shake the feeling that Doreen was less enamoured with her as a running partner.

Though that in itself was not enough to dispel this promising potential association. That was until a couple of other things occurred. They may not have seemed like deal breakers to a lot of people, but for someone who had grown so much in the last year or so and put so much into her personal development, Cayenne had a decision to make. She knew it wasn't deliberate and that Doreen essentially had a good heart and for the most part meant well. However, Doreen was driven by issues of low self esteem which expressed itself in various increasingly irritating ways and were usually heavily disguised by a larger than life exuberance and a tendency to take over the room and draw all the attention to herself. Not that Cayenne minded that part, but overall she became overbearing to be around. She would plan outings, constantly sending reminders in the interim, only to change the details at the last minute or keep Cayenne waiting for inordinate lengths of time. It got to the point that Cayenne was convinced that Doreen was constantly trying to test the loyalty and resilience of this burgeoning friendship. Had they been lifelong friends or at the very least forged some sort of foundation on which to build, then perhaps Cayenne would have felt an obligation to see things through. To not throw in the towel. Unfortunately, at this early stage of proceedings, when neither had much invested in the experiment, Cayenne had felt no remorse at chopping at the root, which had now reduced their association to a pleasant hello and a cordial wave when their paths crossed at the gym.

That didn't stop Doreen from sapping the energy in the room whenever an opportunity arose. Fortunately, Fenton was quite a strong, perceptive character and somehow managed to contain her attention seeking.

Whilst Cayenne and Ella weren't exactly great pals, their similar weight, height and build not to mention experience and ability, made for very well matched sparring partners.

Ella had a fierce right hook which belied the immaculate, well groomed and poised exterior. She approached the classes with the same fierce determination as herself. They were both mature women, wanting to make the best of themselves and made every moment count. Cayenne admired the fact that Ella was always impeccably coordinated. From the purple trim on her trainers to the matching purple headband and towel. This particular week it was a canary yellow ensemble, incorporating yellow and green lycra shorts to offset the canary yellow tank top with a bright green logo. Cayenne tried not to stare at the fact that Ella's legs were always perfectly well shaved and moisturised to perfection with just a hint of a tan. She could remember the days before she had managed to pierce Ella's guarded exterior, when they had first become acquainted at the gym, Cayenne had complimented Ella on her outfit which had broken the ice as they chatted animatedly about their shared penchant for exotic gym gear. She had had to work a little harder each week to keep up the momentum. Going out of her way to cross the room and say hello, to be prepared to be a little overly self deprecating to make herself appear more accessible. Eventually there was an easy companionship between them, although she often caught glimpses of frost on Ella's clipped features, when someone else happened to annoy her and then her pretty delicate little face, framed with golden plaits would cloud over like thunder.

"Come around for a minute and I'm gonna demonstrate the pyramid that I want you to do next". A few groans resounded around the room. "I hear the groans", Fenton was smiling permissively. "...but an integral part of boxing is cardio, so that's what we are gonna work on.

So, I'll use you". He pointed at Adé, a tall broad African guy that had joined a few weeks before who stepped forward readying his pads for the Fenton assault. The two men adopted combatant stances. "So, we are gonna do two jabs, like so". He twisted his waist and arms into a left and a right jab into Ade's poised padded hands.

"...followed by twenty squat jumps, and I want you down low like this, then accelerating into the air twenty times". Fenton squatted low before throwing his arms behind him and jumping up high and then dropping back into a low squat. Effortlessly he raised his hands in fighter mode again, "...then it's four jabs, like so". Ade danced in coordination with his coach, adding resistance to Fenton's punches. "...then it comes down to eighteen squat jumps. Then it's six jabs and 16 squat jumps and so on and so forth until you end up at twen'y jabs and two squat jumps. Fenton was drawing circles in the air with his hand, suggesting a repeat of what he had just said, so as not to have to demonstrate the whole sequence. "...then you're gonna repeat the same circuit but instead of jabs 'n' squat jumps, it's hooks and push ups. Then...." The sound of more elaborate groans, "... we do the circuit again but instead of hooks and push ups, it's gonna be upper cuts and burpees. Is everybody clear?".

Without waiting for an affirmative reply, the pyramid began. "Let's get it!".

Ella and Cayenne grimaced at each other as they knew that they had a tendency to lose count midway through the pyramid and in their eagerness not to come last owing to their equally competitive natures, they were often prone to exaggerate in their guesstimating.

"Finished already girls?".

They would both nod at Fenton with their padded hands on hips panting frantically. "Immmmpressive". Fenton would shrug approvingly.

Ella would glance at Cayenne and Cayenne at Ella, hoping that no one had noticed their sly winks.

CHAPTER 6

"Black Queen, good morning. How was the gym?".

"It was a 10am session today.... Shamelessly, the Queen rose effortlessly above the competition".

"I so wish I was there to see that black chocolate ass bouncing. The ass I want right now in my face".

"Note that it's firmer and tighter.... Unchartered territory for a white boy.... However would you cope?".

"Will try awfully hard to hold…."

"The Queen adores a tryer"

"To pleasure a Queen is such an honour".

"Indeed…. It is not lost on the Queen that hierarchical rivals await… however her suburban white whore has caught her imagination.

None are more surprised than the Queen herself, as suitors who fail to serve champagne with regularity are traditionally extradited.

Does Suburbia not yet comprehend… intermittent trysts to Bond Street ensure a generous flow in her caramel valley…."

"Just got hard remembering how you glided in to the Westbury…."

"Yes I recall…. A little flustered and tardy if memory serves.

I relished watching you squirm over lunch knowing full well that my moist pussy was prohibiting your enjoyment of Mayfair cuisine"

Every fork entry, tantalisingly teasing your cock into premature erection".

"Michelin star cuisine was just an annoyance …. I wanted a different feed".

"So much so… once in the seclusion of the lift…. Your erotic launch paved way for the passion that followed".

"The lift release…."

"Oh my white darling, I fully understand the burden of your laborious yet necessary wait for a cinnamon post lunch delicacy".

"I was straining to get on to you".

"Tingling pussy sensations at the thought of being ravaged. I struggled to open wide enough…. Desire wanting to drive my thighs wider and wider apart to appease your ravenous appetite".

"Rampant and desperate".

"My pussy recognised what was imminent. And so the warm flow began…

Cocoa puss puss is now desperate for a Suburban fingering prompted by the vag muscle memory.

Mmmmm wet patch…. Nutmeg creamy dribbles… the anticipation of the next assault".

"Drench my white formerly innocent face with your fucking black juice".

"The excitement of clandestine white fucking and devising inner city blacking… counting the days".

"I need my secret blacking".

"My Noir valley pussy fails to recognise the innocence upon which it sits...

Cocoa cunt however, detects significant cultural void ... sexual nothingness... sparse dry plains..... vaginal cacti ....

Causing bursts of nourishing caramel coulis to spring forth to feed that which is desolate".

"Fucking use me you evil delicious Black Queen".

"Sudden urge to silence your mouth with hot pulsing pussy cream...

Hunger no more... the Queen has bountiful rivers of delight until your reserves are overflowing".

"I need to satisfy you

Need your cunt vibrating".

"The Queen will supersede feeding…. She wishes to drown and punish… suffocate and torment…. Her aim to fully submerge your face with Caribbean cunt marinade".

"In my fantasies I'm drowning in gorgeous black cunt cum juice. I want to lube my dry white hands and aggressively stroke my cock with your black juice. No rubber, just your juice all over my cock.

Waterboard me with your black chocolate cunt. Racially corrupt me you bitch".

"The Queen needs her release…. Though the harvest is bountiful… and yet more cum juice could surely jeopardise the white whore's respiratory abilities…

But release her you must…. For the tensions are mounting… release the overflow of black berry coulis, locked within the depths of her regal vag.

The Queen will neither corrupt nor contaminate…

But lead her white fuck across the genital equator … deep into exotic climes…. Hedonistic horizons we must explore. Passionate jungle fucking aplenty. Addictive chocolate pussy exploits.... The possibilities are tantalisingly endless".

"I want the rivers to flow...

I want the Queen cumming on my tongue and on my cock....it's only then my job is done".

"I can barely stand to wait for my gateaux pussy licking.... So damned ravenous. Desperate for the racial facial abuse to proceed... my white fuck pussy cushion.

My pussy hungers for your multifaceted touch.... Tongue, finger, cock.

The Queen demands her servicing... tormented by the restraints of white suburbia.

She can hardly wait to perform her regal pussy stretch with her black rounded arse high in the air. Gaze at it from afar, fully bask in it's rare beauty. Then approach stealthily, tongue first... follow the juice trail... don't be fooled by the narrow entry... for a black fondant cream lies beneath, with spellbinding hidden depths... Suburban white fuck must come with his white hose full to the brim.

Fill her cavernous cunt until it overflows with corporate milk.

The Queen's cunt is empty I say.... Who can fill it?

Are there any suitors worthy of the challenge?".

"Where are you?"

"Home.... Knicker-less in a white robe. Pussy airing on the balcony in the evening breeze".

"Shame I can't join to provide a full servicing".

"If only you were permitted across city boundaries...

Alas.... Your suburban heritage, is the bed in which you must lie.

Surely the most a white whore executive can hope for is the occasional mercy of a hungry Nubian Queen...

Let not your good fortune lead to any delusion of black cunt continuity.

That being said... at my request, an expectancy of white suburban penis deposits into a voracious chocolate lubricated pussy remains. For the Queen must not be refused... she must get what she wants... and the pussy must hunger no more.

Can barely tolerate the hours until I can gag my whore with my swollen cunt.... Swollen with intense desire and hunger.

I will surely cork your mouth with my moist labia. Tease my clit with your tongue... I want to witness the feeding. To feed you thoroughly to strengthen you for the load you will unleash thereafter into my coconut creek".

"Fuck I want it".

"Picturing me stuffing your head under my dress in the elevator... awakening your senses with the essence of pussy Dior.

Lining my thong with your tongue, rendering it surplus.

You are fucking consuming my thoughts.

Just don't fucking stop... my black juicy pussy can stand it no longer...

Needs more...

Fuck me Again and again".

"Good. Being your fuck whore consumes my thoughts also.

I want you to face fuck me first.

I will gladly be your slut".

"Yes you will give me the orgasms I demand".

Cayenne arose and closed the balcony door, glancing in at the children as they slept and continued towards her room at the end of the corridor. Sliding in between the tightly tucked cotton sheets, she rolled onto her back and looked out through the gap in her grey silk organza curtains, into the slice of sky just visible between the apartment block opposite and the top of her window.

Their email seduction marathons always seemed to leave her feeling less fulfilled and agonisingly hungry.

She wondered what he was doing at that precise moment. Was he at home now….with her. There had to be a her. She could sense the inner turmoil. The battles taking place in his head. When she had met him he had obviously been scouting for something more, which hinted at domestic dissatisfaction at the very least. But it was as though he hadn't bargained for what he had now found. Finding himself totally unprepared for the depth of feeling that palpably coursed through him and she'd daresay his upbringing and family values hadn't planned for him to develop feelings for a black woman. She had guessed that his hidden Nubian passion was his secret fantasy. That the ogling of black women was something for his private times, for the sly porn moments that THEY didn't know about. The private wanks when no one was around. It was certainly not a feasible option that his family, peer group or conscience would tolerate, any more than there was likely to be a Maasai Warrior in-law investiture at the trooping of the Colour at St James Park.

But he was far from royalty. So what forbade him from the avid pursuit of his own choices and secret desires.

She remembered when he had held her hand in the foyer of the Mayfair hotel and said almost to himself ' if you didn't have any children, I really would be in trouble'. Or the time at Park Lane Intercontinental when he had cursed bitterly, 'it's alright for you, you already have your brood'.

She certainly couldn't picture him as a father figure to her children. Strong black, powerfully minded children. Even if he were the biological father of her own hypothetical mixed race brood, he would likely be one of those fathers that opted for overtime and long working hours and conjure up the occasional hostile corporate takeover to avoid the demands of family time. Anything to avert the challenges of real manhood. If she herself caused him moments of trepidation and he had actively pursued her with relentless determination, it would take a quantum leap of spinal growth and extreme dick shrivelling resistance for him to be considered in any kind of familial mentoring role.

So what was this. Two people that seemed to be developing feelings which were being disguised as sexual wanting. Kidding themselves that they were simply getting their needs met. Not daring to apply perception to what could potentially be happening?.

Or was she looking into things too deeply which was her tendency. During his absence in Zurich, she had sworn to herself not to be taken in again. She knew he hadn't meant to hurt her, but that he was overwhelmed with his feelings and the lack of control he felt which had no doubt driven him to create a corporate story to give himself thinking time or a way of retreating temporarily from the line of fire.

She had come close to deleting his email altogether.

But then he had found her in Chanel café on that cloudy morning and all the angst seem to disappear. When she looked deeply into his eyes, it was as though she could see into his soul. As though he were transparent. He was crying in there. Huddled and small. Arms wrapped protectively around his knees, gazing upwards. But she knew she couldn't reach him. That he would have to stand up and climb out himself.

She remembered warmly how he had fed her. She must have looked so girly and vulnerable to anybody watching, when in fact he had appeared almost helpless as he had wiped her mouth, wrapped her coat around her and held her tightly against his chest for dear life as though scared to let go.

CHAPTER 7

Cayenne arose early the next morning, deciding to forego yoga class and proceed with her own amalgamation of yoga and Pilatés poses. The few that she could recall from a book she had bought once when she was pregnant with Sugar. Though she knew she probably wasn't following the breathing patterns to the letter, she simply allowed her body to do what she felt it needed at that time. A sun salutation of sorts.

Her phone suddenly bleeped, interrupting her cobra. She kissed her teeth at not remembering to put it on silent. Now she would have to engage her mind more intensely in the battle to follow the course of her breathing and ignore it's prompts to find out who was messaging.

"Chu". She cursed, in the same way her mother used to when she was a child, expressing mild vexation. A similarity that Diego took every opportunity to point out.

The battle was temporarily lost as her shoulder press rolled into a stretch towards her bedside table where the flashing phone lay.

"Sorry, my itinerary and whether or not I can actually indulge you tomorrow is up in the air…

Will only be able to confirm first thing in the morning, so that's awkward, we could try for Thursday".

"What a sorry itinerary indeed.

Not at all surprised by this disappointing state of affairs.

Suffice it to say your entire chocolate blacking adventure (at least of the qualitative kind) is in jeopardy.

The whole fiasco is up in the air … and your voyage of cultural discovery equally up in smoke.

Now let me get back to real regal fishing in an altogether more superlative Nile".

"Sorry my Queen – I can't make today work"

"The Queen acknowledges your short comings…vast as they are".

"How is the diary tomorrow?

I know I need to do better".

"Height of busyness… any diversional exception would have to be for an exceptionally electrifying, gift laden Shard culminating alternative".

"Leaving fantasy land of Queens and Knights for a second… how is the new job? Better than the last one?".

"I'm reluctant to descend from my innate Queendom but if you insist….

Considerably better than the kids holiday camp penitentiary, not least because it merely accounts for two hours of my time.

I was under the impression that I would be assisting with the navigation of 600 primary school children during the lunch period.

At times I have to stand back and wonder whether I have been mistakenly transported to a more advanced children's correctional facility. Although, having been here for approximately seven days, it is quite apparent that they cannot hope to find rectification there. That much was clear when I had the misfortune to witness a year 6 child, supposedly one of the older role models of the school, hurling two chairs across the reception area in protest because someone supposedly superior to himself, had had the audacity to prevent him from ignoring the rather significant school rule of exiting the playground via a prohibited fire door. Once one of, or more accurately, three of my colleagues had managed to persuade this particular dastardly imbecile to cooperate, he eventually acquiesced to withdraw from his gang related playground activities momentarily, whilst they escorted him to the headmistress in order to give her the opportunity to address his acute disdain for authority.

I was fortunate enough to be present to witness this highly anticipated (by me at least), grand retribution, preparing myself to see the wretched corpse, annihilated by a severe dressing down from his revered principal.

However, that was not be, as in an act of abominable cowardice, she simply allowed this delinquent to disrespect her by not listening to a word she said, though I could hardly blame him, it must have been incredibly difficult for him, given that Ms Henchbush, seemed to adopt the demeanour of a deer facing oncoming traffic at high speed. Her eyes gave away the fact that she had no clear strategy of how to deal with the endemic behavioural issues that I now know are resident".

"Errm. Ok thanks for the essay. I only asked how you were getting along.

Goodness you do need a treat

Could try and get to the Hilton later to at least cheer you up. I know it's out of bounds for a chocolate treat as my Queen insists upon out of area titillation, so was just thinking a chat over wine".

Cayenne couldn't shake the disgruntled feeling that came over her, whenever he suggested that they meet up in her immediate vicinity. Her home was totally off the cards, and her neighbourhood, strictly reserved for lunchtime beverages. They had established that a while ago, but somehow the thought of him simply strolling over the bridge at South Quay to spend time with her wasn't quite enough. She needed to feel as though he had applied himself. That it was costing him something and taking him far from the beaten track. That he had to make a specific determined effort, put skin in the game. Whilst she pondered his internal proposal, she switched off her phone and busied herself with some tidying up.

Diego's room was atrocious. For some reason, he seemed incapable of even keeping a matching pair of socks in unison. A plate that was at least a day old lay under the bed. Dirty clothes and layers of dust combined with strands of hair formed a colourless layer on his window sill.

She sorted out his clothing rail and rooted through his drawers which seemed to house all sorts of odds and ends that didn't belong in there. Unclean combs, pen lids, a half eaten apple. 'narrrrrsty', she muttered under her breath. She could feel the boiling sensation building up inside which she would store and use to blast the dry skin from his lips with her tongue when he returned home. By the time she had cleaned the room and changed the sheets and sorted a bundle of clothing that seemed to be a mixture of unclean garments and items that she had painstakingly ironed that had not quite made it to their designated storage place, a couple of hours had passed.

After switching on the washing machine, she yanked open the airing cupboard door which even after almost two years, still seemed intent on resisting the thick pile carpet, making it necessary to put full force into prizing it open. Almost every time she did so, she almost wanted to close it again immediately, heaving as it was with half-filled paint tubs and wallpaper paste, a now defunct step ladder and an odd assortment of tools, acquired from various places. Some that she must have forgotten to return, others that she had bought when in the throes of decorating along with a couple of rolls of left over carpet and bundles of wallpaper that she had over zealously ordered and completely miscalculated. This left little room for the items that they required on a regular basis, such as the mop buckets, vacuum and ironing board which seemed to groan in protest to being squeezed through a narrow wedge between the ladder and a stack of Diego's old sports bags.

She set up the ironing board in her bedroom and switched on the iron which gurgled it's parched displeasure. To avoid having to walk to the kitchen to grab some water from the tap or the kettle, she pulled out the bottle of mineral water that she had remembered was still slotted in the side pocket of her gym bag. The iron sighed out it's relief in a misty haze of steam.

Glancing at her phone, the battery light had gone from red to green signifying the charging process was well underway.

Leaning on the ironing board, she scrolled through the notifications, dismissing advertising campaigns and a confirmation from E-quip accepting her resignation.

Then she remembered that she hadn't answered the last email request.

" Have you gone due to delivery failure? I was supposed to be away this week".

Cayenne was in just the right mood to entertain herself.

"Sorely disappointed with SWF.

Seriously re-thinking this particular uniting of nations.

Must proceed to identify quality sources of cunt hunger remedies".

"Black cunt hunger lingers here badly".

"Oh platinum executive… with your vain pussy satisfaction promises…

Oh for the bold magnate to return".

"Where are you babes?".

"Home of course.   Just letting you know you're dismissed due to insufficient email contact. Off with your head".

"I haven't forgotten about you you know…. Unfortunately I can't forget about you, so there"

Cayenne placed the phone faced down on the bed for fear he would see her expression.   Then realised how ridiculous that was as they were

62

messaging. But she still didn't trust it, for surely he would be able to detect the flush rising in her cheeks or the change in her breathing pattern. She glanced around the room as though searching for a way to define what she was feeling. Eyes wide open and free hand on her chest, she panted to regulate her breath.

She felt something. When he had said 'I can't forget about you so there'. In fact, just to be sure, she turned the phone over in her hand and read it again, and then again. Replacing it to face the purple and grey cotton quilt cover, she leaned her head back against the grey buttoned bed head and breathed out lengthy, slow exhales just as Josephine, encouraged them to do in the semidarkness of the yoga studio, allowing her chest to rise fully and then collapse again as her thoughts and feelings saturated the air.

Oh my God, what's happening. She daren't allow herself to indulge the possible answers that were tapping away at her conscious mind, asking her to interpret his words in some way. To define it and distinctly label it.

No, she mustn't. Previous experience had taught her that that would be a big mistake. Especially with a fretful executive who couldn't seem to execute on his promises. Who was clearly wrestling with the task of figuring himself out.

"Can the Queen please confirm next week's diary. Her toy needs to make amends".

His demand jolted her out of the tempting fantasy.

"Fortunately for you, this Wednesday would be a good option for Shard activities although the Queen is at a loss as to quite what amends can be made. The damage sustained is severe and substantial".

"How is the chocolate... sounds like it needs some proper hungry desperate attention".

"This caramel carcass is positively ravenous. It has to be said... you are a whore with regrettably poor form. Is there any area in which you excel? Your virtues are presently well hidden from her Majesty".

"I concur, I have been very bad my Queen.

I need due punishment.

Suffocate me with your boldly delicious cunt.

I think a drenching of black cunt juice is appropriate retribution.

Suburbia has me fucking bored…. I want blacking. Show me what I'm missing… show me that deliciously heavenly black tight form of yours…. Be evil about all the other cocks you tease".

"Perhaps the most prudent punishment of all would be complete abstinence.

For what one fails to value… one inevitably loses.

Delicious black pussy juice is clearly not on your list of priorities".

"That would be hell…

A return to the underbelly has to be avoided at all costs. I notice that you completely sidestepped the Hilton catch up idea… wasn't worth gracing me with your appearance I assume.

Whores have feelings too you know".

"I like the video you sent me before. The white whore was most impressive. Subservient, obedient, incessantly hungry… devouring the black cunt, recognising the honour bestowed. This white whore in the video is clearly of premium underbelly stock.

Regarding your request, I naturally presumed this particular invitation was meant for one of your alternative low grade ethnics".

"I will study the behaviour of the video whore for inspiration so I can improve my Queen….so that I can step up in the hierarchy of underbelly white whores. I must work harder to please…

I still get off on that one where the two black girls enjoy that white girl".

"With regards the local Hilton offer….

I'm afraid unless something smacks of luxury and decadence … it doesn't occur to me that I may the intended recipient".

"I love it… can almost visualise your delicious smile… fuck I want your mouth and tongue right now".

"You refer to the white girl with a hint of desire… a clear indication of your slum grade whoreism".

"Not at all. I appreciate her subservience to chocolate slavery. The way she was getting used".

"My newly honed biceps and thighs would rather like to grab you in a vice like grip, if only you were a well behaved whore... worthy of my cinnamon embrace".

"You've fucked with my natural tendencies – I only look for chocolate and only rise for black cunt now... tight juicy majestic black cunt... despite being a white whore, I have standards now.

There's something fucking delicious about your arms being firm around me so toned and tight".

"Alas, I must upgrade to a more prestigious privately educated pussy graduate... it appears you are of the Ofsted directed academy distinction".

"Brilliant school references babe".

"You speak as a juvenile, low pedigree cunt whore, vastly unseasoned, as though I have rivals and peers.

My regalia clearly escapes you".

"Apologies for my candour ….

I must remember my place….

My sub-ordinance".

"Insatiable uncontrollable untenable pussy hunger abides".

"My cock is hardening for you… it needs to be back inside, immersed in you.

The POWER you have over me is really bad…

I'm desperate for a using by you.

I'm enjoying the pride I feel having been blacked by you".

"Not entirely blacked... but I will take you as close to the molten as you can possibly withstand.

I'm still sore from my last spin cycle class which was closely followed by intense conditioning and abs. My black ass is solidifying by the day.

At least the sessions help to avert the pussy hunger which has subsided slightly. Couldn't help but wonder whether the dribbling, erogenous gym instructors would treat me as appallingly as my suburban fuck.

I'm sure they would be less likely to abandon me for suburban Easter pursuits".

"Bet that firm chocolate ass has some big admirers. Isn't it a shame they don't have platinum status to give the Queen both things she craves.

Must count myself very fortunate that the Queen doesn't get off on underbelly fucking, despite my tendencies".

"Yes, all things considered.... These lowly instructors couldn't hope to entertain me with lavish extravagance. Doubtless the Queen's need to expand on the depths of her pussy hunger would overwhelm mere credit card holders".

"I fully intend to remind the Queen that she needn't look elsewhere and I fully intend to indulge the Queen's appetite for clandestine city PANORAMIC pussy capers. I need your black cunt. I need to have you. Fucking show me that black chocolate delight".

"The lengthy wait and procrastination has almost turned any desire into utter contempt".

"PROCRASTINATION??? …. It's more to do with the exorbitant cost of seeing you these days".

"Serves you right for boasting of high end escapism… your idea if memory serves.

If you are unable to live up to your lofty brags, just say the word and I'll happily offer my regards to suburbia.

Enjoy your scraps at the Travelodge won't you. I'll be glad not to have to make do with low grade counterfeit opulence anymore anyway.

Step aside lame knight and make way for next level luxury, way out of your league….as am I.

Ps. If the Travelodge is fully booked… you could always suggest their communal stairwell. Such class.

Don't bother to respond. I don't even check my spam emails these days".

"Hey you. Yes the luxury was my idea and the plan is to continue. I'm no fan of Travelodge either for goodness sake. Send me a gorgeous picture".

"Negative".

"Guess I'll have to make do with the ones I already have".

What did he mean by that?. 'the ones he already has'. Is he saying that there are others. That she isn't the only chocolate delicacy in his life?. Why did the very thought cause her to feel so injured.

Pursing her lips, she hammered out a response with angry fingers.

"Pray you'll continue with 'the ones you already have.

Waste no more of my time PEASANT".

"Hey, I was talking about your pictures.

I requested a picture, you said you would never give me one again so I said I'd make do with the ONES (i.e pictures) I have".

Cayenne buried her head in the pillow, cringing with embarrassment. Had she been white, she would surely have flushed a healthy shade of pink.

She banged the pillow with frustration. She felt exposed. She knew she must be acting like a spoilt child. Trying to keep up the pretence of not having any emotional connection to what they were doing.

Now he would have seen right through her. Known that she was upset.

She glanced at the abandoned bundle of clothes on her bed and considered the hour or so that she had just wasted on the phone.

Ironing had never been her strong point. She remembered that it had been her mother's least liked household chore also, which is probably why she could clearly visualise cupboards and baskets and suitcases and wardrobes, filled to the brim with un-ironed clothes. Discarded and uncared for yet selfishly imprisoned and hoarded. Somewhere in the back of her mind as a child, this had caused her some unrest, though she could scarcely articulate it at the time. This is why she always made a determined effort to do her ironing on an almost daily basis. To maintain continuity. Wash dry iron put away. In rotation. Keep the home ticking over, don't put things off, it simply made for more work in the long run. It was the same with tidying up and clearing out. The latter of which Cayenne had almost gotten down to a fine art. She relished the fact that under the beds, the space was mostly clear. She would make a point to assess that what was under there had only been placed temporarily and not simply discarded absentmindedly. It was the same with the children's rooms, much to Diego's dismay and on occasion, acute embarrassment. When she had threatened to photograph and Instagram her findings, she knew that there would not be a repeat of her gruesome discoveries.

She generally felt compelled to micro manage her home and continually evaluate what was stored where, so that areas of neglect did not have room to develop. She refused to simply throw things in a cupboard and adopt the out of sight out of mind mentality. Even her heaving airing cupboard was under regular scrutiny.

She placed a leg of Diego's cargo pants onto the ironing board and fished out a crumpled piece of tissue that had been left in his pocket, which luckily hadn't contaminated the rest of the load with it's speckled fibres. She rolled her eyes and began picking at a few strays of fluff and flicking them somewhere behind her, making a mental note to remember to vacuum her room later Before turning the leg over and ironing the other side, she pressed it to her face and sniffed the fabric. The scent of cotton linen fragrance from the fabric softener, wafted pleasingly through her nostrils. She cast her mind back to childhood years and the several trips she would have to make to the launderette with her mother whenever the washing machine broke down which seemed to be with alarming regularity. She remembered feeling embarrassed to be pulling heavy loads of sheets and towels that had been stuffed in black bin liners and squashed into a shopping trolley that looked as though it had been donated from the help the aged society. Her mother had been quite young at that time, but somehow seemed so old as her low expectations and the worries and cares of this life sapped her youth. When the clothes were eventually dry, Cayenne would squirm uncomfortably as the other ladies in the launderette seemed to have such quality items that smelled like sweet smelling flower beds. Whereas the coarse, brittle sheets that she helped to fold, smelled damp and musky. Many of them, she knew had been handed over by Aunt Meg when she had replaced her own bedding with fluffy new quilts. They had long-since lost their original vibrant colours and soft woollen texture.

And now few things gave Cayenne as much pleasure as the smell of fresh clean linen, or the distinct saturation of Febreze as she entered the house.

'Isn't it funny how childhood experiences shape you more than you realise', she said to herself. She would often tell the children when they were moaning about having to vacuum for more than 30 seconds, about the weekend chores that she and brother Roman had to endure, whereby they were expected to clean the carpet in the whole house with a red wooden, seen better days hard bristled hand brush, not a full length broom in sight and a square metal shovel, the likes of which she hadn't seen since. In fact she wouldn't have been at all surprised if her parents had manufactured it themselves, as it often seemed that they would rather that than give someone else the money and so it was perfectly feasible that her welder father had put his skills to good use.

The metal contraption required them to get down on their hands and knees and cover the designated areas inch by virtual, dusty, inch, their mother having sprinkled droplets of her favourite disinfectant around the house an hour or so previously which would fly violently off the synthetic polyethylene fibres in tiny splatters under the gust of each swipe. It would take them hours to complete the task, taking it in turns until the expanse of cut pile, with it's 70's style multi coloured mismatched design was covered.

Her phone beeped.

"Meeting cancelled - want to do 11.30 at Chanel?"

"I am finding the thought of pressing out creases on a bundle of laundry with varying fabrics with a hot instrument, far more enthralling a prospect".

"See you in our booth and NO LIPSTICK".

She smiled at his show of authority which filled her with excitement and she quickly turned off the iron and slipped into her gym gear in preparation for yoga later. Grabbing a wipe from the bathroom cabinet she looked at her reflection, wiping off the nude matt colour from her lips that she had carefully applied earlier within the lines of her chocolate brown lip liner. When it had all been removed, she rooted in her makeup bag for her red Maybelline alternative that stood out as the one that was the most durable. Following the outline of her ample lips so as to make them appear even bigger, she tilted her head from side to side to scrutinise her efforts. Wiping away evidence of a slight slip of her hand, she was now ready to fill them in. She chose her new Charlotte Tilbury hot red edition, unscrewing the gold tubular stick and filling the lining of her lips in generously, taking care to apply as many layers as was feasible. Dabbing the lips with some tissue to blot off the excess, she applied another two coats on top. She smirked mischievously at the thought of his dismay when he walked into the café and caught sight of her act of defiance, picturing the fantasy that would be playing out in his mind, as he spread her over his knee and spanked her bare bottom ferociously until it was sore enough to require the healing balm of his tongue.

Luckily a booth became available just as she walked around towards the open plan rear of the café, as a couple exited clutching their matching laptops.

Cayenne swiped the remnants of their left over coffees and what looked like the remains of macaroni cheese, towards the edge of the table and took out a wipe to clean the residue of coffee stains, sprinkles of sugar and cake crumbs into a ball, tossing the soiled paper into an empty coffee cup.

She had ordered their drinks, coffee for him, a pot of Earl Grey for her, even though this was an honour usually reserved for him.

76

Minutes later, she looked up to see his quirky stroll approaching, his head tilting from side to side as he walked as though straining ahead to catch a glorious glimpse. She had guessed that he had developed his inimitable walk as a child. She could just imagine a pre school Kenneth Halpern-Smith, with a shy bashful demeanour, embarking on his first real reluctant departure from his mother's apron, wandering in late, long after everyone else had already assembled and being introduced via a few strategic 'getting-to-know-you' nursery rhymes. The late arrival, which he would evidently fail to outgrow, would suddenly acquire a deeper colour to his cheeks as his parents ushered him towards the baying crowd who were now sitting smugly in pairs on the carpet in the story corner. Little Kenneth was probably one of those kids who always seemed to find themselves slightly on the outside of things, on the outskirts of the mix, never quite sure whether he fitted in or whether these newly acquired friends would still be quite as attentive if he hadn't continued to petition them with the sweet bribery stash that he had managed to swipe when mother wasn't looking. Would he still be popular if he hadn't been so obliging in allowing himself to be the butt of their collective jokes or been quite so willing to hand over his much coveted, comic books As the years passed, he learned that it was far less painful to simply conform. Make the necessary adjustments to not stand out. To blend and curtail anything that was unique and original about himself.

She supposed he had never quite grown out of that bashful, self conscious walk, and no perceptive adult had thought to knock it out of him, or had the wherewithal to point out that that wasn't actually his walk, just one adopted from circumstance.

Although, looking at the fully grown Kenneth Halpern-Smith, waltzing towards her, adult in some respects at least, she wouldn't have been at all surprised if the walk was another opportunity to flick his beloved long curtain fringe, another feature he should surely have outgrown. The length and style of his hair was certainly a source of comfort.

He looked intently at her bulbous red shiny lips and bit his own in annoyance. She could see the irritation in his eyes that he scarcely attempted to hide. Cayenne attempted to pout as potently, yet subtly as possible.

"Oh you bought the drinks?. I should be doing that. Oh thank you very much, that's very kind. And cake too". He picked up his individual Victoria sponge and looked over at her tart citron.

"You're welcome to have this one if you'd prefer, I really don't mind which one I have".

"No no, this is er…. perfect". He laughed with a sense of incredulity as though no one had ever bought him a cake before.

The disdain at her non-compliance drained away as he basked in appreciation.

She too smiled as the warm glow bubbled up on the inside. It was incredibly endearing to see him so appreciative of such a small gesture.

She stirred her tea, extracting as much of the potent flavour as she could before pouring half into her cup and saucer and adding a handful of sachets of brown sugar to make up for the lack of rum that she would normally add at home.

He removed the lid from his coffee and took a sip.

"I see you totally ignored my request for no lipstick. You did that on purpose didn't you?".

Cayenne picked up her spoon and dipped into the centre of tart citron and licked the spoon seductively before clasping it in her mouth and pulling it out as slowly as possible.

"Well I didn't see why you should be granted all of your requests when I am repeatedly denied mine".

He tipped his head to the side in that school boy fashion as though hoping his hair would be sufficient to hide his embarrassment.

"Touche".

He took another sip from his coffee, not once taking his eyes from her.

"Look….". he stopped short and looked at her, from her hair down to the gym bra just visible inside her khaki mac and let out a deep sigh, which spoke more words than he was able to utter.

She secretly cursed herself for being so damned understanding. Most normal people would simply demand to know what the hold up was, why was he so reticent having invested so much into her pursuit. But something held her back.

"I fully intend to make good on my promise, I assure you". After a lengthy pause, she could see the switch in his eyes and it was at this point that she knew she was about to get the usual spiel. He knew it too which is why he suddenly avoided her eyes and instead looked beyond her, out of the back window overlooking the quay.

"There's been a lot of pressure at work, I've really been having a bad time. The company's going through some changes and head office in New York are piling on the pressure. I have never seen my boss look so stressed".

Cayenne continued to pick at the tart which proved to be a little too tart for enjoyment. She wished she had picked up a little pot of honey to pour over the top to balance out the flavours.

"Look, I don't want to just book it and then find that I haven't got the time to enjoy it properly. Do you understand?". His eyes were pleading unutterable words.

She nodded unable to disguise the heaviness she felt.

His shoulders visibly sunk to match the defeatist drop of his head. She could detect his own self loathing and had no desire to add to his pain, even if it diminished her perception of her white knight somewhat. In fact, at this point, he couldn't look any more distant from the assertive stranger that had grabbed her attention months ago.

She knew that he too could sense the admiration slipping away and he needed to recover the situation with some urgency if he was to hold of his exotic new discovery.

CHAPTER 8

"Geeeeeeently come into Utkatasana, intense pose", Josephine crowed as she demonstrated the challenge of sitting back on her heels and raising her hands to the sky. "It is also known as 'chair pose' as it's like a sittin' back into a chair. Make sure you can see your toes, sit right back. Press your kneeeees and feet togever, tuck your tail bone in to leeeeeeeeenthen the spine". This was an absurd, nigh on impossible adaptation as far as Cayenne was concerned. It felt totally unnatural to her body, which is exactly why she persevered to follow Josephine's instructions to the letter as she was convinced doing so would surely permit her entry into some kind of zen utopia at the end of the yoga journey.

"Hips back, chest forward, aaaaaarms to the skyyy, stretchin' out the fingers to the ceilin', joinin' the paaaalms togever is your option. Tryyyyy to keep the aaaaarms in liiiiiine wiv your ears.

Although it's quite a challengin' pose, it is increasin' strengf, balance and stability in the body. The hamstrings, the quads, the glutes are all bein' strengfened.

Come up to standin' and raaaise your aaaarms to the sky and into a backbend. Foldin' forwards hands to mat, raise the chin to the top of the mat, foldin' forwards again onto the mat.

Come to a squat pose moooovin' your feet out wiiiiider if it's comfortable. Hands to prayer, geeently press the knees outwards usin' your elbows and feeeeeel the openin' of the hips.

Now for those of you that have been practicing with me for some time and are familiar with 'crow', you can go ahead and adopt the crow pose. The rest of you, come with me".

Cayenne loved this part, having discovered that she was getting quite good at it. She marvelled at the progress she had made since the first time she had practised crow and how impossible it had seemed, until it wasn't. She was reminded of the words of the Great Nelson Mandela, who said 'every challenge seems impossible until it's done'.

She glanced in the corner of her eye at the less successful attempts around her and wished she could encourage them that perseverance really was key. Cayenne hardly considered herself a yoga type and looked the complete opposite of many of the lithe limbed slim devotees around her.

She bent over, placing her knees into the back of her triceps and gently hoisted herself skyward. She felt slightly wobbly at first, but willed her wrists to hold out, forcing them into submission. She raised her feet into the air. "For those of you in the full crow pose, joinin' your toes togever is your option".

The rest of you, raise your hand if you want me to come and assist you".

Yet again in the semi darkness, to the earthly hummings and the eastern sounds emanating around the room, Cayenne was flying.

"Home ok?"

"Yes thank you.

Au revoir, my regards to Zurich". He had dropped that bombshell as they prepared to separate outside Chanel earlier, with his hands firmly on her tight ass. Completing the speech he had begun a little earlier, something about difficulties in the Switzerland branch, filling in for someone in his team. To think he actually managed a team?. She hadn't thought he had it in him.

"Send me a picture of what you're doing right now".

"I fear I am unable to recover from this sudden betrayal". She rolled her eyes at herself. 'here I go again' she thought as she could feel her body responding to the hunger welling up inside her.

"You are deserting a woman with famished pussy. Surely you are no man at all.

Enjoy the Swiss bitches… match made in underbelly heaven".

Admittedly she had succumbed to the calling of the bottle of Lindelmans sitting on the work surface on her return from Yoga which was partially fuelling her prose.

"The Queen WILL get to view her realm in PANORAMIC glory".

"If you are going away for some considerable time then I want you to fly me there and ravish me with a Swiss fuck fest"

"Do you still like your counterfeit whore?".

"A little too much". There. She said it.

"God only knows what I see in a whore that fails to deliver and inspires pussy hunger to the extreme".

"I'm glad that we keep to high end rules".

Cayenne rolled her eyes, doubting his sincerity.

"I could have been a depraved local whore this afternoon, not sure that would have been healthy for either of us". He was alluding to the offer he had made to stow her away for the afternoon at the local Hilton. She had declined.

"if you go away when I'm in this hungry state... I actually think that frustration will turn to deep resentment.

Not that I believe that you're actually going anywhere near Switzerland".

"Do you want it this afternoon?"

"I can't see you anymore. Please respect my wishes.

The time has come to end this chapter.

THE END"

" I can't actually help being drafted to Zurich.

I'm booking the Shard... If you want to come by I'd really appreciate it. I will leave it up to you gorgeous".

On her way to pick up Sugar from school, he continued the onslaught.

"I can get out of a meeting later this afternoon. Meet me for a tea. Please".

Her feisty resolve all but gone, "…. Then I'll want a hug… then a kiss… then my pussy will yearn for a touch… then I'll need to be fucked ravenously.

None of which my pathetic Swiss seeking suburban whore can deliver…

Are you still here?. Just go. GO!

Don't even look back".

"SWW – suburban white whore… is actually sad".

"It's been memorable".

"The fun will continue.

Meet me for tea or more?. NTK".

"What does NTK mean?"

"Need to know".

"No".

"Fucking tormented.

Want my hands on you

Want my mouth on you

Want my cock in you. Thinking of you in your hot black dress".

"If you really want it.... all things are possible.

I'm removing my thong... pussy airing time. Think on this mid-flight".

"Fuck this. I want you now. Be at the Hilton at 5.15pm. I'm booking the room. Be waiting. Can't stand it any longer. I shall deliver for my Queen".

Any thoughts of weakness or resenting giving in so easily were fleeting. His masterful demanding instructions caused multiple knicker changes as she rustled up pan fried steak and oven potatoes for the children. Sugar's favourite.

Cayenne glanced anxiously at her wall clock certain that Diego should be home by now. Just at that moment, she heard the faint chime of the elevator signalling its arrival on their floor. As there were only two families on each level, a heavenly advantage compared to most apartment's on the square, chances were high that it was indeed her son returning. She heard his familiar cheerful whistle as he approached their door and the customary multiple successive rings on the doorbell even though he had a key. She was sure that he loved to hear his little sister running along the hallway in her padded socks, where he would wait for her to call out, demanding the family code.

"Who is it? she would ask in her best Judge Judy voice.

The person on the other side of the door would have to say the password in a convincing enough tone for Sugar to open the door. She wasn't quite tall enough for her eye to reach the peep hole, so she heavily relied upon the tone of voice, as the accurate password was clearly insufficient evidence for the astute pre-teen.

Cayenne could just make out Diego's subdued response as he refused to jump to his little sister's lengthy commands of "I can't hear you, say it again. Louder".

Eventually depending on her mood, she would open the door only to be swung in the air, part punishment for making him wait too long and part adoration as though she was a sight for his sore eyes. Her squeals could be heard across the square as she buried her head in her older brother's shoulder.

"Sugar, you're my best friend", he would murmur as they lapsed into lengthy discussions about their current Animé obsession, Sugar being a total tomboy when it came to her leisure pursuits. Cayenne would sometimes listen outside the door barely understanding what they were talking about but her heart warming as they became absorbed in their mythical Japanese world.

"Dinner's ready". She called out to deaf ears as she tipped out a plateful of bronzed potatoes next to the large piece of steak onto Ocean's plate. She set it down on the dining table in front of the half finished jigsaw puzzle that they were currently challenging him with. She could see that the train and the boat in the picture were almost complete along with half of the border. She ruffled his hair proudly and ran to her room to grab her handbag.

She hoped she hadn't got too sweaty in the school run rush. His command had been short notice and hadn't given her too much time.

She sniffed her armpits and dipped her head under her dress to give the fanny a quick sniff.

"ummm it's ok", she determined, giving it a quick spray of deodorant.

Not that he'd have minded if she hadn't. In fact he quickly confirmed, she really shouldn't have. Something about it interrupting the salty smell that was more to his taste.

The essence that was now devouring his senses. Pulling her legs apart and elevating her yoga nurtured buns in the air to allow him complete entry. She placed her hand on his shoulders to encourage him to slow down, go easy, be gentle. Her attempts were to no avail. Gone was the tentative executive and in his place was a newly determined Wharf Knight who was not about to listen to her wails now having managed to dissuade her from her own city limits. Not when he had been forced to listen to her accusations, albeit correct, of his inability to deliver. Now he had her at his whim. At his mercy, she would not escape without full execution of the rules. The terms. Hell the wants.

When he had finally satisfied himself with as much hot caramel as he could desire, the fact that she had managed to come twice during his feasting was simply by default as this had been purely about what he wanted and needed.

She had never known such hunger. Such yearning. Such desperate thirst.

She had had no choice but to succumb. Laying back and allowing him free reign of her vaginal canal. Happily surrendering to his expert handling as he manipulated her flow like a true professional. She allowed him to flip her over and back around, thoroughly enjoying how amplified she was becoming.

The screams increased drastically the moment he entered her. The wait had been too long. The teasing too extreme, the temptation too great.

He plundered her mercilessly, thundering into her, following the path that his fingers and tongue had paved.

Showing absolutely no regard for her hips and thighs as his full weight pressed down on her before rising up again and forcefully pressing in again and again.

She flopped around drunkenly as he flipped her on all fours and grabbed her hips from behind pulling, yanking her towards him, letting out a throaty moan as his cock banged against the tip of her urethra. She was overcome with dizziness as he spun her around again, pinning her knees down with his arms until she found herself in a happy baby pose that her yoga teachers would be proud of. Happy baby indeed, as he rode her like a champion jockey, hurtling ahead of the competition, blinkers on, pressing forward with no distractions. Not even the sound of other hotel guests, or the rattling noise of room service staff, delivering and retrieving the menu requests. Any of them passing room 407, would unmistakably be made aware that the occupants were already feasting. Ravenously.

He was ploughing on like a missile, intent on one destination. The finish line in his sights. There was absolutely no stopping him now.

CHAPTER 9

After working at the Primary school for little more than a month, it no longer surprised her that the reception area was fortified with impenetrable glass windows and the only access was via two double security doors. The behaviour, especially of the two elder years of the school, who were supposed to be the role models, didn't bode well for the younger children to follow.

There was a particular gang of culprits who tried desperately to outperform each other by seeing who could get away with more and who could show the most defiance and disrespect.

Barely a week went by without incident, and Cayenne could guarantee that as she was hanging up her staff apron, gleefully preparing to leave each day, that there would be a string of the usual suspects lined up outside the headmistresses' office, with bored expressions on their faces, knowing full well that any punishment they were likely to receive would be the most minimal deterrent for the same thing happening again the next day.

"What have you done this time Mustafa?", she enquired on her way out to the playground. Mustafa was a defiant, but cheeky young man, with dark skin, curly hair and prominent front teeth, who seemingly despised school and any form of authority, but the more Cayenne observed a hint of warmth in his eyes, she was convinced that his behaviour was born out of a deep unconscious desire for real definitive leadership. He simply shrugged at her and grinned, probably bemused that she was even attempting to question a tradition that had become mythos long before she arrived.

She recalled passing a short lady in reception one morning and overhearing her saying in broken English that she was there to collect Mustafa. She barely matched the average primary school height, as she peered anxiously over the counter and spoke in little more than a whisper. A rotund, circular frame hidden behind layers of traditional linen. Soft timid eyes peered out from the small window of her garment.

Cayenne wondered if there was an authoritative figure waiting for the boy at home but judging by the nonchalant manner in which he had barged out of the reception doors, barely acknowledging his mother's presence, Cayenne highly doubted it. Had Diego displayed this kind of dissent, he would have been shipped off indefinitely on a holy pilgrimage. Destination unknown.

Whilst the boys tended to give her a wide berth, opting to harass the assistants with a far less menacing demeanour, the girls gravitated towards her, much to her surprise. They were usually fascinated with how she had applied her make up that day or what colour she had decided to paint her nails. They often asked about the shoes she was wearing, enquiring where she bought them from and mentioning that someone or other that they knew had some that were similar.

The younger girls often snuck up beside her and took hold of her hand, needing reassurance in the harsh post toddler actuality.

The older girls were already showing signs of the teenage angst that awaited them beyond the primary school gates. Gangs seemed to form relatively quickly, with last week's pick of the month suddenly and unceremoniously ousted, for no apparent reason other than they clearly hadn't followed the rules of that particular week's negotiated uniform adjustment. These disputes proved a little more challenging to overcome, as Cayenne often found herself firmly attached to the evictee for the whole lunchtime period as they served their penance for failing to adhere to the gang ordinance.

Needless to say, she was finding the two hour stints mentally exhausting. She was particularly looking forward to the detour for lunch that afternoon, even though the glow she had awoken with would be all but gone after a harrowing afternoon at the inoperative correctional facility.

"Pumpkins after work?", was his earnest request that morning.

She was aware of the large Wine bar come restaurant on the corner of West Ferry road, largely because hordes of city workers tended to congregate there, especially on a Friday night, no doubt to relieve themselves of the corporate stresses and obliterate the hectic challenges of the week with several bottles of Prosecco and litres of ale. Cayenne could remember strolling past on occasion and almost wishing she could join in the camaraderie emanating from the large outdoor terraces with their wicker tables and elaborate exotic looking plants in huge concrete pots which were stationed around. It was as though they had been working all week towards this moment to relax and let off steam before dispersing towards the DLR or Canary Wharf underground station or to their underground parking bays and hotfooting it out of the city until Monday.

On this Tuesday early afternoon, however, there was no such crowd. There was no one enjoying an alfresco lunch and the outdoor terrace was empty. It almost looked to her as though there may have been some mistake and that it may in fact be closed. She walked past the expanse of tinted windows that made up the front of the establishment, turning the corner in search of the entrance which clearly wished to remain obscured. When she found no joy, she retraced her steps only to find that she must have walked right past the door in her haste.

Stepping into the foyer, a dark stained wooden bar dominated the area which was covered in black and white piano tilling. To her left was a quiet area with several tables and leather chairs either side and a grand piano in the corner. To her right, were lines of larger dining tables, pushed together, varying in size depending upon the number in the luncheon parties they were expecting. A shock of pink caught her wandering eye. Glancing up, the familiar curtain of floppy hair signalled that the arrival of the right honourable Lord Kenneth Halpern-Smith had already taken place. A uniformed gentleman approached her with pen and paper in hand.

"Can I help you madam? Will that be a table for one?".

Cayenne tilted her head and peered around him. "Actually no, my lunch date is already here".

The waiter looked over his shoulder at a smiling Kenneth and escorted her towards the table at the far end of the room. Cayenne became aware that two sides of the room were glazed, which meant he would have seen her strolling past, going in the wrong direction and then back again.

He rose and reached for her hand and leaned in to kiss her cheek before steering her around to the conjoined seating that ran alongside the wall, the full length of the room.

He was smiling and bashful.

She nestled into the deep spongy padded seating that was covered in maroon leather and returned his gaze.

He kept looking at her for a moment, his eyes conveying everything he really wanted to say.

"How are you?".

"I'm good, you?".

"Better now. You look incredible".

"Thank you". Cayenne would normally receive such compliments with a pinch of salt, her nature tending to question the sincerity of the source. But with this guy, she saw such truth in his eyes pertaining to what he saw and how he felt that the integrity, in this context at least, was unquestionable. So much so that all one could do was accept it and absorb it.

"I saw you walking past".

She smiled sheepishly.

"I wasn't sure where the entrance was, so I thought I'd walk around the corner to try to find it not realising that I'd already passed it".

He chuckled, shyly. "I actually thought that you were going to punish me by deliberately walking past in that tight figure hugging dress, your hair flowing in the wind, looking stunning. I thought 'she's actually going to just saunter past and disappear into the sunshine'. I was so relieved when you turned back around".

Cayenne dissolved into laughter at the thought that he actually considered she would be that callous. Secretly she wished she had only thought of it.

A waitress appeared with a pen and notepad in hand and carrying some menus.

"Excuse me, would you be ready to order. Can I get you some drinks?" she asked in a deep authentic Italian accent.

Kenneth pulled his eyes away from her momentarily to glance at the waitress, a hint of irritation emerged that perhaps she had interrupted a moment.

"eerr," he shook his head as though food was the last thing on his mind, but then thought better of it. " are you hungry?". He turned back to her with concerned eyes.

"Very".

"What would you like to drink, red or white?".

Cayenne's tipple of choice was usually a full-bodied red wine, however with the sun shining and tingling in appreciative company, she distinctly embraced a sparkling white mood.

"Prosecco perhaps".

Kenneth glanced at the waitress again, who nodded affirmatively that she could certainly provide a good Prosecco for them.

"A bottle of Prosecco then please, and we will take a quick look at the menu".

"Certainly Sir", she placed a menu in front of each of them before disappearing in the direction of the bar.

Kenneth immediately ignored his menu, leaning his elbows on the table and covering his mouth.

"You do look gorgeous".

She smiled warmly at him.

"Are you ok, how's your day been"?.

Cayenne rolled her eyes in answer, not wishing to ruin her mood with recounts of delinquent behaviour, opting to turn the focus back to him.

"How are things at work?. Still busy?".

"Yeah, well you know it's been hectic lately right?".

There was the slight antipodean lilt again, as he leaned back in his chair, hunching his shoulders slightly. "Look, I don't particularly want to go away, but it's my team, so I have to go".

Cayenne tapped her fingers on the table and smirked. "If you think I believe that story, you're more stupid than I thought. I don't believe you're going anywhere near Zurich. If you were, you'd take me with you".

"There's nothing much to see there Babe". He said with merely a hint of earnest. "It wouldn't match up to the Queen's standards. It's a really small quaint town, a regular hotel. There's a guy who works in the hotel there, Sven, and he usually shows me around and occasionally joins me for dinner". He was smiling as he began to recount the many nocturnal escapades they had shared. Sven evidently made himself instrumental in relieving the British executives post work boredom.

Cayenne raised her hand to him, taking a full sip of the Prosecco that had been neatly placed in between them.

"I'm sure those stories are very interesting, whenever they actually took place".

Kenneth smiled, "Oh so what you're saying is, I'm simply relaying previous experiences to make it sound as though it's pertaining to my upcoming trip out there". He joined her in sampling the cool, refreshing liquid coolant, nodding approvingly, he took several more sips leaving a tiny amount in the bottom of the glass. He clearly had no intention of confirming or denying her assertion, preferring instead to intently examine the menu.

She wondered whether it was a more personal trip on his schedule. One that he couldn't share details about.

"What do you fancy to eat?".

Cayenne felt a sense of immense triumph, commending herself for her perceptive intuition as she glanced through the lists of Italian delicacies.

She eventually opted for the jumbo prawn linguine with creamy sauce which she felt would go perfectly with the wine. He predictably opted for Spaghetti Bolognese which prompted him to relive a university experience relating to a precarious bowl of Spag Bol, involving a pristine white shirt and a stern university lecturer. Cayenne shook her head bemused by the fact that that the experience still haunted him. She imagined that those four years in a distant town away from home at a formal educational institution of his choice, had moulded him as much as any other life affirming event and she suspected that there were horrors that took place, both real and fearfully imagined, that had frozen him emotionally in that time. These thoughts she kept to herself as she knew, he wouldn't necessarily be open to such introspection. That such a man didn't abide on such a self reflective planet and that he would likely be unnerved by any in-depth form of self scrutiny and that such an element did not feature in his great plan to adhere to society's conventional thinking, to follow the conventional path of completing school, advance to some form of further educational college, proceed to university, graduate with honours, and begin a career in either Law or Accountancy, work his way up, retire relatively comfortably, hopefully fit in marriage and procreation and then die.

No frills, minimal drama. Nothing to draw too much attention to himself, keeping his head down as he endeavoured to achieve a life that would meet his friends' approval and satisfy the barometer that university lead him to believe equated to success.

To not deviate from this well trodden path, would be the ultimate achievement and to detract from suburban convention would surely lead to irrefutable demise.

"God knows where I'll end up if I continue to let you rule me like this. You know that I cannot stand to know you're upset don't you?".

Cayenne smiled appreciatively. It was true, his torment whenever they were at odds was palpable. Consequently, when they were speaking again, the relief seemed to wash over him, restoring his equilibrium.

"How long are you going to put up with me, … your errant whore who seems to be adept at failing to fully deliver?".

The smirk resting on the corners of his mouth whilst formulating the question, suddenly disappeared the moment he began waiting for her answer. She could tell he really did want to know just how much time she was prepared to give him.

"It all seems to be too good to be true. I mean, you should…. you must have men queuing up. I don't understand. ".

"I often ask myself why I put up with you", she pondered as she attempted to spiral the tagliatelle around her fork perfectly and place the content into her mouth with precision.

She knew she was guarding her heart as despite the abiding fervency of his pursuit, he was now holding back from her. She could tell his feelings for her were increasing and that that scared him. She concluded that aside from his cultural programming and individuation, he must have gotten himself into some kind of domestic bind which prohibited him from seeing her as any real prospect. That had clearly been ok in the beginning, but it was almost impossible to ignore the chemistry between them. The fact that they laughed at the same things, harboured the same passions and frisky fetishes which they couldn't fathom sharing with anyone else, had all worked to create a deep understanding. She hadn't even known she had them herself, as whilst she may have dabbled in a bit of steamy text writing on occasion, it had stirred nothing to this degree. His eager reciprocation was clearly fanning the flames of her imagination. She sensed that should they examine their feelings beyond this point, they would effectively come to a stalemate.

"I'll no doubt tire of you eventually", Cayenne raised her finger, fork in hand to cover her mouth whilst she attempted to talk and chew simultaneously.

He seemed to straighten with relief "Well of course. It's only a matter of time before someone snaps you up right?, or else you'll get so annoyed with me and brutally bin me off again".

"Well if memory serves, I have attempted to, but you simply keep coming back. Can't get rid of you".

He replaced his fork and allowed himself to fully appreciate his current mouthful without thinking about the next one as he looked at her intently. The thoughts circling in his head, literally causing his head to sway. "That's cos you're fucking gorgeous. I can't seem to keep away". He licked his lips and pulled his shirt away from his body, avoiding dislocating it completely from the waistband of his trousers, but just enough to check if he'd repeated his university faux pas and stained his crisp shirt. Once assured that the shirt remained spotless, he proceeded with his meal.

"This is actually quite nice. Wanna try some?".

They exchanged forks as had become their custom and both nodded approvingly of the other's dish.

They did the same over dessert. Her with warm jumbo profiteroles with icecream which she heartily exchanged for some of his rich chocolate cake. Cayenne glanced enviously at his spoon as he ate the delicious sponge layered in glistening chocolate sauce, topped with a silky ganache. She could quite easily have finished hers and then given him every assistance to finish his. She managed to restrain herself reasoning that she ought not be greedy.

More intense exchanges continued on the stroll home as he escorted her half way, finding a secluded spot which allowed him to explore her up close. He had been dying to get his hands on that ass ever since seeing her swan past the restaurant window as he sat waiting. Her small waist was cinched in by the diminutive size of her garment, generously protruding out to allow for the covering of her ample bottom. He could feel himself getting hard as he followed her out of the restaurant, as every stride caused the rotatory motion of her glutes, drawing the eye, not just by his judgement but the turning of heads around them. He basked in the rise and fall of each glorious buttock.

The moment he finally cupped them in his hands was beyond euphoric. He almost whistled the National Anthem with utter relief and satisfaction, not to mention a smidgeon of unbelief that his nerdy self could be so damned lucky.

"If only". He paused from exploring her mouth and looked skyward, his hands holding firm around her middle.

"If only what?", her mouth hung open as she looked up at him, wanting the exploration to continue.

"If only there were an apartment nearby that we could go to. There's a load building up inside me that needs somewhere to go".

She dropped her hands to her side, a sense of indignance rising up in her chest. Him coming to her house was out of the question. Firstly, that was her children's home. The fact that the apartment was in fact empty at that precise moment was besides the point. She was never going to be that woman that allowed various men to traipse through her home. The memories of feeling like she had to share her own childhood home with dubious characters, was still far too vivid. She vowed never to do that to them.

Secondly, she simply knew that his opportunistic character would immediately begin to devalue her. That he would cease to make as much effort if she made herself easily accessible. That his regard for her would wane unless he applied considerable dog in the fight.

The fact that he even brought it up evoked an immediate reaction. Her once moist pussy, clenched shut and she could almost hear the hardened steel clanging and the reverberating jangling of iron chains ringing out as they fastened up her vagina, refusing a single further drop of liquid gold. Any desire coursing through her veins, speeding up the blood flow, now recalibrated in a nanosecond. She sighed deeply. He did seem to have a knack for altering her mood from one extreme to another.

He knew it too. Sensed the tension in her body. The stiffness as she walked away. He witnessed the sudden altering of her demeanour as she fastened her robe and adjusted her crown and proceeded to saunter back towards her exclusive domain, turning her back on him with cold resolution, he could only wish that his desire for her would do the same.

CHAPTER 10

It must have been around 2am when she became conscious that she was no longer asleep but that frustrating thoughts were spiralling in her mind and had been for some time whilst her subconscious tried to convince her otherwise.

Eventually she lay there, eyes wide open in the dark, only the stream of light from the apartments opposite and the square below squinted through her curtain's narrow parting. She pulled the duvet up above her head to block them out and allowed the scent of Black Pearl fabric conditioner that was now embedded and interwoven into the fibres of her covering, soothe her mind as she inhaled deep full breaths.

Josephine's teaching somewhere in the back of her mind was urging her to remember the equally deep exhales. 'when you inhale fully, allow the breaf to fill your lungs. Feeeeew the back of your ribcage pressin' down into the mat and feel fuw and energised. When you exhale, allow aaaaall of the breaf to leave your body, releasin' any stress or tension, and enjoooooy the feelin' of bein' empty and spacious'.

The French yoga instructor's voice also interjected with her own mantra, 'let your thoughts pass you by as if on a conveyor belt. Be the observer of your thoughts'.

…even Claudine seemed to caress the air with her poetic tones… 'come oooooon, spread your wings, leave it all behind and let's flyyyyyyyyyyy'.

Images of Kenneth, head hanging to the side as though dangling somewhere in outer space, began to fly across her inner vision. Only the top half of his body was visible and his arms were outstretched as though trying to prevent his departure but to no avail. Then another image of him appeared as though he had somehow managed to climb back aboard the conveyor belt, typically resisting her dismissal. Determined to hang on to her thoughts, fighting tooth and nail for his position. The more she attempted to push him along on a breeze of forgetfulness, the more he seemed to repel and clung on even tighter, refusing to release his hold. For every image of him that emerged, another one of her surfaced to join the contingent in the battle over her mind. She refocused her brain on utilising the full exhales to blow him into oblivion making effective use of the practise she had learned in Yin Yoga, where their internal scan allowed them to identify an ache in the body or an area of tension, which once identified could be blown away with the latest intake of breaf.

Charlotte's soft lilt interjected, 'okay guys... it's time.... Just let it all go'.

He seemed to be winning. In fact half an hour later, thoughts of him were still triumphantly, boldly and smugly interrupting her meditation as the other battle preoccupied her mind. The questions that she had thus far avoided any real attempt at answering. Did he have feelings for her? Real feelings? Or were they simply lustful meaningless notions to relieve his boredom or alleviate whatever tensions he was experiencing in whatever circumstances he was inhabiting. The things that came out of his mouth seemed to suggest the latter. However, in their moments of togetherness and occasionally through his written messages, she could definitely sense something else. When they were together, she saw it in his eyes. He spoke it in the way he touched her. The tenderness and sincerity of his hands as they touched her face. The haunting honesty of his soul, penetrated, not only his glasses, but the protective pupils that could not disguise the hidden thoughts. The energy between them informed her that he cared. The nonverbal messages from him were deep and convincing, yet of course the mouth failed to comply. Refusing vehemently to betray his ego which had it's own single minded objective. Protecting him at all costs. Even from the truth. Even from reality. Protect him it must, even from himself. Stand guard of anything, anyone who threatened to derail him from the traditional track he had set himself that had begun to formulate in preschool. Beginning subtly with the gentle coercion to sit with that group, gather in that corner. Be the same as, identify with. It continued into primary and secondary school as young minds are blended together and individuality slowly becomes subdued. It was nurtured in the suburban culture as his parents tried desperately to fit in to their environment. Refusing to put their head above the parapet and despising any form of extreme distinctiveness, of standing out and drawing too much attention to themselves, other than the occasional ego led, envy inducing new vehicle or family travel plans. Making an exception perhaps for being the first to acquire PVC windows at the height of their endemic popularity or a renovated loft space to distinguish themselves from the Jones'. Throughout all of this controlled fear, young Halpern-Smith eyes were watching and learning.

College and university solidified the doctrine. Enforced the conception that life merely presented a few primal options and one must select one and stick with it. Any form of introspection must be evaded, be observed with suspicion and conjecture at best though total eradication was much preferable. Best achieved by surrounding oneself with like minded people who were equally fearful of living on the other side of the limitations of fear.

The beginning of adult life allows for putting these learned beliefs into practice. Join a company, figure out what everybody else is doing and follow along, ensuring you operate within the guidelines, embracing the subtle cues that encourage avoiding any distinctive flair or originality. Keeping safe by ensuring expectations aren't heightened. Demonstrating conformity and regularity and finding a familiar comfort in that, until ones own voice becomes virtually indiscernible. Eventually, one's choices become deduced by what one thinks is best for everyone else, what would be acceptable to the masses, what would be expected by the family and acceptable to the peer group. This may well continue until one finds oneself a middle aged, professional, still seeking the approval that he was informed he could expect if he simply followed along, perpetually awaiting the commendations and applause from a life lived in coherence and obedience to the norm. Reaching for the rewarding sense of satisfaction one can expect by obtaining the predictable lifestyle that was forewritten and inevitably finding oneself perturbed and confused in a society of increasing anxiety wondering how one came to be locked into a life that one couldn't quite remember choosing.

The career, the friends, the relationship, even the hobbies can often seem out of sync. It would become much like finding oneself in somebody else's life, playing a role in someone else's narrative, with no clue as to how one arrived there, much less how to get out.

God forbid one should happen upon something, someone, some unexpected and unplanned experience, forming a curve ball that posed the question why?. Why do you do what you do?, how did this career come about?. Why are you in this relationship? Is this the life you imagined for yourself?. Do you actually enjoy eating Tapas?. Really enjoy it??. Define an authentic Tapa?.

Seemingly for most, these moments of enlightenment were rare and if suspected upon the horizon by the discerning few, one could always divert oneself from possible conflict by using any number of distractions varying from vices, smoking, drinking, mind numbing entertainment or pursuing regular holidays with alarming missionary synchronicity, determining a different destination the following year to infuse a false sense of impetus and purpose. For some it manifested in an obsession with sex, not because it was truly desired, but the false feeling of status it manifested. The promise of acceptance amongst peers had come to form a powerful societal hindrance to the necessary discomfort of illuminating self scrutiny.

(2am)

"You up?".

(2.46am)

"My Queenly pussy closes tightly at the thought of your cruel disregard...

What erectile force will it require to prize open this delicious confectionary lady cavern?...

I can barely contain the waves of ecstasy threatening to burst the restraints of my temporarily pursed chocolate molten lady lips.

But contain it I MUST.

As such callous desertion must not be rewarded with the rich caramel silk, simmering tantalisingly in the cup of my clit...

Desperately seeking a knight with a resolute power house cock thrust and a dynamically heroic spurt to relieve this maddening torture and satisfy this regal pussy hunger...

Oh where oh where can he be?".

(8.05am)

"I'm on the underground, hurtling towards the inner city enjoying this great morning reading... the dilemma was penned so eloquently...

Did you get a release?"

(8.10am)

"The Queen languishes in cunt despair... heightening an intense hatred towards counterfeit white whores who fabricate urgent business trips in the wake of extreme cunt release famine".

"So cheeky... :)

If only the Queen knew what the break has done for the executive black cunt hunger....

He is positively bereft upon his return".

"It pleases the Queen immensely that Suburban White Whore is viciously reminded that the exclusive path to the Queen's ebony pussy enclave is a heavily laden minefield.... A simple wrong turn could cut off it's molten supply....

The Queen sincerely hopes SWW is engulfed in an abundance of colourless eroticism... that he bares the suffocating sensation of a bland couscous pussy horizon in a Tofu spiceless arena... bleak and devoid of life giving moisture...

Tapas like in nature....

For you have sabotaged the rare golden ticket eligibility …. One so seldom dispersed…"

"The SWW is worried…. The Black Queen has fully fucked his senses…. He needs flavour….   He needs seasoning…He needs blacking….He cannot now abide pussies that lack the essence of scotch bonnet cum juice and jerk pussy extract…he is a disgrace".

Cayenne sat on the balcony after the school run rush, drinking her ritual Earl Grey with a drop of 100% proof Jamaican rum.

She tilted her head back and considered his position. The black Queen and White Whore alter egos allowed him to express what he otherwise daren't even acknowledge, even to himself and certainly not out loud.

He really was worried. His desire for her and she knew it was her, not just any black woman, but her in particular, was now affecting him and his perception of what he wanted and needed in his life, causing him to re-evaluate. But would he ever develop the courage to do anything about it. How could he if he barely acknowledged it himself. She doubted he would ever have the daring to ask himself what he really wanted in life. It seemed he wasn't accustomed to doing so.   He seemed used to allowing circumstances to control him and dictate the course of his life and simply opt out and allow life to happen to him and forever lament and subsequently self medicate his misfortune. 'One must surely know one's own mind and voice in order to effectively direct ones' own life', she pondered aloud.

The words he used ' he is a disgrace', although partially in jest, spoke volumes.

Is that how he really felt about himself. Although she wasn't to know whether he was referring to the association with her, or simply his habit of seeking out extra curricular activities in general.

When she had joined him at the Intercontinental, she recalled to her mind something he said as they stood naked in the hotel bathroom.

He had just finished spanking her naked derriere, something which he thoroughly enjoyed and the image of which fuelled his desperation to persist in relentless pursuit of her for three months without response. He was towelling himself down and with a haunted look in his eyes, he looked at this complete noir stranger and said 'how can I stop?'.

It was perhaps at that point that she took pity on him, saw a glimmer of a helpless soul, lost inside and trying desperately to find himself, wrestling with his drug of choice, trying to numb some kind of pain.

Cayenne decided, as was her nature, to inject some humour into his dilemma.

"The Queen would advise, that the SWW refrain from referring to the desire for Premium cunt juice as a disgrace…

Now…your omittance from pursuing bespoke pussy throughout your adult life…. That Dear Sir is your utter disgrace…

Languish now in the ultimate disgrace of your milk white pussy penitentiary…

Dream of long lost forays into the wonders of equatorial seduction from the confines of your suburb au blanc…."

CHAPTER 11

"If you're fatiguing, come to your knees". Gregory was evidently picking up on the weariness that was now beginning to engulf the class as they neared the finish line of the Muscle Pump session.

They had soared through the intense warm up, followed by the heavy weighted squats where as usual, Cayenne topped the class with her fortified barbell using 30kg weights and completing a million reps in sequence with the music. The chest segment came next which was her least favourite, followed by back and shoulders, which consisted of multiple reps of clean and presses straight into shoulder presses.

Lastly, there was the second leg section with multiple squats and lunges interspersed with push ups on the step. Thankfully the loud music all but drowned out the groans caused by tired limbs. It was only when the music stopped that the force of sweaty panting overtook the room. Cayenne fixed herself in the mirror, eyeballing her image intensely, ordering her reflection to push through and to not even think about stopping or showing any sign of exhaustion. The pain and aching gradually gave way to relief and pride as the high tempo beat, softened to the more mellow, cool down music that filtered through the speakers in the ceiling of the gym as Gregory encouraged them to grab a mat if they so wished, and to lie on their backs in preparation for scissor kicks and Russian twists.

After the class had packed away their equipment, Cayenne high fived Gregory and thanked him for another great class before heading downstairs to the holistic area for yoga. One class followed the other with little time to spare, so she quickly stopped at the fountain to refill her water bottle, downing half of it almost immediately.

Josephine was busy arranging the mats according to her exacting standards. She always liked them spaced out just so, making sure they were in perfect alignment and that there were spaces dotted around for her to slot into, to demonstrate exactly what she wanted close up.

If anyone had made the ill-fated misjudgement of moving a mat, even slightly altering the Josephine Parker vision, the dimness of the lighting effectively concealed the death stare daggers that pierced the offender as they lay unwittingly with their eyes closed.

"We 'ave a few minutes before the class begins as we wait for a few more people, so feel free to liiiie back in Savasana, ooooopenin' your legs as wiiiiiiiide as the mat wiv your hands facin' the ceilin' and your fingers touchin' the floor".

117

The late arrivals signalled their appearance with several unceremonious bangs of the heavy fire door, with little regard for the recumbent crowd.

Josephine waited for everyone to settle as she fiddled with the knobs on the music system, until the familiar haunting refrains sucked anything but calming energy out of the room.

"Start to take some deeeeeeeeeep breafs, breavin' in for the count of fiiiive, holdin' your breaf for a moment, then exhaaaalin' for a count of fiiiive. Continue to do this in your own time, tryin' not to beat the breaf. As you inhale, follow the course of your breaf, feeeelin' the belly riiiiiiise, fillin' the ribcage, feelin' full and energised. As you breave out, let all the breaf leave your body and hold for a moment feeeelin' empty and spacious".

Cayenne tried hard to ignore the sniffles and coughs punctuating the atmosphere and forced herself to subdue the irritation rising up within her. Someone close by was jangling keys. Cayenne opened her eyes and looked in the direction of the offensive sound. An oriental looking lady turned to look at her and froze like a deer in the headlights with a stunned expression on her face as though suddenly finding herself in the direct line of a pride of stampeding lions.

The jangling keys were immediately arrested into submission, with trembling hands allowing Cayenne to regain her zen and allow the deer to live another day.

"Start to take some normal breafs", Josephine was suggesting as she sauntered towards the music centre to lower the volume slightly so that she could be heard above the eastern chants.

"Pull your knees into your chest, tuck in your chin and give yourself a hug, rockin' from siiide to siiide, masaaaaaaagin' the lower back.

Rock yourselves backwards and forwards and come to table top". The class manoeuvred themselves onto all fours. "Keeeepin' a neutral spine, make sure your hands and legs are equal distance apart, then come into downward facin' dog".

"Start to walk the dog out sloooooowly, try to keep the movement in time with your breaf. Come up on to your tip toes at the same time, pressin' the opposite heel to the floor.

Now find some stillness in the pose and we are gonna take 5 breafs in downward facin' dog.

As you breeeeave in, lift your hips in the air and come forward to plank. As you exhale lift your heels and hips and come back into downward facin' dog.

Continue this process for a few more moments in accordance with your own breaf.

Now come back to downward facin' dog. Look between your hands and step forward with your right foot until it is between your hands. Straighten your left leg and come up to standin' with your hands raised to the sky. Look to your hands. Turn your left leg outwards if this is open to you, otherwise remain facin' forward making sure your hips are square to the front of the room. Put your hands to the floor and step or jump back into plank". Whenever Josephine provided them with an option, Cayenne always challenged herself with the more difficult choice. A private internal competition to push herself beyond any previous level of achievement.

"Place your knees on the mat, stretching out your feet and bring your chin and chest to the floor, or take Chaturanga. Come forward into cobra or up dog. Nice!". Whenever Josephine approved or was impressed by their efforts, she would gasp 'nice' barely audibly under her breath and simultaneously clap her hands lightly, almost in applause to herself as well as to her students for a job well done.

Cayenne channelled her energy into strengthening her arms in the crocodile pose, lifting her body weight up into up dog, raising her chest proudly and turning her face to the ceiling.

"Now come back to downward facin' dog. Nice!".

Josephine guided them through this process on the left hand side of their bodies, balancing out both sides before taking her position at the side of the class in front of the mirrored wall.

"Turn to face me and stand with your feet wide apart and your hands on your hips. Tryyyy and keep your hips square towards me. Turn your left foot to the left and your right foot slightly inwards. Bend your left knee and sink doooooown into it as low as is comfortable today. Place your hands behind you, claaasp them togever, try and press your palms togever. Push your shoulders down into your back, relax your shoulders and dip doooown diagonally in the direction of your left knee. Try to keep your back straight, leadin' wiv your chin and chest, dip downwards, raisin' your hands behind you as high as is possible.

This posture is called the humble warrior as we are bowin' down, surreeeeeeenderin' to the mat and to this practice. Nice!".

Cayenne lay down on the thick carpet of room 325 on the third floor of the Hilton Hotel. Her breathe was deep and full as she prepared herself mentally for the next posture. The intimate room was dimly lit, only by the bedside lamps either side of the Queen sized bed with it's royal blue intricately woven cover, with gold tassels around the edge, draping down onto the floor.

She reached her hands behind her head and dug her fingers into the thick pile, readying her bent knees, her feet tucked in towards her buttocks, she hoisted her thighs into the air until only her hands and feet remained grounded, thus completing the full reverse table top posture. Simultaneously, Kenneth hovered over her, hands and feet, arms and legs splayed in downward facing dog. His face levitating above hers, his hips lowering slightly to touch, their torsos facing each other. He was encouraging her to lift her hips higher according to her instructions, whilst she guided him to lift his hips high too, reminding him to bend his knees slightly and lengthen his spine. He began to pant as his body felt the cardio-like effects that the posture was creating in his system, blood coursing through his entire being. Her arms too were becoming increasingly aware of her body's weight and began to bow at the elbows in protest. He quietly challenged her to straighten her arms, telling her she could do it and assuring her that he would reward the rejoining of their hips. Indeed as she summoned the strength to push through her arms until they were almost straight, reconnecting her hips with his, she detected an additional limb that must have subsequently grown in the moment of her temporary weakness. As he pressed his hips towards hers, the full length and girth of his cock, throbbed beneath his loose shorts. Teasing the lace fibres of the slip of fabric between her legs, which soon began to glisten with the moisture now defying gravity and oozing upwards despite her deep back bend. He moved over her, backwards and forwards until involuntary droplets of his juice seeped steadily, forewarning of the imminent avalanche.

He placed his hand under her back and lowered her gently towards the floor, rewarding her effort with miniature butterfly kisses to her brow on her descent. He reached for her hand, raising her to her feet until they stood facing each other. The room was warm, the hazy glow from the dimmed light creating synthetic heat in the atmosphere. Hands on hips she directed her feet toward the right, standing slightly to his left. She guided him to stand tall in mountain pose, spine straight, feet pressing down into the ground, head held high with proud fingers splayed until his whole body was active. His penis was the only element that refused to align itself vertically but rather protruded fiercely outwards and then upwards in a defiant sign of promise. She bent down low into the front knee, sinking downwards, resting her chest slightly above her bent thigh until her head was in line with the tip of his cock.

She glanced up at him bemused that his gaze remained straight ahead in deep concentration or anticipation. His eyelids began to flutter until eventually his eyes rolled downward and their gazes met. Her eyes communicated stern cooperation was expected and that he must now pay acute attention to every detail of her posture in order that he may replicate it shortly afterwards.

Taking a deep full intake of breath, allowing her chin to lead her down still further, raising her clasped hands behind her, she felt the soft warm touch of his hands as they embraced hers.

Opening her mouth wide and allowing her salivating tongue to encapsulate as much of his penis as was comfortable today, moving her head the length and breadth of his manhood, opening the neck muscles whilst enticing the inner volcanic stirrings beyond his lower abdomen, she surrendered herself in submission, like a truly humble warrioress to the semi naked mountainous monument standing before her. He gripped her hands, guiding her head back and forth in accordance with urgings deep within his scrotum. He moved his free hand, resting it suggestively above the crack of her bottom and fingered the delicacy surrounding her anus. They both closed their eyes savouring the intoxicating effects.

Once her submission was complete, though his hardness indicated, his hunger was not, she rose to standing, feet wider than hip width and rested her hands to her sides to embrace her own mountain stance.

She saw a slight nervous glint in his eye, which was quickly overtaken with a look of hungry desire as his eyes followed the trail of liquid silk to it's source in the natural parting of her landing strip.

He instinctively bent down to sup as one would dip one's head to a water fountain, but her sharp exhale alerted him that he must follow the proper procedure if he wished for full reward.

He squinted whilst looking upwards, trying hard to retrieve from memory the pattern that she had just shown him but that was now elusively drifting from his mind's grasp.

Gradually he turned his feet out to his right, slightly to her left. Trying desperately to ignore the milky moisture which was attempting to lure the attention of his eyeline. He sank deeply into his right knee and placed his hands behind him, fiddling awkwardly as his palms refused to meet. Taking a deep inhale of breath, he bent down rapidly, before pulling back slightly to readjust his posture and ensure his spine was straight and that he was leading with his chest and not his head. The effort that this demanded, challenging his centre of gravity.

He could scarcely hide the smirk creeping onto the corners of his lips as his loins sensed the satiety of immediate consumption.

She edged her feet out wider and tilted her pelvis to both elongate her spine and assist in bridging the gap from her lady lips to his tongue.

His warrior submission was as lowly as it was intense. His tongue foraging with light, progressively deepening strokes, striving to seek but not wanting to thwart the journey, preferring a scenic rummage through her womanly forest in search of the base of her mountain, the origins of her river.

She reached behind him and covered his hands with hers, pressing his damp head further towards her as his lips and tongue paved the passage for the thick caramel honey that he was certain to find.

Realising he needed no aid and that the passion of his pursuit was sufficient to stir her concentrated flow, she closed her eyes, placing her palms together at her heart's centre. "Nice!".

CHAPTER 12

"Gaucho? I leave at the end of the week. Would be good to see you".

She knew that the moment the elevator doors closed that an attack was imminent. She could have cut the tension with a knife even though his eyes avoided hers and hers his.

She squeezed the living daylights out of her pelvic floor in the hope that she wouldn't embarrass herself emerging from the elevator leaving a trail of coconut cream in her wake.

She needn't have worried, for before the elevator, taking them from the ground to second floor of Gaucho could properly close, he was on his knees supping on her nutmeg fondant, devouring her sweet papaya, leaving little room for the proposed steak lunch. She grabbed a handful of his hair and thrust him fully beneath her hem, resting one leg expertly on the opposing elevator wall, she pussy fucked his face with immense fervour, showing no mercy on the refilling of his lungs, using the tip of his pointed nose to part her couture cocoa flaps, smothering him in a steamy Heston Blumenthalesque froth. So it proved that he spent the entire afternoon pushing his Sirloin around the plate, barely nibbling the fries that were standing tall like little soldiers in their individual metal rack. She knew it wasn't that she had made the wrong menu choice, having allowed her to order for him, rather unbeknownst to the waiter, she knew he would need those moments to recuperate from the brutality of his ferocious face fuck.

Cayenne on the other hand, happily munched her way through her own truffle mash. Thoroughly enjoying her rib eyed steak, helping herself to large handfuls of his fries whilst simultaneously swiping generous portions of hardened cock beneath the table.

As usual the restaurant was almost empty at lunch time. She wondered whether it was any busier during the evening hours. Not that she was complaining. The scarce ambience allowed for barely disguised fondling. Just the touch of the pointed tip of his dick almost brought her simmering molten to the boil, assuring a double helping of chocolate ganache, only one of which requiring a spoon.

Just knowing and seeing the effect her strokes were having on him, turned her on even more. She had to force herself not to whip up her skirt, pull out his load and sit on it, rocking both of their tensions away under the breeze of the art deco air conditioning.

Instead she had to make do with a fingering prelude over their shared peach cobbler.

Delighting that the white cotton table cloth was concealing the fact that her legs were spread as wide as she could manage, unveiling the subsequent odour that would have been an ideal accompaniment to her native exotic Ackee fruit, as he tenderly massaged the softness beyond her bush, their eyes clinging to each other, both emanating pain of some sort. The pain of longing and of unexplored feelings.

A pain that they hurriedly strummed on their descent back to the ground floor.

"Home safely?"

"Just about to shower".

"Wish I could watch. Want to see your body glistening under the water. Show me".

She positioned her iphone gently on the soap rack, propping it up with folded flannels to prevent it from slipping into the tub.

She videoed herself rinsing her skin of the afternoon and freshening her crack with delicately scented strokes. Turning around seductively, she bent over to scrub her lower leg, deliberately exposing his second sighting of tight rump barely an hour after the first. Most of which had been returned to the kitchen uneaten. An unthinkable prospect for her own sizzling booty.

The video he had sent her in response, showed that he too was in the shower and by the jerky movements causing his whole body to vibrate, it was obvious that he was getting off on the images of his real life chocolate after eight.

CHAPTER 13

By the time she had changed and headed out of the door for the school run, she was running late. The clock on her phone told her it was 3.28pm which meant that she had exactly two minutes to run to the end of Glover street, a quarter mile distance from door to door. Cayenne always tried her best to avoid leaving her daughter standing alone with the teacher for too long as Sugar would tell her in no uncertain terms that the last thing she wanted to do was stand in close proximity to Mrs Khan who she could barely tolerate during school hours surrounded by the rest of the class, let alone be the last one standing at home time.

"She's weird mom". Her daughter would lament. "Sometimes, she leaves the class and then I'll glance up and she'll be just standing there, hiding around the corner listening like this...". At this point, her daughter, the great imitator, would stand up and hunch her shoulders and allow for her long black hair to fall over her face like Yoko Ono, with two small dark piercing eyes, staring out from behind.

Once she had crossed the main road, she broke into an all out sprint, swinging her arms to propel her forward, remembering the images of Michael Johnson with his back perfectly straight whilst dominating the 400metre heats, with unnaturally high knees. She quite enjoyed putting herself under pressure like this, firstly she knew that the distance was manageable and that she wouldn't' tire too much, and truthfully, she quite liked showing off and darting past several other moms who would never dream of walking too fast, much less run. To be able to leave them in a cloud of dust with relative ease gave her no end of satisfaction. Cayenne forced herself to straighten her back and slow to a gentle jog to the finish line. Sugar was standing with two other Beatles of tardy parents and she could tell by the glare in her daughter's eye that there would be a price to pay for this show of irresponsibility.

Year six children were actually permitted to walk home alone if their parent's sanctioned it and a few of Sugar's friends were allowed to brave the main road by themselves and make their own way home, even during the shorter winter days. Sugar periodically asked whether she could do the same but her mother's intuition, decided that she wasn't quite ready or confident enough yet. She knew Sugar was secretly relieved at the fact that either her mother or Diego would be waiting to escort her home.

Diego made sure he maximised big brother posturing whenever it was his turn. Often wearing a scarf over his mouth or hunching his shoulders authoritatively, ensuring that everyone knew that his little sister was

130

adequately protected. The following day Sugar would report that many of her peers had commented on how 'hard' her big brother looked. Cayenne was sure that this was one of the reasons Sugar had avoided any major issues with some of the dominant characters in her school year. An unsmiling mum that spoke very little and was capable of running like Merlene Ottey and a big scary "hench" looking brother, clearly put paid to any opportunistic playground egos.

"We've got letters", Sugar mumbled rooting in her pink rucksack for a wedge of paperwork that the children had been handed.

"What are they?", Cayenne tried to disguise her lack of interest.

Sugar glanced at them one by one. "Well...there's a school trip to the Natural History Museum next week, we are doing a project on the Romans", she handed the top sheet to her mother.

"...and another trip to a Mosque in North London, as part of religious studies", she handed her mother the second sheet.

"and a leaflet about parent groups, there's loads mom".

Cayenne had seen the leaflet before and had only ventured to attend one course regarding communication with teenagers which she hadn't found particularly useful. It seemed to be all about not saying the word 'no' and negotiating with your children once they were into their teens and the harmful effects of being too authoritative once they came of age. Cayenne hadn't agreed with a lot of the philosophies that the course was attempting to instill and she had told Diego as much. Quoting her

131

favourite mentor Judge Judy, she had reminded him 'as long as you live under my roof, I own the air you breathe'. She may even have said as much during the course, much to the course leader's disdain. She had decided after that that these courses clearly weren't designed for a free thinking person like herself and had deliberately avoided them ever since. She scanned the list in case something of interest caught her eye. Just then something did. Tennis lessons. Wow. Tennis lessons. Cayenne had loved watching tennis since she was a child and watching Wimbledon and the smaller events leading up to the historic tournament, was one of the highlights of her summer. When they had lived in Torquay, she had taken advantage of the large back garden and erected a tennis net and acquired some tennis racquets. The children loved playing after school and visitors were often found wrestling for points on her back lawn rather than sitting in the house. After getting fed up of losing balls to the neighbours, they had eventually taken to using Badminton shuttlecocks instead which were considerably harder to lose. The idea that they could actually be taught by semi-professional coaches dispatched by their local Borough Council, was exhilarating.

Jill Hopley was the group coordinator. Cayenne had met her before as she was the driving force behind the numerous courses for self development that the school ran which made this particular Junior and Infant school one of the most proactive in the entire borough. Jill worked tirelessly and selflessly to petition for funds to encourage parents to participate and improve themselves, which had made her a much loved member of the community. All colours and creed gravitated

132

towards her and were happy to break their traditional codes of discreet conduct, to embrace her warmly.

From basic maths to internet awareness, parents from far and wide flocked to the old school keeper's house that had now been converted into a development centre on the school grounds, to sign up for extra curricular classes to either support their children or to expand their own experience. The walls in the hallway were dotted with pictures of the parents enjoying jogging, sailing and football, knitting and baking for mums and dads.

Part of what made these courses successful was Jill's engaging personality. She seemed to possess inexhaustible energy that could not fail to infuse otherwise lethargic or despondent parents into action. The school's internet website, proudly boasted the many achievements of those parents that had chosen to commit themselves, many attaining recognised certificates for sailing or completing Jamie Oliver healthy eating programmes, knitting and even ceramic textiles.

Cayenne and the children had often walked past the expansive side by side tennis courts in the middle of St Edward's Park minutes away from their block. It was gated and appeared to be closed most of the time which Cayenne was now learning was due to the fact that court time had to be pre-booked via the website, which not only ensured that the courts never became congested, but invariably deterred the site from degenerating into a playground for aimless delinquents. As a result the court remained clean and ready for practice at all times.

Jill and the two tennis instructors were waiting inside the wired fenced court on the morning of the first practice. A small number of other mums had begun gathering also, most of whom were adorned with their native scarves and hijabs, their tennis shoes and trainers barely peeping out from beneath their conservative garments.

One or two of the ladies looked familiar to Cayenne, their paths most likely, having crossed on one of the other courses. But most of them, she hadn't met or could even remember noticing. She wasn't likely to know many of them closely as she tended to stand alone when waiting for Sugar. The only other parent that she had taken the time to get to know was Sandra, the mother of one of the only girls to befriend Sugar when they first moved to the area. Lucy was in Sugar's year and for the first few months, her daughter and Lucy seemed virtually inseparable. Looking back on it, Sugar was probably grateful to have a friendly face to show her around and accompany her as she found her feet in a new school environment. Gradually though, Sugar must have become aware of Lucy's reputation as a bit of an outcast. She certainly looked unusual compared to her peers and most lunchtimes according to Sugar's recollection of her days when her mother enquired, consisted of groups of spiteful children pointing out Lucy's differences as though she must be totally unaware. Most days, she seemed to have to endure being taunted about her recurring nits, or her peculiar hairstyle which looked as though a family member, not particularly skilled in the practice, had been enlisted to perform. Her clothes similarly, had no sense of coordination or evidence of prior thought or care. It often looked as though she had simply woken up and grabbed whatever lay in her path to the front door and pulled it on without considering how it may look or even it's appropriateness to the weather conditions or seasons.

Despite her mother's encouragement to not judge her classmates according to their popularity or lack thereof, or perceive someone by the actions of others, Sugar's delicate stage of development, adding to the fact that she was a new person in the school and did not relish any unnecessary attention, meant that she gradually began to pull away from Lucy and her name was mentioned less and less at home. Cayenne thought this was a sad outcome but knew that her daughter would learn those social intelligence principles and vital lessons with maturity and perspective.

Perhaps in response to this and partially to set an example for her daughter, Cayenne seemed to gravitate more towards Sandra who not unlike her daughter, stood out in the playground for less than favourable reasons.

Her mop of grey hair, which loosely maintained it's similarity to a bob, could be spotted from a mile away with it's brutal stance in the midst of blondes, brunettes and natural dark shades. Every so often, a sharper edge was discernible just above the collar to suggest that scissors had been introduced at some point, even if the evidence was cloaked in obscurity. She wore thick grey rimmed glasses that looked ancient had clearly not been cleaned with regular efficiency, judging by the green substance gathering in the corners of the lenses close to the bridge. The clothes, as with her daughter and every other member of the family that Cayenne had either been introduced to or had witnessed around the neighbourhood, had a staple familiarity to them that bore little or no relation to the seasons. Horizontal rain, sleet and even light snow, would see Sandra standing in the beige, A line skirt, bare legged in her tan buckle sandals which made her skin tone appear paler still. They were the type that were popular when Cayenne was growing up in the 1970's. Sometimes she would wear her purple coat which looked as though it could scarcely manage an autumnal night let alone frosty wintery conditions, but generally, owing to the fact that 'she never felt cold', the skirt would be matched with a light tee shirt and baby blue knitted cardigan, a colour which just so happened to make the silver in her hair, pop. In the two years that Cayenne had been acquainted with the school, she had perhaps only seen one variation of this outfit. Likewise, the other members of the family she had met, seemed to have adopted a similar lifestyle of giving little thought to seemingly unnecessary thoughts, such as a change of attire. An elder son who acted as his mother's constant companion, wore the same head to toe brown outfit, which happened to match the brown grocery trolley that he was surgically attached to, every single day.

Yet Sandra, once comfortable around a person, gradually began to beam with a generosity of spirit, leading Cayenne to discover that Sandra was one of the most charming, warm and humorous people that she had come across. Their conversations, though usually concerning the day to day toils of family life, were always interesting and thought provoking and somehow, these seemingly contrasting characters,always managed to find something to chuckle about. Any dire situation that came up would be given a comical spin by the time they bid farewell to each other along with a 'see you tomorra'.   Cayenne found it interesting to observe Sandra with other people though, such as during the parent's social get togethers organised by Jill in the old School Keeper's house, where the upstairs room was dominated by a huge table and as many chairs as they could gather, with an array of confectionaries, cakes, and home made delights that generous parents had cooked at home and brought in. These would be mostly of the Asian variety, English and Black folk tended not to share food around as was customary in other cultures which always gave Cayenne pause for thought.

Their neighbours either side in Torquay had both been Asian, from Pakistan and Bangladesh respectively. At seasonal times in the Islamic calendar, Cayenne would be inundated with food from both sides as was their custom. Typically Biriyanis and samosas of every kind from the Pakistani side and a less familiar assortment of Dhals and Panta Bhats from the Bangladeshi side. Cayenne would often marvel with Diego that one of these fine days, she was going to return the favour and deliver, Rice and Peas, Ackee and Saltfish and a large barrel of Peas soup sufficient to last for days, on each neighbourly doorstep with her good wishes, along with the hand gestures and commands of 'Eat, Eat Eat'. Diego would give his mother a stern look, fully acknowledging the jesting tone in her voice, knowing full well that the Eastern culture of sharing food tended only to work one way and that the Pakistani and Bangladeshi cultures had no intention of feasting on her Caribbean fare.

At these organised parties, Sandra would look out of place, uncomfortable and on edge, her wary eyes darting around from one person to the other with learned suspicion. She would refuse any offer of food or drink in full Eastern fashion and stay, loitering on the outskirts of the room, for a polite few minutes before disappearing, virtually unnoticed, back to her scullery existence. Cayenne could picture the exact same expression on a young Sandra's face. When she was perhaps a similar age to her daughter Lucy, wandering around the playground in a friendless orbit, not even attempting to fit in, the futility of the exercise, glaringly obvious. Remarkably, just like Lucy.

Whenever Sugar would recount a particularly cruel exchange that Lucy had endured where someone had criticised her clothes or her odour, Cayenne would always enquire as to Lucy's response to such acerbity, to which Sugar would reply "she just shrugs, as though she's not bothered".

Cayenne would marvel at the tenacity of the child who from observation, was not fabricating this resilience. It was as though she had endured so much that she was now impenetrable or else she was innately immune in the face of discrimination. Knowing that her own daughter would be traumatised by such a daily onslaught had she been subjected to it, made Cayenne's admiration for the little girl and her family, all the greater.

Cayenne rather doubted that tennis would be to Sandra's liking in the long run. She would inherently be too self conscious, a trait that Lucy had found the wherewithal to dispense of. Cayenne predicted that Sandra, would be lacking in confidence to even attempt such a sport, subconsciously choosing to be otherwise consumed with catering to all her other family members' needs and making their concerns her own, even the ones that had long since flown the ramshackle nest but still relied upon their worn down, neglected mother, who it seemed knew no other way but to follow the path of least resistance.

The final count on the tennis court was a group of twelve moms. Most of whom had no extensive experience or had even thought about playing before. Cayenne was surprised to learn that most hadn't even watched the game or could even name a prominent player past or present. She appeared to be the only avid follower of the game even though her own devotion could be described as casual at best.

It looked as though their instruction for the next few months would be in the hands of Jefferey, a tall curly haired young man whose glasses suggested a studious individual who once had aspirations of tennis glory. Jefferey had a calm and relaxed demeanour and it was obvious to her that he possessed an apt personality for teaching youngsters as was his usual profession when not schooling parents on his day off. His lanky long limbed build made him appear octopus like on the court with an elastic ability to catch shots that would otherwise be out of reach.

Frida, his female colleague, was diminutive and fast paced and the stronger personality of the two. Cayenne could just imagine watching her on the big screen in a big league tournament. A dark haired, stark woman, with Eastern European features that perfectly complimented her accent, casting a no nonsense, pragmatic tone over the group, though her warm crinkly smile took the edge off her dark intense eyes which spoke silent truths.

"Come over here ladies, once you've signed in with Jill, grab a racquet and make your way over here, we are going to warm up", Frida beckoned the women over to the left hand court and stood facing them directing the eager group into a semi circular form.

"Yeah, don't forge' to sign in please, cos I gotta send the names in to the caaaansul". Jill bellowed in her fierce cockney dialect.

"Awwright Lubna, good to see you giwwwwl... should be fun shu'n't it". Jill's warm enthusiastic chatter, calming the nerves of the many first time athletic venturers. The bonds she had built within the various communities working to full effect.

The young Asian girl smiled with an unsure look in her eyes.

Frida held her tennis racquet high above her head and was bending over to her left and right, guiding the women through their warm up.

"Now bend over and place your racquet on the floor, then reach up the sky, then bend over and pick up your racquet and raise the racquet to the sky and alternate".

There were a few groans as Frida demonstrated the reaching over of their racquets first to their right legs and then to the left until their bodies were warm and ready for the drills ahead.

By the time the ladies had completed their volley and serve practices, interspersed with running exercises, they were more than ready for doubles matches to complete the hour. Their inexperience rang out throughout the court as their wild, misdirected shots hammered the wire fencing and a few balls found themselves lodged in the neighbouring trees and the communal foliage of the nearby estate.

"Ooooh, oh my Gaaawd, I've only 'it it over the fence 'int I?", Jill guffawed, before running off to retrieve the stray balls outside of the court.

Cayenne stopped for a moment after delivering a sharp backhand shot across the net, watching it fly past her opponent who subsequently ambled after it.

She glanced upwards into the near distance and gaped in wonder at the juxtaposition of a life size tennis court surrounded by an array of sky scrapers, a stone throw from the iconic, stainless steel frame of One Canada Square with it's distinctive pyramid pinnacle and the neighbouring newly erected Baltimore Tower with it's visual twisted outer design, accessorising the world renowned skyline, standing 42 floors above Canary Wharf.

"It's yours!". Kathy was shouting that the ball was heading swiftly towards Cayenne's court.

Snapping out of her day dream, she jumped into action and calculated that if she sprinted she would just manage to get the ball before it had bounced and sprung towards the line. Pushing hard and accelerating towards the ball with her arm outstretched, mustering all the power she could in her right arm, she watched the ball bounce up and knew she had to reach it before it hit the ground again. Pulling her arm back slightly, she whacked the ball to her left, tilting the racquet up to ensure a swift cruise above the net. She had covered the distance quickly and watched as the ball sailed into her opponent's corner, just shy of the line, leaving no room for them to retaliate.

141

Frida was ecstatic at this amateur show of unexpected skill as she shared a knowing glance towards Jefferey. "Advantage Richards!".

CHAPTER 14

Laying awake in the early hours, thoughts turned to Zurich and what the stranger would be doing at that precise moment. She gathered it would be a similar time there, give or take an hour. That's supposing he was even there. She somehow couldn't shake the niggling thought that he had concocted another sudden executive crisis as an excuse. Perhaps the lady in his life was putting pressure on or had sensed that he was somewhat distracted. But why lie. Surely it wasn't necessary to go to the lengths of creating a whole troubleshooting expedition. He had given her enough detail about the small town on the Rhine River in the North West of Switzerland and the late night escapades with his assigned guide and driver, Sven around the Marktplatz Square, to convince her that he had in fact been there. That there had in fact been cause for him to rush over there and take the helm at some point, she just wasn't convinced that the scenario was as current as he was making out.

It had been several months since the fateful day of their first encounter and yet there had been no mention of exchanging numbers or seeing each other outside of office hours.

But hadn't she herself stipulated such an arrangement at the very beginning?. She could scarcely start complaining now. Now she knew the score, even if it remained unsaid. There was someone in his life. There had to be. The fact that he seemed so imprisoned by the situation suggested that there was something serious enough to protect and that whatever was happening elsewhere, must not be jeopardised.

Cayenne began to feel a familiar unease. She had been here before and had vowed never to be here again. Although the dynamics were different, somewhere along the line she had crossed over from venturing into a little bit of fun and socialising to developing feelings. Feelings as yet unexplored. She knew he was battling the same thing. That he had probably pursued fun on the side in the past within the safe greenbelt of his life, but with her it had begun to get deeper, encroaching upon the real estate on which he lived. This had invariably frightened him, which is why she could sense him backing off. Yet he would also be the first in pursuit following their many breaks of contact.

Her phone beeped in the darkness with an accompanying flashing illuminous green light, letting her know a message was pending, splaying it's reflective specks across the darkened ceiling.

She reached for her phone and swiped the screen.

"You up? Save me from this…."

This wasn't the first time that he had reached out to her in the early hours. His yearning tone revealing much more than his words. She wasn't sure how to interpret this. Save him from what?. She knew it would be pointless to ask. She intuitively understood that there were questions he couldn't answer.

"Yes I'm up and I'm here".

She couldn't think what else to say other than to provide vague assurance from a distance. He didn't respond that night and it was several days later before she heard from him again.

"How is the caramel?".

"You're a mind reader it seems".

"Flavour my day".

"How".

"Have you looked at the Shangri la?"

"Briefly".

"Tell me how to bring you off".

"How I'm feeling right now, I'll be dripping at the very sight of you, let alone a touch".

"I want that Westbury feeling again".

"I'm struggling to recall the date of our last hotel tryst... absurdity that you should retain your title".

"The passion and the filth".

"Fucking ravenous right now.... Thoughts of shagging the fucking Zurich out of you".

"I'm your hotel whore. I want you to fucking indulge. I need re-blacking. Re-using. London will view our interracial fuck fest of pure indulgence from on high".

"Blacking?... you'll be fucking charcoal by the time I've finished with you. Interracial fuck fest...sounds fucking divine. Can hardly wait to smother you in my potent rum potion, massaging it into your pale skin like a self tanning mouse, until you are well and truly smothered in my regal soot.

"I needed this adrenaline rush. The blood pumping to my dick as you fucking corrupt me.

Are you juicing?".

"I can certainly detect the onset of erotic trickling. Knickers will soon be sodden. Will have to remove them and lie naked to allow the river it's natural course".

"God, I hate the fact that I'm missing it. fuck!".

The urge overwhelmed her. She threw her phone aside, bundled up several plumped up pillows and threw herself over them, raising her hips allowing her to straddle her legs wide with space beneath. She visualised his head in that space. Created the image of his long tongue beneath her, poking through the copse of her pubes like a farmer cultivating his allotment, hastening the seasonal search for ripened crop. Very shortly after, her imagination gave way to the pulsing sensation emanating from deep within her vagina. It was coming. The orgasmic rush was heading toward the open air, causing involuntary shagging thrusts as though she were a man on top of a woman, her fingers, simulating his flicking tongue, were already coated in her sugar cane icing. By the time the avalanche began to peter out, she needed a towel to soak up the dampness. She would change the sheets, first thing in the morning.

"Hey, what happened to you last night?".

Cayenne was rushing towards the gym as she was almost late for her morning cardio class.

The elevator was taking longer than usual to arrive and she could hear the sound of multiple presses on the control panel, suggesting that someone on another floor was holding the lift against it's will.

The robotic announcements could be heard throughout the lift shaft, 'door closing, door closing'. Eventually whoever it was that was holding it up was promptly delivered to the ground floor, releasing the lift to respond to her own 5th floor request.

The stench from the bins on the underground disposal bays, bombarded her senses and the general unkempt condition of the lift told her that the regular cleaner was yet again missing in action.

Once she had crossed the forecourt and her phone was able to pick up a signal, several messages awaited her response as she typed in her answer.

"I was overtaken by hunger and in the absence of a decent whore, yet again one is compelled to satisfy oneself. As a result, I find myself in the throes of the constant negotiation of waves of utter resentment and contempt… the remnants of which abide".

"Your white whore feels privileged that you still give him the time of day".

"As well he ought".

"Momentarily I thought that your sudden disappearance last night was another cut off. I was fully prepared to crawl on my knees and beg for forgiveness if needs be. How I want to worship at the Queen's feet.

I sincerely hope that the Queen is aware of my incessant desperation for face sitting and drenching".

"Her Majesty is very aware..... though unfortunately, your position is precarious".

"Mmmmm your white whore, always ready to exploit openings senses a chance to get back on the right side of his Black Queen.

Shard. Still want it?".

"I seem to recall a reference to 'high end treats' and a ' birthday celebratory itinerary'...

With our previous Tapas experience in mind... it is clear that one's interpretation of 'high end' is relative...

Therefore... the Queen would insist upon perusing said high end treat proposals and itinerary draft in order to determine the prospective Shard experience.

The Queen's mounting diary prohibits the week of the 25th and the following week she is required to oversee tedious youngsters for a mere pittance".

" Ha ha... the tapas never to be forgotten. Is there no way you can do the 25th?

I'm relieved that you haven't consigned me to your spam file".

"You were seconds away from eternal spam confinement.

The fucking AUDACITY of a hopeless underbelly scouring whore...

To even suggest you are eligible or worthy of my time in Panoramic Utopia... when to even be considered, depends wholly upon the quality and EXECUTION of the itinerary and prior presentation pitch and approval of PROMISED 'high end gifts' worthy of a Queen...

If I have to repeat myself yet again...

Swiss frost will be no match for the punishing icy conditions I will inflict on this pathetic excuse for white whoreism. Persist with this disregard for the Queen's divine status and I shall be forced to use you as an instrument to lick an orchestral symphony on the narrow ledge of my clit.

"The Queen's mercy... such a delight...

Evil mistress.... I can't wait for you to face sit me. I will revise the plan until such time as it satisfies Your Highness' regal tastes".

"You do know you are treading on remarkably thin ice...

Sheiks would seldom be so tiresome. It would simply not be in their subcontinent nature to simply talk the talk.

Hopeless Caucasian city execs... what a low rent exercise in absolute designer pussy futility.

The Queen feels the need to temporarily disable her email app whilst in recovery from low class exposure.

Return date unknown..."

"Seriously..... stay with me on this... I will deliver immediately upon my return.

Fuck!... I am caring that you may be upset.

Please give me some dates that suit birthday week.

Queen please save me from this:

Sorry, the last message and viewing was incredibly weak".

His pleading video depicted a white man in a business suit being set upon by a trio of white hungry women. Pawing at his manhood and having their way with him as he lay helpless to their demands.

"A truly abhorrent scenario".

"The Queen is back….

In addition to how my role as your executive white toy hardens me… two images have given me a lot of release fun recently in this dank existence.

1. The fact that the Queen can harden me and almost bring me off with just her feet. (memories of you stroking me under the table with your foot). The fact that I allow her to subject me to such corrupt behaviours appeals most strangely…

2. Regal black arms – toned, powerful and muscular.. being clamped in your vice like grip (the Westbury), assessing your gorgeous tight chocolate biceps hardened me… a reaction that's completely unique… that piece of the body has never been viewed sexually by this whore before…

What weakness that this dirty whore admits such things and hardens in the process".

"Not at all... the Queen admires such honesty and is excited at the prospect of you seeing a more finely honed physique.... Many hours have been spent staving off extreme pussy hunger by pumping iron to define the biceps for such another sensual hold. Limbs have been elongated in yoga and many hours have been spent sweating in strength class in order to sculpt an athletic form...

Such defined muscle must be closely examined and extensively studied.

My white whore would be prudent to increase his stamina and elevate his prowess if he is to retain his position as the Queen's primary courtier.

The Queen has altered her daily cuisine to complement the gruelling exercise... her resolve to become royally ripped from head to toe, come the height of summer... her ultimate motivation.

Thoroughly enjoyed toe wanking your succulent white cock... I only wish I could have witnessed the pulsing in your pants and the subsequent projectile somersault cum that you no doubt unleashed in privacy.... so hot... so delicious... so juice inspiring...

The Queen is extremely pleased to be the one to introduce her white whore to the unknown territory of curves and steel muscle. Definition and body substance. Extinct in suburban regions.

Ps. I've never heard someone refer to the woman in their life as 'Dank'.

Interesting... sounds cold...unrefined... dry and carcass like. An inevitably bereft terrain, devoid of moisture, sapped of nutrients creating irreversible bodily crevices".

"Cheeky.... I wasn't referring to anyone... I was referring to a town. The Queen does not need such arrogant prose... the fact that I'm a whore to her chocolate juice, feet and arms should tell everything she needs to know".

"My mistake....

I mustn't let your obvious craving for mixed spice cunt juice and your absolute slavery to my black honed form, lure me into jumping to hasty conclusions....

I must refrain from allowing your unfed disposition to lead me to casting aspersions...

And we won't mention the desperate soul I encountered in the underbelly…

None of the above should necessarily be any indication of desolate hopeless longing and extreme pussy depravation. Cunt deficiency on another scale.

How could I forget that Zurich is indeed a place?

For I shall never forget the place that denied the satisfaction of my most intimate urges… nor the sudden dank executive urgency that caused it".

"I can just see the smile on your face as you write…fuck… I wish my tongue was in your mouth right now.

Will the chocolate regal majesty get wind of her white knight on his return to her locality?

Will she want an accurate and precisely extensive rundown of his executive adventures over a lunch where she can also acquire knowledge of the plans he has arranged for her?".

"Talk of what you will arrange for the Queen sounds absolutely divine.

I fully anticipate an aggressive attempt to troubleshoot my vaginal short circuit. Apply the same dedication, extra hours, burning the midnight oil, prepared to travel at short notice to far flung climes, ensuring you find an executive solution.

I trust that I won't be disappointed. Will the White Knight get hard under the table as the Black Queen turns up in yet another figure hugging outfit?

Let us pray that your recreational tan subsides in the hope that the Queen swallows your counterfeit Zurich fairytale...

Panorama may yet be in jeopardy".

"Considering the Queen's calendar, I was thinking Wednesday 31st May or Thursday 1st June. Which suits?".

"I'm certain the Queen had aforementioned prior engagements from 28th to the 2nd June" according to her royal schedule.

"Oh of course. The 25th definitely out right?. I'm not in a position to take time off next week so won't get to enjoy properly".

"Not to worry. I'm certain the Queen can enlist a willing Sheik to entertain her for her birthday".

"Your White Whore toy will do all he can to prioritise the Queen's diary.

The Shard! Fuck!!....mmmmmmmmm. This white whore cannot wait to repay his Queen for her mercy with thrust after repetitious thrust".

"Fascinating how SWW cannot seem to resist getting ahead of himself...

The Queen will sanction the Shard including up close and personal proximity to newly honed black physique, subject to approval of the itinerary and PROMISED HIGH END TREATS, reflective of SWW's appreciation of the miracle of her birth...

Gifts and itinerary will be perused over the proposed toe wanking Michelin Starred lunch".

"The gracious Queen will be looked after on her birthday".

"The Queen anticipates handwritten proposals on an ancient scroll in your finest calligraphic feathered handwriting".

"The Queen has been scarred by the tapas experience hasn't she?.... and now constantly questions whether her whore will deliver the standard required".

"Though she is reticent to confess to such weakness as it is most unbecoming, the implications of SWW's poor initial culinary choices and his culturally unrefined palate have undoubtedly brought his pedigree into question...

The fact that your pussy palate has now been elevated significantly along with your couture cunt consciousness, gives the Queen hope that potential lies therein...."

"Michelin Starred treatment last time for both food and cunt licking.... Cheeky.

Has the Queen had any other suitors trying their charms".

"The Queen is somewhat overwhelmed by male attention...

Particularly when strolling around her vast estate clad in mere uber tight gym gear…

The city lunchers are aghast at the toned, perfectly curved derriere, the bulging biceps and emerging toned stomach muscles.

Whatever is a Nubian Queen to do?".

"Lap it up Beautiful Queen… they should look… and be brave".

"Alas, bravery is in short supply…

However, SWW has given one hope that suitors can indeed arise from the ashes of their undeveloped esteem and not leave a finely honed Nubian to chance…

Hope that in future, they will be not quite as desolate, under nourished and bereft as the current underbelly loiterers, as any unfortunate soul who would endure such vacuity is unlikely to appreciate my regality, as the Suburban White Whore has disdainfully proven".

"I wonder how many underbelly loiterers there are secretly seeking to be blacked. Wanting to be face straddled by a delicious wet tight chocolate cunt. Longing for caramel drenching, yet afraid to take that first step, that initial cultural \societal quantum leap. We should be helping them, offering kind support and encouragement rather than mocking them".

"The Queen has quite had her fill of loiterers....

She has since learned that such depravity leads to poor regard for Heads of State.

The Queen has been utterly dissuaded by the constant attempts to justify her Nubian prestige and the exhausting practice of nurturing any hope of perennial high end treatment...

A Sheik, would surely consider beautiful jewels and designer gifts as par for the course".

"Any fun viewing lately?".

"Strangely No. Apart from the early morning one you sent"

"That was pretty tame... hotel options too vanilla unsurprisingly".

"Tame?. What's your favourite?".

"I got off on the two black girls using that white princess if I'm honest. You?".

"Yes agreed. That was probably the best one. Unmistakable pussy hunger... such a fucking turn on. Clit sucking... licking... drinking...salivating with no hint of hesitation. God I'm about to get wet".

"The control they had over her.. the racial filth coming out of their mouths...)

Can hardly wait to taste you and have you dribble all over my face".

"Yes... loved the dominance... forcing her to eat it... fucking hot. It reminds me of witnessing white people eating authentic West Indian cuisine for the first time and watching as they are blown away by the concept of thorough seasoning.

"Blondie looked hungry for chocolate... she liked being their whore... perhaps that explains my affinity with the video".

"Dreaming of face sitting my SWW...

Getting absolutely comfortable straddling my hot pussy over your lips...

The Queen is questioning the White Knight's pussy devotion and will demand absolute famished licking".

"Dreaming of being under you, tasting the caramel juice as it dribbles down.

Being your hungry whore".

"Not yet convinced of your hunger.

Curiosity perhaps... peckish at best.

But unparalleled thirst I've yet to see".

"Yes.. the Queen is right. The video should be played and the SWF should be made to note where he can improve before he gets to the task".

"Thoughts of smothering your face with my unique caramel spice cocktail and drenching you in a Dunn's River shower".

"Desperate... mouth so dry. Feed me Queen".

"The Queen is almost orgasmic at this suggestion. Creamy knickers already...

Yes watch and learn SWW.... Fucking feast on the cunt or your generous plate will be removed".

"Yes yes, straddle my fucking face until you are done; remind me that I'm your fucking whore toy and I will lick and taste until the Queen is satisfied".

"The Queen can certainly produce a chocolate fountain... though she cannot make you drink. Perhaps the Queen has been too lenient... force feeding may be in order".

"Blacken my face my mistress Queen.

Own your whore :) ".

"The Queen's desperation interspersed with mounting frustration at her SWW's shortcomings…may lead to brutal savagery. I will fucking own this opportunity to get my delayed release.

You will receive your own personalised charcoal face mask".

"The Suburban White Whore should have his hands tied so as not to distract from face sitting duties. Make me feel your toned chocolate biceps. I want to be smothered in your cunt juice. This needs to be a punishment blacking. Cannot wait to have my hands all over your ass".

"I especially want my black Queenly ass mauled incessantly… though your hands may be small… place this black firm bottie in your grasp and squeeze for your dear suburban life.

Punishment indeed… such will be the intensity of your torture…. You'll be begging for mercy in Swiss German by the time I've finished with you.

Touch me all over… drink me in with your senses before you bludgeon me alive with your hard white cock".

"Disgracefully, I'm actually thinking about having my lips on your regal black ass. I'm as stiff as nails... you will get banged hard and brutal".

"SWW must consider his already privileged position...

Currently the singular invitee within the Queen's inner court with exclusive access to the crown pussy jewels...".

"He is indeed very privileged... his desperate rampancy will prove this".

"My black ass will threaten to smother you entirely... only a poke of your finger in any chosen orifice will force it to give way for your inhalation.

No more Spag Bol' for you...your fingers will be smothered in pent up Zurich infused vag' bol'...

Double portions will be available for your consumption".

"So fucking desperate for a taste and a smell of your cunt juice and gorgeous black ass... my unrubbered white cock wants to be drenched in chocolate pussy dribble and submerged. It will provide whatever the Queen wants filling. Want to see you totally getting off on me".

"The Queen is now drenched"

"Good.... whore toy still has use.

Shame I'm not there to mop it up orally".

"SWW is certainly arousing his Queen today.... Perhaps her faith is somewhat restored....

Simply cannot wait to be banged unceremoniously.

Not much longer to wait... excited to look down and watch the divine consumption.

My hungry pussy is positively yearning for a touch.

It is most unjust that a regal pussy be addressed so infrequently..."

"Yes I think after face sitting... white whore once fed, needs to step up like a Knight and give the Black Queen the proper hard strong fuck she craves.

Plans afoot to address this. White Whore toy should provide his Queen a local succour on a convenient week night…".

"Your tentative nature has certainly denied the Queen her cunt rights".

"My need for blacking becoming incessant.

How awful would the Britannia Hotel be?".

"I can just imagine your incessant yearning. Quite how you endure the dryness of the suburbs is beyond my comprehension".

"What are your thoughts on a local weekly supply, or should we resist to ensure the anticipation of Panorama is utterly fuelled?

SWF was simply thinking of a need for a weekly base to satisfy a regal Queen.

High End activities will not be impacted.

Simply trying to ensure regular blacking and compliance of this white whore toy".

"Your recent cancellations have indeed thrown us off kilter. The Queen's patience with your executive schedule is wearing decidedly thin".

"I would like to fuck next week. Are you ok gorgeous?

I think I'll watch something".

"Oil looks good on black.

https://www.redtube.com/3tdheyt

https://www.redtube.com/ehgy3

Couldn't resist another viewing.

https://www.redtube.com/shsj3

Think it might be this one actually".

CHAPTER 15

Cayenne looked at her backlog of executive emails.

"Sorry haven't had time to view, navigating pancake making and trying to prepare for the gym.

Gym at 10am and again at 1pm.

Sun's trying to shine.... Wouldn't it be lovely to be invited to lunch?

Hopeless whore. Agreed. Oil makes my newly honed muscles pop..."

"Baby oil on list for the Shard.

Let's find a new lunch place this week.   You didn't seem impressed with Tomkins".

"I positively adore your conscientious attempts to keep me contented.

Tomkins is fine... they are sure to have an assortment of alternatives on the menu I assume.

Besides... it's just a short enough distance from home to rock my mini bodycon dresses and high heels safely".

"I'm only doing what a whore desperate for his next blacking should be doing".

"Absolutely!".

"Perfect... you do turn heads.... I harden knowing that I'm the one you're coming to see. I'm the one getting it. And that's the truth".

"Privileged whore".

(14:10)

"Any jealous crones in the gym this morning".

"Pitiful spineless plebs (male)

Glaring sullen pale bitches (female)... before I've even moved a muscle.... They know they're defeated.

Just seen the second video. You really must up your tongue game as my appetite increases".

"The whore is aware he must do more to avoid the Queen's castigation.

He looks forward to spraying for the Queen's delight".

"Your words betray your incomplete technique....

if you observe the video closely (white slave video)

It is infinitely more than licking you ignorant whore...

The tongue must pursue it's own voyage of discovery...

my pussy must be given the same level of attention and diversity. Smell, lick, poke, suck, chew, probe, pummel... don't deny my puss puss what it needs lest you will be instantly replaced".

"Points taken my Queen – I will make sure I study this video more closely... I will indulge the racial slurs and hone my technique".

"Did you notice the animated commercial when viewing the slave video?

171

The woman holds her victim captive between her thighs, one arm firmly holds him in place while the other wanks him to a frenzied climax.

Cannot wait to vice grip you with my huge chocolate well oiled biceps and thighs and bring your delicious white cock to it's roller coasting magnetic crescendo".

"Smell,

Lick,

Poke,

Suck,

Chew,

Probe,

Pummel

I will learn the proper art of blacking.

I want you to use me as your fucking whore toy. I am in complete and utter submission to the Queen.

"That majestic squirt of yours…. Heavenly to witness on the one hand…

Though puss puss cannot help but be envious at having to observe from the sidelines and not be part of the immersion".

"Want me to fill you with my cum?. How could a white whore ever be so fortunate".

"Pussy is throbbing in anticipation of your white cock pummelling …. Slow and then fast pokes… deep and probing pokes and shallow ones, just pipping the pussy post….

Want to watch your hips thrust urgently and rhythmically, overcoming any cultural coordination short comings and making a non verbal point of possession and temporary ownership.

You ask a poignant question.

On our very last encounter, we will both know that the blacking exercise was incomplete and somewhat futile…

Like some sort of erotic rehearsal…

Tedious…."

"Will be good to take that ownership… the Queen now on all fours… the platinum exec now in charge, getting his blacking how he wants it".

"A Queen at times tires under the weight of her awesome position…. to acquiesce to occasional submission is imperative to hold her interest and provide diversity… as long as the territorial aggression is convincing…

The Queen abhors anything counterfeit".

"Don't worry, the desire to have you and enjoy you as I want is not counterfeit…. My true desire will be very much on show …. With PANORAMIC views beyond, I will take charge and fucking indulge myself in all of your chocolate glory.

With such a magnificent view of London provided for her amusement, the Black Queen really ought to get on her knees and let her white toy take a nice cool dip in her regal mouth.

A white cock face slapping high above London would be particularly pleasing".

"Thoughts of my cunt filled to the brim and overflowing….

I was watching a film last night about a man that stalked a woman before approaching her. Sound familiar?.

It did make me think twice for a brief moment".

"Oh for goodness sake cheeky".

"I wondered whether all the years of scouring the depths of the underbelly had honed your stalker skills.

Did I by any chance, look particularly vulnerable whilst browsing the aisles of Waterstones?

Or is the bus stop one of your designated chosen vagabond pick up points?"

"You! vulnerable? Come on... I think I could have made this much easier.

Your highly disciplined nature does not suggest vulnerability is one of your personal traits. Unlike your penchant for high end treats".

"I wonder if you could positively identify high end treats as several months on, since said 'pick up' and high end treats are yet to materialise.

I ought to warn my fellow womanhood about such underbelly slickers…

'don't believe a word of it' shall be my cry…

'He will ply you with the alternative wine to which are accustomed and within weeks, after convincing you of the deserving treatment that he assures you will manifest, soon you'll be carrying a packed lunch to the Travel Inn most convenient to his place of work, that is unless he can convince you to sneak him into your communal stairwell' ".

"I suppose it's all relative… you are certainly not your typical lady jumping the bus….

This does seem to be messing with your head a little though babe… want me to drop off and make thing easier for you.

Have you found a higher class of executive whore to play with?".

"Yes, thank you that would be great.

Enjoy pickings".

"Sad face".

(3pm)

I can't do the underbelly anymore and you fucking know it.

 (3.15pm)

don't go".

"From whence does this arrogance derive.

I have no competition... therefore I shall leave you to your chocolate confectionary assortment".

 (3.25pm)

"I am fully aware of the calibre of this Black Queen.   Underbelly far too easy... doesn't provide the same thrill as it once did. Blacking for this corporate platinum exec needs to be majestic and regal... more Mayfair as opposed to Tower Hamlets".

 (3.50pm)

"hey!".

"The Queen finds your obvious expertise as you expound upon the inner workings of the underbelly rather off putting...

Your depravity both betrays you and contaminates you.... Suburban Sally, it is now clear, is the perfect antidote to your addiction.

Seedy underbelly by day (lunch hour)

Tranquil bland suburbia by night.

Your horizon appears safe... if not exactly.... BRIGHT.

Adieu".

"Any other sexual conversations ever been so depraved yet so fun?".

"How very infantile. The Queen is now reconsidering her eagerness to consort with depraved unfulfilled, low grade white folk...

She sees the error of her ways in associating with white deluded city execs.

They are to be employed as servants and courtiers... Not to be socialised with.

That distasteful sensation of the North Greenwich experience is returning to my palate.

My first instincts are usually remarkably intact. The Queen would be prudent to remember this as she recalls the moment she was exposed to the theatrical yet ineffective prance around the hotel room, posturing like a man who had attained sexual prowess, but rather gave her reason to withdraw in regal haste".

"I am your servant.

Mmmmm, however bad her memories now are....she was still happy to share her full chocolate glory for her white executive fuck when he was back at his office... even tried filming herself to make it clear what black beauty he had walked out on".

"Even servants must come with a degree of decorum   to this end...you have failed abysmally.

Yes, this was totally out of character behaviour for the Queen.

Your narcotics of choice (slipped into my drink) must have had the desired effect. Once it kicked in, coincidently towards the latter end of the rather uneventful parade".

"Mmmm wow!. That's an amazing drug to get that kind of behaviour … wish I knew what they were.

You wanted to tease. You got off on blacking me – just like I got off on you doing it".

"One doesn't usually run for the hills for three months in the face of a relentless barrage of daily requests, from events that one gets off on…

And for the record, you are no more blacked than I am whited… not that I would want to be.

Heaven forbid that I should be devoid of culture and class, not to mention curves and skin enriching, wrinkle evading melanin".

"You are fucking gorgeous hence the persistency:

See you for lunch next week?".

CHAPTER 16

As usual, Cayenne and Claire, were the first to arrive at the enclosed tennis courts in the middle of St Edmunds Park complex which also consisted of a Basketball court, a lily pond, several floral arrangements and a large recreational area housing a concrete climbing wall leading to a huge winding slide, as well as swings and monkey bars.

Claire lived just outside of the borough, so perhaps wasn't able to pop home after the school run during the spare three quarters of an hour between the beginning of school until 9.30am when Tennis lessons were scheduled to begin, whereas Cayenne could easily go home and have a quick cup of tea, or nip to the local shops, but in her eagerness to get to the court, much preferred to sit and wait on one of the benches outside, no matter how cold the weather. Together they would sit and chat with their cold hands stuffed in their pockets. Cayenne was secretly pleased that Claire always turned up early as the instructors would encourage them to warm up by rallying the ball to each other and fortunately, Claire had a good solid serve and seemed to have a natural ability to barely skim the net with a devastating forehand, not to mention a fierce backhand and rarely sent the ball careering way out off the court. She was the only one who could return a shot with such velocity that made it extremely difficult for the opponent to counter. Cayenne knew that her game was much more likely to improve playing with someone more skilled than herself and so relished this one on one time rallying with Claire before the wild battalion arrived.

"Sorry", offered Claire as Cayenne allowed the ball to roll past her towards the far corner of the enclosure as even with her hands cocked over her brow in an attempt to block out the morning sun, she still hadn't been able to locate the ball until it was too late.

"No that's okay". Cayenne quite enjoyed the chasing and secretly welcomed the extra challenge of having to wait until the last minute to respond to the ball. She appeared to be one of the few that didn't simply wait for the ball to come to her but relished the opportunity to have to outrun it and knock it back to her opponent.

There were a few others who at least attempted some control over the ball, but the vast majority of the primary school moms turned would be tennis pros seemed to consider any contact whatsoever as being a triumph, regardless of whether it was directed accurately or not. Cayenne was almost certain that some of the women saved up all of their pent up domestic frustrations and used this hour of tennis to unleash it back to the universe. Their shots being so vicious and manic that they rendered the red and orange Council provided tennis balls as weapons of destruction. As more and more women turned up and signed their signatures on the attendance sheet, Frida rounded them up and guided them through the warm up routine, incorporating the tennis racquet in the stretches and warm up poses.

"Ok ladies, first we are going to work on our serves. I'll put one basket over on that court", Frida was pointing to the court that was on the far right of the two. Then I'll place the other one here and I want you to form two lines on each court and one by one pick up a ball and serve to the diagonal service box on the other side of the net. Don't bother collecting the balls for now, just serve and go to the back of the line and keep serving. Remember the foot placement and the toss and after you have served, alternate from the forehand queue to the backhand queue".

"Yeah, if the toss isn't right… start again". Jeffrey confirmed.

Cayenne positioned her feet at five minutes past three as they had been shown. She rested the ball against the centre of the racquet and eased up to straighten her back as she glanced across the net at an imaginary opponent before glancing at the spot in which she intended to place the ball. Squinting slightly, channelling Serena Williams whom she rather thought shared her own venomous glare, she bent over the battered, overused, council provided ball which had seen better days and doubtless much better talent and stooped lower than usual to make up for the lost bounce ability. She was vaguely aware that the other women were wondering why she found it necessary to adopt such a serious stance in what was supposed to be a casual activity for inactive moms and housewives.

It was the same during the drills when the coaches served the ball from behind the net and the women queued up to run forward and take either a forehand or backhand shot, then run in to the net for a volley. Cayenne's approach was always the same. Serious, strong determined as though Serena herself was poised on the base line preparing her return. She noticed the same look in the eyes of the coaches as they too recognised that her approach was different. That for her it wasn't simply a friendly game but just as in the gym sessions, for her it was more than just a way of appeasing dietary guilt or passing time until the school run. Everything Cayenne turned her hand to, was an extension of her champion mindset. Her essence had to be in it. It was who she was and who she was, turned up in every situation.

She tossed the ball up high but knew instantly that it would not fall in the best place for her to angle her shot. So she caught it before it bounced and prepared a second attempt.

"That's it, " Jeffrey pointed out, reiterating his earlier caution. "it's all about the toss, so if you're not happy with it, take it again".

Squinting conspiratorially over to the far court, she repeated the futile exercise of bouncing the lifeless ball before throwing it up into the air with more accuracy this time and waited for it to fall within swinging distance. Swinging her bat gently above her head, she knocked the ball in the direction of her gaze, remembering to complete the swing so that the bat ended up behind her left shoulder, just as she had seen the professionals do it. Then watched in silence, for the moment, unaware of the activity around her, the mindless chatter, the gossip, the triumphs or failures of the other team on the other court and even the queue behind her awaiting their turn. She stood and watched as the ball sailed across the net, landing dead on the line of the service box before catapulting off towards the corner of the enclosure.

CHAPTER 17

The sun was beginning to break through the clouds, casting a soothing balm across the quay as Cayenne strolled past in her off the shoulder black blouse tucked tightly into her tight wide leg crumb catcher waist trousers, glancing in the reflection of the glass fronted stores and feeling very pleased with what she saw, considering his spontaneous call asking her to meet him for a drink at the newly refurbished Novotel building, had left her little time to prepare after her gym session.

The thirty minute strength class was one of the hardest on the gym schedule, as it was designed to leave very little recovery time. Baz the black, very athletic instructor had assured them that they weren't meant to be able to complete it, but to aim to do more each week but somehow in the heat of the moment with the music blaring and pumping loudly and the audio voice counting down the last few seconds of each particular segment, the compulsion to push as hard as possible and not be left behind in the class was overwhelming. Cayenne often found herself face down on the floor desperately trying to regulate her breathing by the end, questioning why on earth she was putting herself through this.

Part of the reason that this was one of her favourite classes, though she would never admit it, was Baz himself. Medium height with a stocky build and a slightly larger upper body than his frame required, he exuded a magnetic personality which is why his classes were almost always full. He was typical white girl totty as any strong sense of culture was remarkably well concealed. Street cool and suave, with a walk that was timed to an innate beat, with a point of a finger and a wink of his eye, he could reduce women to varying shades of flush crimson and his smile could top up many a fading white gyal tan.

His personality livened up the atmosphere and his sessions were mostly characterised by his obvious love of music. In fact, it was his personality more than his looks, that made him more attractive to Cayenne's mind. To pass him in the street, you would simply overlook the slightly too short guy in his baseball cap and oversized earphones, unless of course he happened to flash his diamond smile which in Cayenne's experience, he seemed to resolutely reserve for working hours only but there was something in the way he encouraged and inspired his charges when the pain of exertion overtook them or when their bodies faltered with fatigue. A touch on the shoulder, an encouraging word. Often, he would stoop next to a dying soldier as they strived to finish the complement of burpees required, urging them not to give up and sometimes mirroring them, executing the same exercise, right beside them as though almost literally taking them by the hand. Unlike many of his gym colleagues, Baz wouldn't hesitate to join them in the trenches, adding a dose of energy to inspire them to find more. More strength, more grit, more self belief, until suddenly the previously wounded casualty would find a second wind and push through until the countdown, infused with the spirit of Baz.

Cayenne secretly relished when he would hold a fist up in the air from across the room, "Come on Cay'", he would shout, which would give her all the impetus she needed to zone in and get it done.

Once or twice she had wondered whether to read anything into the frisson she sometimes detected between them, but at other times, he would pass by as though he barely saw her. She would chide herself for getting carried away. 'Of course he wouldn't be thinking of you in that way, he's in his early thirties, you're mid forties with children, not to mention the fact that by any stretch of the imagination, you're far too dark for his European tastes. Much like some of her own extended family, she rather suspected he was one of those black guys who would be clueless as to how to handle a black woman. Perhaps they had been tainted somehow during their formative years by the discrimination in school or amongst their peers and had subconsciously determined that their selection in life would reflect their perceived ideals. 'Don't be ridiculous'. Much like the executive, Baz struck her as the kind of guy whose mate selection would very much be influenced by what his peers would consider acceptable. Not quite having the strength of character to know and stand by an individual choice. Not that she seriously considered him as a worthy prospect outside of the energetic buzz of gym life. She would never be able to wear the vertiginous heels that she so loved for a start, not to mention the fact that he only ever seemed to have one topic of conversation available to him... music. Any attempt at an in-depth conversation would be met with indifference and acute discomfort.

Some of their conversations had revealed that he was accustomed to dating olive skinned, Mediterranean girls. She recalled him mentioning a Spanish ex girlfriend as the reason that he was currently learning the language in his spare time and many of their early conversations were repeatedly punctuated with 'my ex'.

Overhearing some of the girl chatter which seemed to be preoccupied with his personal status, she learned that he was also prone to dating younger girls. That had made Cayenne question whether there was an underlying confidence issue.

There was also the fact that, quite opposed to when they were around other people, when he would almost treat her with a warmth as though she were an extension of his family, if she happened to see him in the area, perhaps at the local shops, you would have thought that they were complete strangers as he passed with barely so much as an acknowledgement.

Diego had scolded her for this, as he considered it to be an unreasonable assessment, as having worked in the service industry himself, he attested that the on and off duty Diego were two entirely different people, and that any customers that had considered themselves endeared to their on duty server, need not be fooled.

Still... harmless flirting and the occasional voyage into the realms of her imagination wasn't going to harm anyone. How could one not wonder just how he applied his boundless energy in the boudoir. His high jumps and gymnastic infused burpees certainly set her curiosity alight which would be just as well, as from close observation of his gym shorts when demonstrating the appropriate posture for a straight legged dead lift, he didn't exactly seem hung like a horse which was perhaps another explanation for the youthful, Mediterranean penchant. Would the acrobatics that he was clearly capable of, render the sizing irrelevant?. She could only speculate.

Kenneth was bound to ask her about the gym instructors. She thoroughly enjoyed winding him up with exaggerations of their feigned interest in her.

"How was the gym", his question was predictable. He embraced her and kissed her cheek as she emerged from the elevator of the 39th floor of the hotel which was dominated by the double storey restaurant bar and sky terrace. "Still eyeing you up are they?".

Cayenne ignored the question as her eyes took in the stunning 360 degree views across the London skyline where the prominent outlines of the Gherkin and the Shard were clearly visible. Inside was dominated by exposed bricks and the and open ceilings revealing metal pipework which gave the space an utterly contemporary feel, whereas the numerous pieces of Moroccan style furniture and dimmed copper coloured lamps provided a contrasting traditional warmth.

"This is so beautiful". She gasped as he led her by the arm, weaving through various settings and seating areas to a quiet corner of the large outdoor terrace where the summer breeze whirred around them.

"I remember you liked it the last time. Sorry about the short notice. I just thought it would be a great for us to meet up for a quick drink before I go".

She tore her eyes away from the exotic surroundings and looked at him curiously. She couldn't quite pin point it but there was something about him that was bothering her. Was it her imagination or did he seem different somehow today and was she developing some sort of deep seated paranoia or was there something strange about the way in which those men had looked at her. Two men dressed in city attire had been huddled at a table as they had made their way through the restaurant and Cayenne was almost certain that they had stopped and looked at her with an air of recognition as she passed. Kenneth hadn't outwardly acknowledged them in any way to suggest that he knew them, so where on earth did she get the impression that he did and that they somehow knew they would be there. Had he been boasting about her perhaps. Did he orchestrate for them being in the bar simultaneously so that his colleagues could check out his new piece of pigmented totty, or was her imagination now running deliriously wild. She wasn't usually given to such suspicious thinking although she had always considered herself rather more perceptive than most.

It wasn't just that though. She could tell that he was on edge, more so than usual and that he was resisting dissolving into a relaxed state at the sight of her which was the response she had come to expect. The more agitated she became, the more on edge he got as though her lack of cooperation was going to be hard to explain to the comrades back at the office. Either that or she was certain to be going completely mad.

"What's wrong with you?".

"What do you mean what's wrong with me?. Nothing's wrong with me. Why do you keep asking me that?".

"I just thought it would be nice to see you for a quiet drink that's all".

"That is what we are doing isn't it, having a quiet drink?".

He looked exasperated and highly offended which only served to fuel her suspicions.

He slumped sulkily in his chair like a man defeated. Rather like a man with a thwarted plan she mused.

They sat in complete silence for the longest time, sipping their cocktails absent mindedly, though in spite of the frosty atmosphere, his hand which began by stroking her bare shoulder had now managed to find it's way around her back, under her arm and was comfortably fondling her bare breast under her blouse which Cayenne was loath to admit was causing a rapid defrosting below her waist. The soft strokes of her nipple almost caused her to gasp aloud, though if he was aware of her arousal, he certainly wasn't showing it, preferring to stare gloomily into the distance, seemingly unaware of the electrical sparks flying in her knickers.

Earlier he had cheekily, cautiously asked whether she might like to peruse another one of the newly unveiled hotel rooms below as they had done on their visit shortly after the official reopening. Her chilly glance had silenced any further enquiry.

Totally oblivious to the fact that within the hour, she would be rather enamoured with the elegant coving on the newly painted ceiling of the suite on the 20th floor, admiring the ornate porcelain carvings around the light fixtures and the splinters of deflected rays of light forming a pattern above them as she lay on her back with her legs in the air, humming the tune of her ecstasy as Kenneth rummaged in her coconut honey crack. His fingers pulling her apart to aid his erotic scavenge. She groaned loudly as he hungrily slurped in and around her private tuft, using his tongue to weave her intimate strands into a vaginal corn row, seeking with digital accuracy, for the morsels of defrosted cunt juice, leaving no part of her inner lips untouched.

She flapped around with a deliberate display of helplessness as he raised her intertwined ankles high above her head with one single arm, using his free hand to lift her hips higher still so that his face was in a direct line with her butt hole. She had read about the sensitivity that surrounded the area from which could be derived much pleasure. Now she could confirm that what she had read was indeed true. Hard to describe but the sensation of his tongue circling and delving in and around her anus was a feeling somewhere between the frustration of a tickling itch and the soothing pleasure of perfectly executed scratch.

She experienced something else new. The refreshed atmosphere goading them to push beyond boundaries previously observed with caution. She sat on the soft carpet in front of the bed and sat on her hands as instructed and there were moments she was sure to positively choke as he fucked her face with his enlarged dick. Thrusting with force, exposing a throat capacity that she never knew she had. All she could do was suck with the full force of her tongue to attempt to counter his velocity. She was somewhat relieved when the thrusts took on a furtive urgency, indicating that his flow was en route. He seemed to lose control as the convulsions of his body took over until they slowed right down as his hips tilted forward, delivering a mouthful of cum to the back of her throat, with every lunge, until she could feel droplets falling delicately on the back of her tongue. She swallowed gallantly, savouring the saltiness and creaminess of him. Rubbing her tongue back and forth across the tip of his softening manhood, teasing every last drop out of him before allowing him to taste of himself as he kissed her mouth hungrily before finger fucking her until dusk clouded the windows, and the lights of the London skyline glistened anew.

CHAPTER 18

"Mooooooooom!". The booming sound of Diego's rapidly deepening voice echoed along the corridor, bouncing off the walls and resounding through to the kitchen.

"Whaaaat!".

The hyenic chuckle of her eldest son which was infectious at the best of times, vibrated buoyantly across the airwaves.

"Come 'ere. Mooooom".

Cayenne quickly washed the seasoning from her hands and covered the jerk chicken she had been preparing and hurtled towards the largest middle bedroom which was now the teenager's domain, noticing that a smile was beginning to form on her lips in anticipation of the comical source causing the hysterical commotion. Knowing Diego it would be some senseless meme currently trending on social media, the humour of which often eluding her.

Turning the corner into his room, she pushed open the door which was once white but had since taken on a distinctly dark matt finish, although the paint on the handles had begun to wear away exposing the stainless -steel origin. Diego and Sugar were huddled side by side on the double bed pouring through countless pictures from their early childhood and finding the images of their mother in various stages of her self discovery and fashion experimentation, highly amusing.

From Diego's overly dramatic laugh, most people would have deduced that there was some significant drama occurring, though Cayenne knew only too well by now that her son was given to theatrical overreaction.

His loud, demonstrative cackle was hard to ignore and thoroughly engaging to the point that you would find yourself in hysterics long before the object of his laughter became apparent.

Sugar, her profoundly more reserved daughter, clearly found the images equally humorous, though this was merely evidenced by the slight shrugging of her shoulders as she attempted to contain the amusement stimuli bubbling up within her ten year old self-conscious body.

After several attempts to stifle his laughter long enough to be able to speak and to show her the current picture under scrutiny, Diego finally managed to sit up off the bed and with one hand on his abdomen signalling the effects of excessive howling and the other holding up a picture of his much younger mother holding a toddler like Sugar in what was clearly Cayenne's experimental skinhead phase. Her head was turned towards Sugar as though she was about to kiss the little girl on the face, exposing the side of her head which was shaved close to the scalp in a way that suggested it had been executed by her very own hands. Sugar's hand was pointing towards the camera and the delight on her little face made it obvious that her beloved older brother was behind the lens.

Cayenne's mouth dropped open in abject horror wondering what on earth had possessed her to have given herself such an unflattering hairstyle, let alone immortalise it in a photograph for generations to ridicule. She cast her mind back to the many attempts to apply permanent chemicals to her hair refusing to pay money for something which she was convinced she was quite capable of performing herself. The pictures begged to differ. A fact that provided her elder son with much entertainment and clearly he hadn't finished, as another image produced from an old photo album that had long since been discarded and remained obscure through many a house move, and would have remained so, but for an inquisitive ten year old who enjoyed nothing more than rifling through items that had been packed away well out of view of day to day consumption.

The great thing about Diego, one of the things that she really admired about him and that she suspected he inherited from her, was his ability to also laugh at himself. Interspersed with her photos, were a few of him when he was in the depths of his own self discovery. Various shots of him wearing clothes slightly too big as he tried desperately to emulate his older cousins with strange expressions on his face as he tried so hard to be cool reduced his family to uncontrollable convulsions as they rolled around on the floor.

The images that they enjoyed the most were the unrecognisable portraits of a preteen Diego who was clearly in the throes of his Ice cream discovery phase, followed by the multiple Snicker phase, evidence that he was consuming too many calories, even for his advancing hormones to keep up with were clear to see in his bloated face and bulging cheeks told a vivid story.

"I don't know how Social Services didn't intervene and whisk you away when you were looking like this". Cayenne and her son mirrored each other as they doubled over and allowed the laughter to envelop their whole body.

The next image that had now rendered her son limp with exhaustion, crumbling off the bed onto the floor, croaking as though in deep bodily discomfort, was a picture of Cayenne standing in the park. She remembered it well as it was customary practice of her and children to set out on curious adventures when they first moved into a property as a way of familiarising themselves with their new environment. Not long after they had moved into a dream of a home in Torquay, they discovered that there was lots of woodland nearby. The kind of places she would have frequented as a child with the gang of kids from neighbouring blocks. The endless summer days that seemed to go on forever, when parents scarcely worried about their children's whereabouts and seemed to have little concern for when they would return home. She would wile away hours playing tracking and getting lost amongst the trees and hidden groves and jumping on stones across green slimy creeks, riddled with tadpoles and tiny little objects that scarcely resembled

198

what a frog was supposed to look like according to the vibrant colourful pictures in the books at school or in the library.

Wandering through footpaths and dodging overhanging, untended branches and dark brown twigs that were bright yellow inside when twisted for use in cave making or den building.

Walking for miles through the forests allowed her to give her children a glimpse into her own childhood and she delighted in seeing them appreciating their natural environment as much as she did, watching avidly as Diego scooped his younger sister on to his back when she tired, or holding Ocean's wary hand to lead him down to the stream for a closer look at the water.

It almost felt like reliving her childhood only having come back from the future with three besties in tow.

The photograph brought back memories of a hazy summer afternoon when the children had complained about being bored and she had whisked them off for one of their weekly treks in an ensemble that had momentarily detracted from her usual smart casual style. A long t-shirt with blue and white stripes combined with a sleeveless white gilet, black leggings and white trainers which did little to compliment the shaved head and oversized sun glasses she was sporting as she posed next to some swings that Sugar was clearly enjoying in the background.

She tried to recall who she was in the picture. What her mentality was and how she viewed the world then. It didn't take long. It was around the time when she had retreated into her safe place. A place with room for only three other inhabitants and a couple of resident cats. A time when her brother had admonished her for always acting in a detached manner as though it was her and the children against the world. She remembered standing by the window where the landline phone rested on the sill and holding the receiver to her ear and staring out at the street beyond as she replied, "That's how I always feel". The exasperated sigh at the other end of the line told her that he didn't understand her mentality at all. Looking back, she could see why, but at the time she was still reeling from old wounds that had erected a battle wall around her and the children. The strange thing was, she was convinced that that was what she had to do. That it was a good and healthy thing to be isolated and self sufficient. To not have to need or rely on anyone else. It was how she felt safe. Fortunately, since then she had recognised that this wasn't a healthy way for her children to grow up and that she needed to learn that how she viewed the world, started with her. Once she began to do the inner work on herself, changing her reading material, working out, exposing herself to more enlightened minds, her children and those around her began to see the difference in her personality. She too could look at her former self and laugh along with her children.

Later that night, she could still scarcely stifle a chuckle at the memory of the how much fun they had had simply laughing together. She had decided to repaint her nails which was always a tricky time of day for this particular pursuit as should she fall asleep too early, which she was ever prone to do, she would invariably wake up to chinks of imperfection strewn across her otherwise perfectly executed French manicure. Cayenne had always been very particular about her nails. Even through her various cycles of style discovery, her nails were the constant flawless element in an otherwise mismatched ensemble. Years ago they would grow faster and stronger and almost all the old photographs of her holding the children through their various stages of growth, depicted her perfectly painted talons, usually coordinated with whatever outfit she happened to be wearing on the day.

She navigated her dewy nails carefully between the glass of wine on her bedside table and the stack of books inches away and using her knuckles, just managed to sift the phone towards the edge of the table to make it easier to pick up without ruining her manicure.

"Hey! You ok?"

The following morning whilst seasoning large slices of salmon for dinner, her phone signalled again.

"Please just let me know".

It was days later before she felt any urge to acknowledge his messages, perhaps prompted by the sense of urgency emanating from them.

"Firings happening on Monday. I appreciate you not wanting to talk but perhaps I can buy you lunch?... I think I'm safe but the team are getting decimated".

Cayenne recalled him telling her, following his apparent emergency trip, that changes were afoot and how they were desperately trying to salvage the situation and minimize the corporate damage that was looming.

His relief that she had agreed to have lunch was obvious in the way in which he hugged her. The way his eyes clung to her across the table as the waiter poured the wine.

"So are there a lot of people that you are having to….. let go of?"

She could see that real life executive decision making , as opposed to the executive pussy footing around that usually consumed the office hours, was weighing heavily upon him and he looked even more stressed than usual.

She quietly considered his job as being much like that of the pilots that she used to work with in her Cabin Crew days, or perhaps that of a Goal Keeper in a deciding qualifier. For the most part, it may appear that they were simply on the sidelines, watching the action in the capacity of an overseer until critical moments, where they really earned their money, would suddenly bring their purpose to light.

For a moment he rested his head on his folded forearms. She sat opposite wondering whether or not to give him a reassuring touch. It remained a thought.

"Well there's one guy in particular", deep sigh, " we got on quite well, so .... I can't help feeling guilty about him. You know, he's a good guy and he was okay at what he did". More sighing and running his hand through his hair. Then came the inevitable justification, "but he'll be ok, I mean, his mortgage is paid off and he's bound to find something else".

"So was it your decision then?".

"eeeerrrr, well.... Certain decisions needed to be made and you know errrrr....".

She looked at him, letting him know that the real answer was now obvious.

"More coffee?". He changed the subject abruptly.

"So you said you were safe, was your position really in jeopardy?"

"Well, it's a possibility at the rate things are going. Is it bad that I almost couldn't care less".

"Really?. So what would you do?"

"Dunno. I figured I could relax for about a year before I would need to get another job. I could travel or consider a complete change of direction".

"Like politics?"

"Well, yeah that would be great right?, but well… it must be difficult".

She shook her head, wondering exactly how many times a day he deliberated on decisions and promptly talked himself out of them owing to their perceived difficulty. She pictured a future version of herself in possession of a vast fortune and enlisting a financial institution that she could entrust with her newly acquired wealth. She made a mental note to discern and seek out those that had developed a healthy self image. Those that bore the battle scars from taking dominant action as opposed to strutting around on the side lines and looking the part whilst looking over their shoulder in fear of a qualified successor.

"I don't think people that become successful consider how difficult it's going to be. I would have thought it was just a case of following your passion and having the courage to just go for it".

He was nodding profusely although she was sure he didn't really believe it.

She wondered what, in addition to modern society in general, had happened to cause him to second guess himself and pursue the path of least resistance.

"I hope you don't mind me eyeing up your toned body".

"Not at all, I took considerable care in deciding which outfit would best display my hard work for that very reason".

"I see you have your shoulders out again". He was referring to the black shoulderless top she had worn at the Novotel which was similar to the floral lycra crop top she was currently modelling, that also exposed her toned shoulders.

"I rather enjoyed your soft kisses on my shoulders and the delicate massaging of my breasts. Every time you softly pinched the nipple....." she paused and rolled her eyes at the sensuous memory of the lubricant after effects.

He too rolled his eyes but with more than a hint of sarcasm, "Yeah despite your utter indifference to my banal chat last week, I did like being able to get to grips with your gorgeous supple breasts. My tongue wanted to follow my fingers circling your nipples.

I wanted your indifference gone

I wanted to get my way

I wanted to be in charge".

"Well, you did get your way eventually. Your discreet fondling must have thawed my resolve".

He smiled greedily, " Yes, the intensity of making up after such annoyance... the executive whore utterly desperate to please the Queen. I hope you could sense my willingness in every lick".

Later he sent her a video to express his continued want of her.

https://www.redtube.com/347yt

He certainly did not disappoint in the fantasies he forwarded in their shared penchant for the reverence of the black pussy. As usual, she enjoyed them at first, until the hunger they inspired became untenable.

"Can barely stand to watch anymore... fucking greedy black bitches. It's clear judging from the white whore's attire... he has no urgent executive schedule to ruin this delicious enjoyment. No apparent time constraints... no executive urgency or suburban pull....No deluded deployment to the Swiss Alps.

Not a phone in sight...

These fucking visa dodging immigrants can really let go, knowing there is no threat of three month Baselesque abandonment….

No air of white competition to cause their pussies to close tightly and their mood to deteriorate…

There's nothing else for it…. either I abdicate to the continent forthwith or I enlist a whore with relaxed work ethic and a strong sense of black pussy prioritising….".

"So you still haven't forgiven me for Switzerland have you?

That was a brilliant response cheeky…

These viewings don't really help me do they?".

"No. I highly doubt you have the exacting tools in your trouble shooting arsenal to solve this apparent predicament…

Nice while it lasted".

"I do really like you though, as you annoyingly know….".

"I rather like you too… yet still no resolution in sight".

"Let's remain available for each other's counsel. A friend who understands the dark side of ones character. Not a bad thing. Perhaps no need to dispense with 'us' entirely, unless that seems selfish".

"It most definitely sounds selfish and you well know it. Anyway, judging from the last several mostly barren weeks, my confidence in your so called 'availability' is shot.

I'm no fool… please don't presume I'm on the white suburban spectrum".

"Don't we know it.

Although I'm glad, as the underbelly holds no desire now".

"Excellent news…. Though I pity you for a time when a more indulgent suitor appears on the horizon".

"You do deserve indulgence – it's your birth right."

"Absolutely…. Of this I shall remain steadfast…

I deserve the utmost single minded devotion in order to unleash my erotic confectionery in all it's glory… from this I refuse to deviate".

"Completely fair… it's such a delight … I still get a rush thinking about it being available to a lowly Caucasian".

"I am sensing your utter remorse at such missed opportunities…

Forever yearning for an unhindered plumage into the underground of my bespoke lady garden…

A life without regrets is a life well lived…

How hellish for you… some sort of half lived endurance….".

"Hunger is building again…".

"Meanwhile, rogue immigrants are getting it from every angle… how wretched. How horrendously unfair…

So tired of being side lined…

How I hope my fortunes are a-changin'.

What a mediocre squirt this white whore manifests"… Cayenne had resumed viewing of his video erotica.

I am dripping whilst dreaming of your sweet dynamic somersault cum….

Fuck! Stealing a hidden finger fuck in the privacy of my room".

"Have you seen the news babe? Not looking good out there – London Bridge and Borough Market terror attack".

"Oh no! not again. What the hell's going on". Just months previously, they had shared their most intimate encounter to date at the Park Plaza Westminster where a horrific threat to national security had occurred just at the very moment he was attempting to burst through his own racial barriers and penetrate Nubian territory.

"I can see it now, Right Honourable M.P Kenneth Halpern-Smith. Perhaps it's time for you to take your place in the House of Commons.

Our country is in need of strong leadership…"

"Reckon so.   Whoah this is getting crazy.   Guys jumping out of vans with knives !!!".

It seemed he was whiling away this Sunday afternoon watching live news.

It was days later as they recounted the terrorist events and the names of the perpetrators were revealed, that his hidden prejudices emerged at the sound of the Islamic names.   "Typical".   He had muttered under his breath, though he instantly tried to deny it.

CHAPTER 19

Later that week, Cayenne was approached by Fenton at the gym who informed her that she had been chosen for a 'Member of the Month' accolade.

"We had a team meeting and four or five of us named you as the number one candidate".

Cayenne had been a little overwhelmed and touched at the thought that she had clearly won the vote and whilst she was flattered, this was the first she had observed any such membership analysis. From her casual assessment, the gym didn't appear to be particularly efficiently well run to have a consistent appraisal of the hundreds of members and attendees. It certainly wouldn't have been evident that there was any form of monitoring going on when it was glaringly obvious that even maintaining an adequate complement of cleaners was proving to be a challenge. If there had been a member of the month award the previous month or the month before that, she would surely have heard about it. Come to think of it, she did recall seeing someone holding up a certificate on the Gym's Facebook page but that had been from at least six months before.   She couldn't ignore the randomness of it and the fact that it wasn't a procedure that they maintained with regularity and therefore barely cared about, took the shine off it somewhat but she was flattered nonetheless and could hardly wait to tell the children. "So what do you get?", Diego enquired hopefully, probably anticipating a free pass for friends and family.

"Errrm, I think they said something about a photo call and a certificate". She ignored his expression showing that he was clearly unimpressed, unlike the would be M.P who was positively ecstatic.

"Wow impressive!", he had responded when she told him. "Well done you". His pride emanated through her phone.

"Is midday ok for tomorrow?".

CHAPTER 20

"Look, I can't stay long. Something's come up". He had come rushing towards their usual den in Chanel Café, carried along on a gush of urgent energy and literally rolling back his sleeves as he spoke as though addressing his young team ahead of an imminent corporate task. As it turned out, the crisis appeared to be more personal. "There's an elderly lady we know, a family friend in the Lake District, Agatha. She must be around eighty something and she's an incredibly close friend of my parents. Apparently, she's suffered a bad fall and my mom just happened to be there which was upsetting as you can imagine. So I'm leaving work early and heading up there this afternoon".

"Oh no. I hope she's okay", Cayenne was touched that he was sharing with her, sharing something from his life, something personal. One of the few times that she felt a little more inclusive. As though he truly valued her involvement. It was also a closer glimpse at the sentimental side she had seen flickered momentarily in his eyes, during their more frosty moments when he quivered in the firing line of her venom. A compassionate side of the corporate man.

"Did I tell you, Mom lives up in Scotland at the moment with her new boyfriend".

"I think you did mention it. He had previously told her about the fact that his parents had divorced just prior to him going away to University, a particularly vulnerable period in his adolescence, and whilst he hadn't confessed as much, she was sure that this had impacted the precarious density of his backbone. So, she has a she has a new boyfriend?".

He sighed heavily as though she were encroaching on his least favourite subject "Yeah, she met him on an online dating site actually", Cayenne's eyes widened in surprise given her own not too distant experience.

"How long have they been together?", she was enjoying this normal conversation about family. The sense that he was letting her in. He shrugged nonchalantly " 'bout eight months I suppose".

"What's he like? Do you approve".

Another shrug "He seems ok although I have to have a heart to heart with my brother about him first before I come to a final decision".

She smiled approvingly of his protective nature.

"I just think…", he was screwing his face up as though searching for the correct description from an assortment of undesirable options, but deciding, in the end, to withhold such harsh judgement. "I mean, what's the hurry?".

Cayenne smiled inwardly and imagined that he tempered every situation with that very question. She wondered how long he had been keeping his current squeeze hanging on. Supposing there was a squeeze. He was probably hoping to silence any commitment requests until just past the child bearing years in the hope that Safe Sally would eventually tire and do what he lacked the fortitude to do.

"We're going up there this weekend, my brother and I. It's mom's birthday too so 'he's' invited us all down. My sister lives in New Zealand so she can't make it. Agatha was due to join us but we will have to see what happens".

"Aaah" she thought, that's where he gets that antipodean lilt from. Just as she had observed, he was probably the kind of person that, not having solidified his own true identity, tended to pick up elements of other people's that appealed and simply adopted them as his own.

"Sounds like a nice guy, inviting you up to the Highlands like that. Clearly, he didn't have to".

The expression on Kenneth's face suggested he wasn't convinced. She got the distinct impression that he wasn't as close with his mother as he was with the father and uncle whom he brought up in conversation frequently. He would mention now and then that he had taken them to watch a football game at the weekend or that he and his uncle had gone to the pub, and she could tell from the warm tones in his voice that he was very fond of both. A warmth that was noticeably absent when he spoke of his mother.

"So what have you bought her for her birthday?, be sure to make it something special.

His face was a picture of indifference. As though he couldn't much care for the finer details of the conversation.

"Dunno, a scarf or something". He chuckled as if to inject an air of uncaring. She wondered if somewhere, seeping from deep within his psyche, he doth protest a little too much. That his complex feelings for his mother had thus far eluded the appropriate introspection.

This was the beginning of him opening up to her just a little more. Over the coming weeks and months, he would go on to share personal details, albeit discreetly so as to alleviate any disloyal guilt, of how much his family relied on him, being the elder of his siblings and how much he was expected to help out. All of which was expressed in a sort of wearisome tone as though he were powerless to change it. Perhaps that explained why he was so desperately seeking an outlet for the turmoil that he couldn't express elsewhere. Or at least that was what he had intended for her to be, but it would seem he felt more than that now. Not that he could ever admit it in any coherent way.

In the cosy comfort of Chanel, all too soon it was time for them to part. Spinning on their heels they walked in opposite directions as usual. Only this time, a few steps in, she turned to glance back at him. He wasn't looking her way at all but kept his head facing in the direction of Canary Wharf, cast downwards slightly. She watched his profile against the backdrop of the iconic business district, hands in pockets head down.

She turned back around and faced the direction of the gym and the Lotus floating Chinese restaurant ahead, either side of the well worn pedestrian pathway.

He held his head down for as long as he could, resisting the temptation to stand and gaze at her as she walked away again, which he was secretly prone to doing. When his resistance gave way, he lifted his gaze from the pavement and turned and glanced in her direction. She was quite a way away by now, but he was glad she was still in sight. He looked longingly at the way she sauntered confidently. Her bulging butt cheeks lifting in sequence with her stride. Her flawless silhouette standing out amongst the dull crowd. She always stood out. Even now, he wanted to race after her and take her by the hand and command his ownership. He could see she was garnering the attention of some of the passers by who couldn't resist a sneaky glance once they had passed her, her defiant demeanour discouraging a hasty stare or another sidelong gape at that ass. A surge of pride rose up to his chest which puffed out a little in response. Knowing that he was the only one within reach of her touch right now. That despite her taunting, he had reason to believe that he currently stood alone in the quest for her hand, the singular elite forerunner with exclusive access to the royal chocolate dipping pool, which would have made the remaining walk back to his depressing offices more bearable but for the fact that he couldn't fully allow himself to indulge. Yet there was a skip to his step all the same, somehow he was coasting just a little.

He wasted no time in berating her in his messages, for being the deliberate cause of his afternoon torment locked in to back to back meetings. "The tight shorts and matching crop top!... Really? I mean just how am I supposed to cope with that. You damn well know that I was in torment. Oh God, so inviting".

"I wanted you to touch me today. Nibble and stroke, like you did at the Novotel. I could see the hunger in your eyes which gingerly nudged at my pussy's muscle memory. Hopeless whore ignored the signs.

Preferring to see his Queen languish in torture and pussy peckish torment. As always… I get home and another perspective kicks in…

Yes I deserve to have my needs fulfilled, but how to balance that with not wanting to be someone's tart on the side. An executive afterthought. A corporate option. All of which are unacceptable.

It's a dilemma that I can see escalating and would much prefer to avoid such a sour conclusion".

"I understand completely - I seem unable to act as a true gentleman, always falling immediately to temptation and selfish indulgence".

"As do I. In today's mood… a local spot would have decimated my resolve completely"…

"Just as well… isn't it certificate day at the gym?. Enjoy your moment later. It is well deserved".

Not for the first time, she was touched by the details that he always seemed to remember.

"Suddenly I'm in no mood to change into gym attire. I think wine relaxes me beyond use".

"You looked absolutely delicious.

Divine".

"Fuck the certificate. Book the Novotel now. Drag me into multi storey seclusion and release this damsel from her frustration.

Going once….

Going twice…

Gone.

Fine fucking toy you turned out to be. 'I will deliver'. Bullshit".

"Sorry only able to respond to this now. I had meetings remember?.

Irritating".

Her apprehension towards his excuses prompting a vicious diatribe.

"I guess you were right… your insistence of living in a fantasy world does not compute with my innate realism".

She was alluding to the conversation they had once shared regarding the iconic Wizard of Oz. A film he admitted to having an affinity for.

She had told him of her love of documentaries and she had been alarmed to learn that Judy Garland, the star of the iconic legendary tale, had endured a horrific experience at the hands of her fellow cast members who were jealous and threatened by this successful young starlet. The documentary had hinted at the trauma of the experience for the impressionable young woman.

"Oh thanks very much, you've just ruined my memories of a childhood favourite".

They had laughed at the time, however it was a mark of her tendency towards the hardened truth and his preference for all things make-believe.

Furthermore, by your own admission you are of the protoplasmic type that seeks to use people for your own gain with no regard for their feelings, seeking to take cruel intentional advantage.

Utterly selfish... the city terrorists are more humane...

Scotland Yard ought to question your whereabouts over the weekend and attest the validity of your alibi...

Wouldn't put it past you to have masterminded the weekend's events".

"Hey! That's rather harsh".

"I am a woman with three children...Have some respect.

Find a street tart for your poisonous exploits...

Someone selfish and narcissistic like you.

Goodbye".

"I think you are great and I'm so sorry if I've given you any other impression.

I wish I had been free this afternoon.

Well done again for your gym award tonight".

CHAPTER 21

"Just lie down on your mat. You are all super early today". Céléste the French yogalates teacher sat cross legged on her mat at the front of the class and silently clapped her hands in glee as she glanced at the wall clock behind her.

Céléste was a small, spindly woman with a healthy toned body that exhibited many years of dedication to her craft. The toning from her previous preference for strength and weight training, still visible in her yoga honed physique. She had shoulder length wispy blonde hair which appeared slightly tussled as though she was accustomed to washing it and leaving it to dry naturally. Her appearance overall was of a simplistic nature, with fresh faced skin and loose casually classic clothes with a nod to Parisian chic. At times she seemed to adopt a slightly hostile air, making the class feel as though an Army Combat Officer were at the helm. Fortunately, Cayenne had not experienced her frosty side directly though she had witnessed a few terse moments when Céléste would make it clear that elle n'a pas souffert les imbéciles volontiers. Whether that was someone complaining about the temperature of the room, which was usually colder than most would prefer or a newbie not paying attention to her exacting commands, which if left uncorrected, would manifest in poor posture. Cayenne couldn't help but recall a Japanese lady approaching her after one of Céléste's more intense sessions and with a look of wide eyed terror, her fingers gripping Cayenne's arm, she whispered, "There was no….. zen".

She had always been warm and friendly to Cayenne and whenever she arrived early, they would often chat animatedly about their various pursuits. Hers varying from learning to surf somewhere off the southern coast, learning to play the piano and electric guitar, to swimming in the Channel on her summer visits back home in Biarritz, whilst Cayenne would share her stories of her tennis exploits or the children. In return Céléste had offered many insights and observations in her experiences of special needs and what she thought might help in their various discussions about Ocean and his challenges.

She sat upright and smiled a little too sweetly at the congregation.

"Close your eyes and relax. Breath in and out slowly. Feel the breath making your abdomen rise and fall. When you breathe out relax your back into the mat".

Céléste spoke in a heavily accented, clear and concise manner and every class was almost identical and ran like clockwork. If they so desired, a class member could predict the routine almost to the letter, punctuated with several drawn out silences, which could often be so prolonged that one couldn't help but begin to wonder, 'Is she still here, has she fallen asleep or temporarily disappeared?'. The fact that Céléste was the only teacher that refused music in her classes, added to the sense of eeriness. Few dared to open their eyes to peek, as their curious gaze would be certain to be met with a deathly intuitive stare in return. Cayenne had experienced this once, to her detriment, when during a spinal twist when the class had been instructed to turn towards the back of the room, with their legs facing the opposite direction, the seconds had seemed to drift into minutes and Cayenne considered that there would be no harm in glancing back to the front of the class out of curiosity, found herself eyeball to eyeball with Céléste's contemptuous gaze. She held her breath and whipped her head back around to the rear of the class vowing never to move again even in the midst of acute discomfort, until Céléste instructed her approval. She remembered feeling distinctly as though she had become ensnared in a scene from Paranormal Activity and resolutely refused to move a muscle no matter how long the silence or the how loud her muscular protest.

Céléste seemed to relish having a congregation lying very still in her presence, cloaked in semi darkness, with their eyes closed. She seemed

223

to enjoy silently, observing everyone closely without the danger of having them stare back. Perhaps it gave her a sense of power or perhaps she was simply taking advantage of the few opportunities that life presented to observe people at close quarters in the midst of a bustling capital city, without penance.

The class lay still and silent with only the sound of soft breathing and the hum of the purple strip lights filling the space, allowing for the energy created to define itself.

After what seemed like an age, the heavy French accent permeated the room, breaking the silence. "Start to bring some movement back to your bo'dee. Move your fingers and your toes. Bring your knees to your chest and roll from side to side massaging your lower back. Then roll backwards and forwards and you caaaaaaan seeeeet uuup". By the time everyone arose and sat upright, Céléste was sitting with her feet up, bent at the knees and her back straight in an effortless v shape. The class attempted to adopt the same pose with varying degrees of success. By the end of the 45 minute class, Cayenne was exhausted by the umpteen number of side planks that characterised Céléste's sessions. They had certainly earned their Savasana and Cayenne lay back on her mat gladly as the lights dimmed a little more and once again they entered into their own private worlds to the sound of slightly more laboured breathing patterns, permeated with sporadic vibrations of distant movement in other parts of the building, exposed in the silence. At this point, Céléste wandered around rubbing the palm of her hands together creating warmth and energy, administering lavender oil on each person's temples before pressing their shoulders down onto the mat and at the same time, guiding them through a meditation to bring their entire bodies into a completely relaxed state.

"Reeeelaaaaaax. Reeeeelaaaaax your feet, your ankles. Reeeeelaaaax your bottom and thighs… Reeeelaaaaax Reeeeelaaaax", Céléste cooed as she meandered around the room. "Reeeelaaaax your head, your neck, your shoulders. Reeeelaaaaax. Focus on your breathing". Cayenne could have sworn that the instructor would hover over her for a split second longer than most. Admittedly, the make-up she wore to class and her elaborate selection of head gear were the possible cause of the real or imagined ghostly pause.

Finally her voice faded to silence as they lay in the darkness for several more minutes.

"Ok you can start to wake up your bo'deee, move your hands and your fingers and your toes and your ankles… aaaand you caaan seeeeeet uuup", she would sing like an Parisian soprano. This time, the class would arise with adjusting eyes blinking open to find a fully draped teacher, complete with hat and scarf, clutching a bulging rucksack, fully prepared to race into the elements, heading across the capital on her bicycle complete with front whicker basket, to her next freelance appointment, deliberately leaving little time for conversation and unnecessary pleasantries.

After a quick "Thank you for coming, see you next weeeek", in a saccharine tone designed to incite a loyal return, she would dissolve virtually unnoticed from the bustling room and seemingly float

225

metaphysically to the upper floor and disappear on her bicycle into the flow of city traffic.

CHAPTER 22

"How have you been?".

"Oh my God!. You're alive". Their contact had waned somewhat and before long several weeks had passed.

"All good…. thought you might be better off without the let downs".

His considerate nature once again gave her cause to reflect. "That's very thoughtful of you".

"All good your end?. Any fun stuff?".

"Extreme withdrawal symptoms following an abrupt end to my routine frisky Mayfair capers…

But every cloud…. It has simply honed my skills at identifying Execs with the competence to 'deliver".

"Fuck!. Those frolicsome exploits continue to appeal".

"Oh really?".

"Yes…. Despite the stress…".

"Stress? From moi??? Whatever do you mean?".

"Regal demands".

"Regal demands were in response to the 'high end' offers detailed in the terms of engagement...

Offers that now appear somewhat disingenuous".

"What you wearing? ...and watching?".

"Stark..... not watching anything... resting my weary overly honed limbs....".

"So..... a Mayfair return would be desirable?".

"I simply could never trust you or your word until you redress the sworn matter of 'I have your birthday gift and I want to take you to the Shard'..... that thus far remains unresolved.

A Mayfair return will only be considered once faith has been restored.

I have to say.... At this point... a rather distinct sour taste of the Intercontinental lingers..."

"Understandable.....

I have this lingering image of you from South Quay... your beauty.... Your wanting.... The juice... pretty unshakeable".

"... Yes a similar memory endures.... Barbaric abandonment in the midst of acute cunt hunger...

You are consistent at least.

Your cold dismissal however has it's virtues… as I resolve never to succumb to cunt depreciation again".

"No knight rescued you from this yet then?…

Hunger for your cunt has not gone".

" I am in the enviable position of allowing quality courtiers to pursue my attention…..".

"So you should be gorgeous Queen. How are the honed limbs?".

"Positively popping and sizzling… even women are either appreciating or coveting my obvious dedication to the cause…"

"Mmmmm sounds interesting… you intrigued by the attention?.

Hey?

Have you gone for the night?".

"There was a delay in receiving your message... Yes... it is flattering most certainly.... Hard work must be rewarded".

"The Queen should be adored by all....I am wanking hard... you are the images in my head".

"Admittedly, just the image of you almost brings me to a climax....

I'm sorry I missed your unique lateral cock squirt... remembering cupping you as you came. I've missed the sensation of you hard in my hands....

What is it about you that seems to release the unbeknownst blockages within and stimulate my caramel canals to flow like never before?....".

"Glad to hear this... I harden knowing I still have impact.... I miss not being your whore toy... I want my place back at court...I want my interracial fuck fest. I want my chocolate juice drenching.

You must be looking very fine in this glorious sunshine".

"Wouldn't you like know...

Feeling fatigued.

Perhaps I've been overdoing it at the gym...

I am resting and filling up on protein to rebuild the muscles...

Lady of leisure needs a little more concentrated leisure".

"How many hours have you been doing?".

"There's been a few occasions where I have done between four and five classes a day totalling around three hours… in addition I had an hour's personal training where I managed to dead lift 120kg. Then I had boxing and then yesterday I ran three miles followed by boxing again".

"Wow babe, perhaps a day off is not a bad thing especially with this current heat wave.

I could pop by early next week if you're around?".

She reflected on what she had written and had to admit she had been pushing herself a little too hard.

She lay back on her unmade bed considering that particular marathon gym weekend.

Diego had agreed to join her at the gym taking full advantage of the occasional free pass that her fitness company advertised as a way of attracting fresh clientele by inviting non members to come in and sample some of the classes.

Diego who was resolutely frugal with his hard earned money refused to join her otherwise, unless of course she was paying the standard £15 daily fee.

After a warm up on the treadmill, and few rounds of pushups, squats and burpees, they had headed to the heavy weight section of the gym in the basement, making the weight station their starting point.

"Let's start with deadlifts and then squats". She suggested.

Diego was eyeing up the weights warily. They had been to the gym together several times before but at times she could tell that it made him a little uneasy to see this side of her. To realise just how strong his mom had become.

Starting at 40kg, they took it turns to do ten deadlifts. The gym had a lively buzz as the Saturday afternoon regulars put themselves through their routines and the sound of unidentifiable background music blasted out just a little too loudly.

Jett Blackstone, a muscled big bear who was waiting to use the barbell, observed them with curious amusement.

"Mate, you wanna keep the bar as close to your legs as possible as you come up". Jett had stepped forward to advise Diego and offer some constructive correction regarding his posture.

"That's it. Can you feel the difference?".

"Yeah I can". Her son replied. "Thanks man".

After Cayenne had managed to deadlift 120kg, Diego stepped forward for his own maximum lift of 80kg. He just managed to lift three out of the five and dropped the bar with a frustrated grunt.

Cayenne smiled to herself, knowing how much he would have wanted to beat her.

After Cayenne had squatted 40kg, she hoisted the bar over her head and lowered it to the floor. As Diego was about to proceed with his own squats, Jett interjected again after returning from the water machine with his newly refilled bottle in hand. After taking a long, thirsty guzzle, he placed his bottle down and approached them at the weight station.

"Do you now what mate?, You see your mom's back, she's developed these muscles here". He pointed to just below her shoulders as Cayenne turned her back to them. "That's where the bar should sit. Tense that muscle for a minute and squeeze your shoulders together". He instructed Cayenne to stiffen the muscles at the top of her back as she squeezed her shoulder muscles together producing a defined and sculptured muscle shelf.

"See that?".

Diego was nodding with an intense expression on his face. "You haven't quite developed that muscle yet". Jet was squeezing just below Diego's shoulders now. When you do, you'll find it much easier. Cos you'll rest the bar right here". He pointed to an imaginary horizontal line on her son's back. Then it won't hurt so much. I could see you flinching a little. But before long, you'll see what I mean".

"Cheers man". Diego shook hands with Jett in his usual friendly manner. "I appreciate that".

After selecting a protein shake each from reception, they headed to the upstairs studio where some boxing gloves and pads were bundled into a corner.

After a few running drills, Cayenne pulled on her pads and braced her hands for Diego's punches.

"Whoah. Steady. You don't have to punch that hard". She protested, trying to grip the floor with her feet to withstand the force of his hooks. She wondered whether it was payback time for having one upped him in the weights section.

He narrowed his eyes menacingly and continued to throw her jabs from all angles unabated.

Cayenne decided that she may as well get on with it and tightened her stomach muscles against his hooks and guarded her face as best she could. She remembered Fenton's cautionary prompts from boxing class, to lower her hands slightly to protect her shoulders from the full impact. He caught her with a quick right hook followed immediately with a left jab.

This was enough to push her buttons and with all the pissed off gusto she could muster, she charged forward, and used the full force of her weight to push him backwards. At first he resisted and only stepped back a couple of steps. She braced herself again and forged ahead adopting a no fail mentality. Diego suddenly lost his footing and began chuckling as he stumbled backwards towards the far wall. Cayenne sensed her opportunity and seized the moment, eyes blazing, she leaned towards him with all her might, forcing her feet into the ground to garner more leverage, pushing him back until he fell to the floor in submission.

He was laughing. She wasn't.

CHAPTER 23

"Let's meet up later in the week".

"Sure. How's everything at work?"

"Team of 9 reduced to 5….I'm one of the unlucky 5".

"Wow! Is that how you really feel?. Sorry to hear that. You only live once… from what I gather, you have no significant dependants…

Why don't you just live… go and do something you have always wanted to do.

There's a commercial I've seen on the TV, where an ostrich stumbles upon some virtual goggles that simulate flying through the clouds and therefore decides that he can fly. To the bewilderment of his fellow ostriches and after many failed attempts well into the night, he eventually lifts off and flies into the sunset to the soundtrack of the brilliant Elton John's rocket man…

So get your goggles on and go fly bro'…

You know you can….".

"Good advice gorgeous x.

Do you miss you white whore toy?.

Scarily I'm missing being it...perhaps it's because I'm hot and thirsty and we both know what my favourite juice is".

She wondered what exactly scared him. She had gathered that most aspects of daily life seemed to cause him slight trepidation, that was his nature, but she also wondered whether, pertaining to her, whether part of it was his inability to conceive that a black woman could be significant to him which she could only imagine was a wholly unexpected development. She pictured him with his old university friends and being frightened to reveal his secret passion. He was definitely the type to limit his appeal to what he considered acceptable to his peers.

"I can't get fully away from this need to be fucking filthy".

"I'm not at all surprised by this... merely perplexed that you've lasted this long without it".

"The rush, the hardening of my cock as I write, it gives me something.

It gives me a feeling of arrogant superiority even though I'm a whore – what a contradiction".

"I must admit... I couldn't fathom engaging in this filth talk with anyone else... surely they wouldn't understand it...

Arrogant superiority is totally understandable given the priceless chocolate whoreism that you are temporarily privy to.

Your unique white cock and it's antics justify your arrogance...".

"Fuck! I want you to use me again. Be that bitch that just wants one thing from her toy".

There he goes again, she pondered. Emphasising that she only want one thing from him. Either he was trying to ward her off from developing feelings for him, from demanding any more than he could give or he was simply trying to get her to invite him to her place and alleviate the cost of seeing her, or perhaps he was responding to pressure from elsewhere.

"I look at the poor souls in this office who don't realise the fucking delights I've enjoyed".

He sounded like a schoolboy sometimes, that had discovered some sort of secret stash that if revealed would grant him the secretly longed for notoriety that he never quite managed to attain at Uni or amongst his current peers. To be known for something other than being the weird nerdy guy, the uncool one, and yet the very fact that it was a secret gave him a healthy surge of testosterone.

"I want you to use me like those black bitches used that white princess in the video".

"Your absence of late makes me question your desire....

I've just had the sweetest message on one of the dating sites... so sincere and honourable, asking to get to know me... I was just about to reply when I registered the height. 5"3.

Goodness, my cat is almost that height.

Am I terribly shallow?".

"You have a cat? You never mentioned it".

"Yes. Temple is her name. My Pussy is a Temple. How remarkably apt. We've had her since she was around 6 weeks old along with her brother Mountbatten. Unfortunately, Mountbatten ran away.

My son says that Temple is a lot like her mother (as in Moi). Very anti social. Likes her own company. Quite prepared to nibble the hand that feeds her".

"Sincere and honourable won't do you long term, I assure you. Let's hope the diminutive knight has a dark side....

No harm in meeting up I suppose... not sure he will have the presence to moisten you in a lift.

Am I stuck with this need to engage in such filthy antics?".

"Not at all.. I'll meet you in Zurich".

"Did I mention that there's a possible return due to recent events?".

"Yes, you did mention something.

I think you're right.... honourable would be a bore....

I'd have to discern pretty quickly whether they have an unparalleled respect for Nubian regality and have acquired an insatiable thirst for cinnamon cunt juice".

"You would…

Anyone not liking juice drenching or face sitting really shouldn't be at the same table as the Queen.

I'm hungry for your black clit… I can just imagine you flicking it, teasing it as you consider eligible suitors for your coconut cunt milk".

 "Here here old sport….

Anyone who has not acquired the nose for it has simply revealed an unrefined pussy palate.

They should be relegated to the dungeons along with half wit whores that fail to maximise their limited opportunities when they arise…

Hence my recent whore resumé perusal.

In my white whore's abrupt absence… I have allowed myself to fantasize of the potential cunt gymnastic possibilities of a certain gym instructor…

Such a shame he seems to lack the necessary arrogance to move things forward…

Pitiful…".

"Half wit whore needs to sort it.

Seriously!? … a non arrogant gym instructor??? How do you find them babe?.

Had any one to one sessions with him yet?".

"Oh suburban half wit… calm your jealousy. 'don't be mad when you see that he wants it'. You had your chance…

With yet a little patience… it's only a matter of time before the instructor yields to the desperate urge to copulate the very buns and guns that he helped hone…."

"I see what you did there 'yoncé. Is it another pale prospect?".

"No. He is deliciously caramelised in fact. Coated in supreme Melanin. I rarely do Personal Training sessions now, but his classes have become my favourite. We may linger after class from time to time, a little chat as I ask advice and he willingly gives it… a little stroll to the stretch and cool down area…

Gently, gently does it…

I have faith he will soon man up and seize the day… no half witism detected.

The watching pale secret droolers speak with their eyes and body language alone".

"Sounds like a viable prospect. Annoyingly".

"What's annoying is the dress I had specially prepared for my Shard encounter that is still hanging, unchristened in my closet. Serves as a reminder to avoid half wits"

"Show me. It WILL get the outing it deserves. Surely you won't get the same thrill with him that you derive from blacking an innocent".

"I have no idea what delights await…."

"I may have to arrogantly step in and give you a fucking high end white corporate treat that poor gym instructors can only dream of delivering…."

"Time is of the essence….

Off to seek attention from my strength instructor…. I do hope he is proud of my elevated, rounded glute gains…

Must go… need to reserve my place front of class. Auf Wiedersehen!".

CHAPTER 24

The long corridor on the middle level of the gym, lead directly to the main studio. A large irregular shaped room halved into the larger expanse which had a mirrored wall where the instructor usually faced the class alongside a slightly narrower half where all the equipment was dotted around in their various places of storage, leaving a smaller workout area for those that were a little more self conscious and insecure and with largely less ego as not to want to parade around in full view. Various doors lead to other parts of the building, mostly only permissible for staff, whilst others lead to large storage spaces which a more forward thinking floor planner may have utilised better. Just behind the door was the sound system and the dimmer switch to adjust the lighting.

"Why is it so dark in here?". Barrington called out as he entered the room, biceps bulging from beneath his silky grey vest which were tucked into long baggy shorts.

He would smile as he turned the lights up to its full capacity to the groans of most of the women who rather preferred their reflection with a more forgiving light setting.

Barrington Cole, the East London cardio instructor, could often be seen wandering around the room nodding his head to whatever track that he was blasting out through the loud speakers overhead. It was obvious that music played a huge part of his life and you rarely saw him without a pair of humungous earphones on his head. He even walked as though he was moving to the tune of something funky and you half expected him to break out into a contemporary dance at any moment. Like many young men that Cayenne observed, especially in the illuminating gym environment, he seemed to use music as a way of buffering the distance between the unsatisfying reality of his real life and the prospect of a life that they hoped for but had no real conviction of attaining.

When he had first arrived at the gym, there was nothing to suggest to Cayenne that he could be anything other than just another gym instructor. After being around the gym for some time, it was obvious that instructors tended to pass through fairly frequently and whilst there were a few that formed a stalwart backdrop, there also seemed to be a constant flow of coming and going and new faces would pop up frequently, which was perhaps one of the reasons that Cayenne had settled into a routine headed by a select few of instructors that she had become familiar with. There was no obvious appeal about Barrington to speak of although she would certainly describe him as pleasantly attractive. Just shy of being categorised as short and his rippling biceps made a loud statement of a level of dedication to his craft.

As time went on however, the personality he brought to the classes and radical levels of energy he exuded, definitely enhanced his appeal. He had a way of engaging the whole class, giving everyone a sense that he was aware of them by encouraging them just at their point of need.

What Cayenne particularly liked was that he remained the same in every class. If he was ever down or discouraged or bored or uninspired, you would never be able to tell. His enthusiasm showed no sign of waning which couldn't always be said for some of the others.

Cayenne giggled to herself when she remembered sharing with one of the other girls and demonstrating how Baz, as he liked to be called, often signalled the end of one gruelling segment with a raised finger and a loud exclamation, "WAIT!". Clearly he could sense the united sense of relief coursing around the room as they were lulled into a false sense of security, certain that he had responded to their pain and that the torture was over. Then Baz would turn his pointed upright finger to the right, almost identical to the way Michael Jackson did on stage, to signify he had come to the end of the good old Jackson five tracks and now there was about to be a change of tempo. 'the new songs'.

"Round 2!" Baz commanded, laughing off the stifled groans with a winning smile that ensured he would be forgiven for pushing them to their limits. "Come on, Come on". There was no dramatic authority in his tone, more like a supportive older brother, not wanting them to give up on themselves.

In his demonstrations, he leaped around the room with a boundless energy that the class could only covet, and more than once, Cayenne had been flagging with exhaustion in a pool of sweat, trying desperately to recover her breathing pattern, when she would hear "Come on Cay", and look up from under her dripping brow, to see Baz on one knee with his outstretched hand open as though in the midst of a romantic proposal, waiting to pull her back into the game. Her chocolate skin disguising the fact that her cheeks would be burning with bashful euphoria.

243

She had to admit she secretly loved it and she knew there was no way she could convince the rest of the class that she wasn't doing it on purpose, which was actually true but if she had her way, every class would end with Baz on bended knee with his hand waiting to take hers.

Baz was now demonstrating his next move, jumping down into a plank with an unparalleled energetic force, followed by a push up, he then sprang up in the air straight into a high knee jump.

He would repeat this several times in high energy, leaving the floor effortlessly, bouncing from one position to another vigorously.

Before long the class would be passed out on their mats for the cool down period which was usually to the tune of Sade or H.E.R. or to the runs of some modern Jazz.

It was here that Cayenne could get away with some sneaky close up glances at her instructor as from a post workout position it was much easier to ogle the chunky, chiselled thighs and protruding calves from this lower angle without being caught perving. Her favourite, was when he would demonstrate a recovery pose after a particularly gruelling bicep round, he positioned his arms in the air, almost with his hands to his ears, cautioning them to pull their shoulders back. It was here that the full glory of his biceps and chest was on show, only with a glistening sheen of perspiration, forming an enticingly shiny ganache. If she was particularly tired, her mind would wander to an image of herself licking the silky topping from his pecs, imagining the feel of those very same biceps gripping her in a vice like hold and any resistance she may have had would be instantly sacrificed on the altar of lust.

After class, Cayenne would put her own equipment away and then assist Baz in replacing his. She knew that it would seem like she was doing this for attention, but she really wasn't. She had always encouraged her children that in a class situation, always be prepared to stay behind and help pack away. To always be mindful to give value and that someone has to do it and it may as well be you. After her gym classes was the perfect opportunity to practice what she preached.

"Good to see you peeps", she could hear Baz cheerily waving his weary class out of the door single file. Cayenne would be way ahead by then, speeding towards the cool down area, giving anyone who cared to notice, no reason to speculate that she had any cause to linger.

CHAPTER 25

"Well…. Did his resolve crack?"

"He is far too professional for that, so not quite…. However, my need for appreciation and attention were duly satisfied with glances and smiles…

Every little helps…".

"This whore hates this honourable resolve which is turning the Queen's head".

"What on earth is a Queen to do in times of extreme famine...

I have you to thank for opening up this newly developed need to be admired...

But your brutal withdrawal inevitably exposes deficit...

Deficit that yearns for fulfilment again... by any means necessary.

Amused...

You persist in referring to yourself as a 'whore'.

At which point, even long after you retire from accounting, will you stop referring to yourself as ..... 'an accountant'?"

"I remain a dirty whore...

We can discuss in person next week".

"Yes, let's discuss the eligibility required to be considered my personal white whore....

I must advise you that you are entitled to appeal the final decision in

writing within 14 days of the face to face discussion".

"Your need to espouse racial superiority will always require a white whore to be available to kneel and lick".

"Your arrogance neglects to acknowledge that not any white whore will do..."

"I like the hard ons that come with my arrogance".

"Granted. That very arrogance is what caught the attention of an otherwise untouchable Queen".

"Yes. Arrogance, yet with an inexhaustible subservient desire to be absolutely used.

I wish you would walk into my office, short skirt, pantyless... and just motion for me to kneel, then pull up the skirt and let me drink from your divine cordial.

Absolutely no talk.

The poor ignorant suits I'm surrounded by would cream".

"You have virtually described my own vision...

After months of enduring pent up Suburban White Whore half witism....

I walk into a room with you drooling pitifully behind...

I throw my things on the bed and grab your loosened tie and force you to submit...

No talk, I've certainly had my fill of your spin.

'just kneel peasant and let your tongue do the grovelling'. I assert.

When…and only when I am sufficiently spent of every last drop of cunt concentrate and all my frustration is expended… will I even acknowledge your entire presence.

Then, depending on my mood… you will either be dismissed or if in all unlikelihood, you excelled yourself with your clit grovelling… I may let you put on one of those newly advertised intense pleasure condoms, using my own personalised flavours, Caribbean cunt, 100% proof rum and Sugar Cane and let you pummel my clit mine for more precious stones….

All whilst secretly despising your pathetically futile expectations for your own pleasure enhancement and for not prioritising her majesty's.

Any of those 'pathetic suits' at your office, happen to be at a loose end by any chance?. Any that you can recommend with a healthy appetite and a spicy, refined pussy palette. Discount those that are merely inquisitive like some kind of dabbling vegetarian, however

the ones that you can identify with an urgent hunger for the aromatic can form an orderly queue".

"Let's just act that out next week".

"I'm sure you could introduce me to one in the lower end of the spectrum... the one least likely to be head hunted for executive trouble shooting in Switzerland".

"Too weak. You like to use a toy with prospects".

"True. I will therefore defer to your superior knowledge, oh arrogant one".

"Just remembered the Novotel when the arrogance was simply removed".

"The five course meal next week had better be exquisite".

"Of course. We will always do high end when we do actually play".

"There you go again. SPIN. High end has been largely lacking of late....".

"Ok agreed. Will try to avoid spin although it's bound up in the character of this whore you are using".

"Deluded Dan resurfaces.

I wouldn't be tempted to whore surf had I a reliable executive harlot in the first place".

CHAPTER 26

Family dinners were rare in the Richard's family calendar, so Cayenne made a concerted effort to attend her cousin's birthday dinner that coming weekend in Torquay. It also provided her and the children the opportunity to revisit a place that was close to their hearts. Where they now lived was a complete contrast to the traditional British seaside resort with it's vibrant, cheerful towns, set at the very heart of the English Riviera on the South Devon Coast.

Having spent the morning attending to Ocean who was due to spend the weekend with his respite facility, she could now devote some much needed time to deciding what to wear.

Ocean loved going away for the weekend to Identity House, an organisation that took care of children with disabilities for short bursts every few weeks, both to allow the families to plan events without the challenges that living with disability entailed and to allow the child to access facilities and explore their capabilities within a more sympathetic environment. He would have the opportunity to socialise with around four or five other children of similar age and with similar challenges, although, just as in school, Ocean tended to enjoy the company of adults rather than his peers.

Cayenne liked Identity House, the moment she had first walked inside. Admittedly the outside resembled an abandoned building, being based on the ground floor of a seemingly rundown tower block which seemed to be constantly adorned with scaffolding. But once inside, the neat, clean little maze of small corridors and compact

rooms lead around to an open plan kitchen diner where the children spent most of their time. The large windows allowing for maximum light to flood the space, leading out to a small paved garden which was dominated by a trampoline which had Ocean's name all over it.

The majority of the staff were Asian, as well as the cooks which suited Ocean down to the ground as there was no shortage of Biriyanis or any other concoction of meat and rice for him to feast on.

It gave Cayenne much pleasure to pack his case meticulously, ensuring he had smart clothes and nice fragrances and whatever he needed to maintain his grooming. She prided herself that her son would not look like some of the other special needs children she had witnessed whose families seemed to think didn't deserve to have pride in how they looked, as though they had little comprehension of their appearance. She spared no expense making sure he had the best she could afford and felt immense pride as she watched him from her bedroom window, being escorted by two assistants towards wherever the grey minibus happened to be parked. He looked tall and handsome and immaculate. She loved his confident stride as though he had already decided that no matter how the world would view and label him, he was his own person. He walked like a 'SOMEBODY', with the only tell tale signs of his challenges being his occasional jerky movements which he at times seemed unable to control, though it was his mother's mission to DIE TRYIN' helping him to curtail.

Another unfortunate and annoying tell tale sign that this smart young man may have unique layers to him, was the fact that his conventionally trained assistants, both of whom were dwarfed by Ocean's height, had firm hold of each of his arms and had found it necessary to pull his carrier case for him as though he were incapable of doing so himself. Whilst she could appreciate, that owing to his size and mischievous inclinations, they undoubtedly felt more secure by controlling him and had been trained that it would be for his own safety, it was a pity that they hadn't managed to insist upon Ocean electing to choose the behaviour that was most appropriate for himself and either rewarding or punishing him accordingly to reinforce the lesson.

Glancing at her reflection as she inspected her asymmetrical leopard print two piece frill trimmed combination, teamed with sparkly brown sock boots, she pulled her stomach muscles in tight, but could still detect a slight bulge in her midriff. She lamented silently that despite many hours sweating in the gym, turning up when others failed to, putting in 100% when others considered simply turning up was effort enough, that the results didn't always come fast enough. She had denied herself breakfast to avoid the immediate bloating that ensued and with this choice of bodycon dress, she needed to be able to hold it in and save a little space for her cousin's signature Jerk chicken.

Dabbing touches of her plum coloured lipstick on her cheeks and accentuating her cheek bones with a glittery highlighter, she strutted into the children's bedrooms to check on their progress. Predictably, Diego and Sugar were slumped on opposite sides of his double bed, engrossed in the latest level of their current video obsession. They were enthusing so loudly in what appeared to her to be a foreign language with Diego demonstrating what they had just watched, squealing Japanese statements in a high pitched voice, whilst sugar lay calmly showing no visible signs of the excitement that she equally shared. Cayenne often mused at the differences in their personalities which did nothing to dissipate the many things that they shared in common.

"Sugar Sugar, did you see that Sugar". Cayenne once counted the amount of times he called his sister's name at the height of their excitement. "Sugar Oh my God, did you see that? That was siiiiiiiiiiiiiiiiiic". To which Sugar would simply smirk in agreement refusing to exert herself and conserving her energy for much more appropriate matters.

"You're not wearing that!". Cayenne cast a disapproving eye over the un-ironed green and black tracksuit with matching long sleeved T shirt that she had bought Diego for his birthday the previous year. Whilst she was glad he was getting so much wear out of it, it seemed to be his go to outfit for all manner of events, although typically to do with college outings with his friends.

"Mi se mi naaaaaah change eeettttt", he barked in response in his deepest and most acute Jamaican accent. Having never been to Jamaica and raised in a second generation home where patois was scarcely used, she marvelled at how he had taken to imitating it so well. She laughed heartily at his impersonation which he executed in a thunderous deep baritone, much like the older generation Jamaicans tended to do.

"It's not even ironed. It's a party. Wear something else". She demanded.

"Will you iron it for me then?". He blinked at her as persuasively as he could and adopted a bugs bunny expression, attempting to emulate the innocent face of his childhood. She threw him a sideward glance. It seemed the older he got the more he demanded her to take care of him. Not because he wasn't capable, more that he appreciated the things he used to take for granted and was now determined to revel in the longevity of it at every opportunity.

Sugar had opted for something equally casual. She, much like her brother, was loath to dress up too smartly for any occasion. She must have been around four when she refused to wear anything remotely girly. There wasn't a single dress left in her wardrobe which was a now a keen reflection of her boyish pastimes and an abhorrence of anything pink. Conversely, in every other way, she was extremely ladylike and seemed to inhabit a grace and femininity that belied her youth. Even when she was lounging in the living room, she had a demure way of sitting and carried herself with an innate elegance and poise that her mother could only achieve with a concentrated effort. Casting a critical eye over her daughter's choice of outfit, she conceded that the metallic tank top over a long sleeved black tee-shirt and black leggings would just about suffice as a smart casual outfit.

As it turned out, many of the other guests had a decidedly more casual look in mind also. Jeans and tee-shirts seemed to be the order of the day. Cayenne had the familiar sensation of being overdressed as she observed the relaxed attire around her.

She leaned back in her chair on the terrace to the rear of her cousin's large detached home, which was spread over three levels with concrete steps along one side leading down to ground level where Diego was holding court, no doubt sharing a humorous meme or story as within seconds everyone around him was howling with laughter as he spread his amiable spirit around. The middle terrace had a large arrangement of chairs set out which were draped in white covers complete with cerise bows at the back, with an aisle space as though prepared for an outdoor wedding. Knowing her cousin Marguerite as she did, she rather suspected that the look was deliberate in a last ditch attempt to twist her long term partner's arm into finally popping the question. The three large wooden tables on the patio were heaving with food, most of which was simmering in heated containers with dome like lids keeping in the heat. The aromas emanating from the spicy, coconut fragrances, filled up her senses.

Cayenne gazed longingly at the glass canisters full of almost every traditional Caribbean drink, from the deep pink homemade carrot juice, bright yellow creamy pineapple juice drink and her favourite Guinness punch which were all gaping invitingly at her from the other side of the lawn.

She could recall enjoying them as a child with her brothers and being introduced to a whole range of traditional Jamaican delicacies with weird names like 'duckunu' and 'blue draws', the names of which nobody seemed to be able to explain. Back then, their mother even made her own hot chocolate from what looked like a huge piece of chalky coal. Those were the good old days, back before their mother became distracted. When she used to make time for all things motherly. Sewing, baking, hair plaiting…

Her phone momentarily pierced the nostalgia.

"How's the family party?".

"Running terribly late... it's a common trait of black folk".

With her phone in hand, she surveyed the expansive lawn and the guests that were mingling and posturing in suspended enjoyment of what was to come, holding on to their drinks and nibbles as children raced mindlessly back and forth across the perfectly manicured grass.

"Miniature undisciplined irritants running around causing mayhem, of course the parents are oblivious. As children, we were often told that kids with mixed blood were prone to delinquency or in my mother's tongue 'dem half breed pickney dem rude you see'".

"Don't tell me... by pickney you mean kids right?".

"Well done astute scholar.

... judging by the red skinned pandemonium I am witnessing, there would seem to be some truth to this mythology.

Secretly longing for the quiet secluded confines of a Central London hotel....".

It was clear she wasn't the only one reminiscing.

"Good I'm glad the longing remains...

White Knight is equally bored in suburbia – I'm longing for it too.

Any white toys turning the Queen's head at the BBQ?".

The next morning, his was the first message on her phone.

"Morning – how are you?".

Cayenne paused for a moment to consider quite how long it had been since she had awoken to this question from anyone else.

"Is there a good park in Crossharbour to eat a sandwich outside?".

"Ginal!!!. Sandwich??? Outside??? Park???"

"Not at all, I am well aware that a sandwich in a park is beneath the Queen's lofty expectations. I just thought it would be nice to take advantage of the lovely weather and have more time together locally. That doesn't make me a 'ginal' as you put it. I am far from a trickster as my credit card bill will attest".

"Just so happens there is a park one stop from Crossharbour (mudchute) or a ten minute walk away".

"Care to join me?"

Cayenne stood leaning against the low wall next to the steps under the bridge leading to the ticket machines at Crossharbour, examining the gleaming red trainers which matched her bright red lipstick perfectly, ignoring the curious glances of pedestrians roaming up and down the stairwell, topping up their oyster cards and getting on and off the constant run of light rail carriages.

She glanced up towards the row of shops in the direction from which she knew he would emerge, certain that any moment now, he would turn the corner. She could guess almost exactly how he would look. Office attire that had become more and more casual as the morning had progressed. By now his tie would be either loosened or removed altogether along with the blazer. The top few buttons of his shirt would have been unbuttoned shortly after his arrival at the office, once he'd gotten the low down from his secretary or after the first meeting of the day was underway. He usually wore typical office type leather shoes and she observed more than once, how he appeared to love the clicking sound they made as he strutted around posturing in accountant-like fashion. His trousers would be tightly belted as if to emphasise his narrow waist. He would appear with his mouth slightly agape and his eyes widened as he furtively looked for the caramel Amazonian figure in the crowd, that he hoped would be waiting for him. Then there would be a moment of exasperation, hoping that she was there, that he would be on time and that she would at the very least be bearing something that resembled a smile. How he loved that smile. That smile could either make or break his day and the annoying thing was, she was fully aware of it.

A few minutes later, the form of him appeared from the assembly of midday shoppers, travellers and residents of the neighbouring apartments. Just as she'd anticipated, his pale pink shirt was unbuttoned and tucked into his narrow trousers. His tie had clearly been abandoned alongside his blazer and she could almost hear the clipping of his court shoes against the concrete as he strode down the slope towards her with two paper carriers in his hands, which no doubt contained her order to the letter. His body swayed from side to side in synchronicity to the movement of his feet, causing his hair to soothingly flip side to side in the breeze. She could picture him doing this as a child. He perhaps modified it slightly when conscious of it, but little escaped this discerning woman's lens.

His face visibly relaxed as he registered the sight of her. His forehead, now smooth, glistened with the perspiration from rushing to see her. He'd been nervous that the assistant that had kept him waiting for his order was going to be the cause of his annihilation. A smile broke out across his lips, giving a glimpse of his crooked teeth. She smiled at his failed attempt to conceal his delight, which caused the corners of his mouth to twitch.

"Hi, you look gorgeous".

She was now fighting to contain her own smile as her esteem was reinforced by the sincerity of his words. Something in the way he said it, resonated truth into her psyche.

He kissed both her rouged cheeks and ran his fingers nervously through his hair.

"So where's this park then?".

They walked together in the direction of Mudchute Park & Farm where herself and the children had whiled away many hours exploring the grounds and observing the animals.

She was aware that they must have looked an unusual sight. An office attired white accountant, looking as though he could barely spend the time to grab a quick sesame seeded sandwich before rushing back to attend to the demands of his corporate agenda, walking alongside a bronzed, gym attired fitness enthusiast, cooling down and strolling post workout in the afternoon sun. She eventually slowed her pace down to match his, settling into an uncustomary relaxed stroll, him making sure to stay half a step behind so that he could steal the occasional glimpse of the glutes that he was already imagining being cupped rigidly in his hands.

They took the short cut through the farm, the large expanse of animal trodden terrain that came into view at the top of the steep stoney steps off the main road, leading to a small hilly plain. Cayenne turned in the direction of the park, not knowing quite where the alternative path would lead. He had other ideas and tugged her hand which was already clasped in his from aiding her ascent and pulled her gently in the opposite direction. She could tell that devouring the healthy lunch options he had painstakingly sought out, was far from his mind, the consumption of an ethnic aperitif was a far more favourable choice.

Even as they strode through the overgrown wild grass along the footpath, leading farther and farther away from the sounds of the city, he began licking her bare shoulder with long slow strokes, savouring the taste and scent of her and her own unique cocoa essence that infused his senses like a drug.

He glanced over his shoulder, gauging his freedom, assessing the scene whilst his hand disappeared into the close confines of her tight gym leggings, enjoying the pressure and resistance from the elastic waist band which aided the pressing of his hand closer to her panty line. Tucking his finger into the base of her knickers, enjoying the sensation of moisture and heat, taking advantage of the space between her legs that every stride provided. They approached a wooden gateway at the foot of another hill and before she could proceed through it, he pressed her against it and closed the gap between them, gripping her with both arms now, one arm settling across her chest, fondling a gym bra caged breast, squeezing and tugging at the imprint of her small dark nipple, leaving the other hand free to continue its heat seeking forage. Delving deeper now into the parting, allowing the silkiness to guide him through to the priceless orifice that was now pulsing magnetically, expressing her hidden desires, pulling him further and further inside the molten cavern, hidden beneath her furry curtain. She groaned and whimpered, rendering herself helpless to the building fermentation inside her. As her body shook, he tightened his grip further still, becoming more and more ferocious in his crusade, unapologetically savage, knowing that she needed him to push through. That he could scarcely afford further penance for failed delivery. Her Majesty's patience was wearing decidedly thin of late. She would be glad of the release as long as he refused to relent, pushing her to her limits. His reward would be borrowed time with an aloof Afro monarch.

He could feel the outline of her abs as he pulled her towards him, the hardened muscle from her iron willed routine, creating a steel like response in his willy, making him want to immerse her in the charged liquid pulsing through him like mercury, gauging her internal temperature.

Her obvious satisfaction with his rampant probing bolstered his esteem, his chest broadening at his own mastery.

He was never happier than when he had pleased her, than when he had managed to evoke an elusive smile from satisfying her culinary and sensual desires.

She pulled her hooded jacket out from her rucksack and tied it securely around her waist. The leggings she had chosen to wear, now bore witness to her complete satisfaction.

263

As they continued navigating the hilly fields and turned onto the horse's trail leading to the park, they became aware of dog walkers, joggers and a small class of pony riders ambling through the tree covered tunnel where streams of light burst through any gaps in the branches like torches. His hands were in his pockets and she could tell from his stride and the flipping of his head that he was feeling immensely proud of himself. His competence in pleasing her seemed to counter the inadequacy he felt in his other life, at the office, around women in general and even in his personal relationships.

Finding a quiet patch of grass overlooking the main park, they nestled into the warm, dry turf, to the excitement of a few loitering pigeons, delighted with the prospect of discarded sesame seed crusts.

Gazing around, Cayenne could see couples strolling and lone joggers circling the oval shaped pathway on the perimeter of the green. In the far distance, parents pushed their toddlers on the miniature swings and waited for their descent on the early years slide.

"Which sandwich would you like?".

He was opening the one of the brown paper bags and positioning the contents in an artful display before her. He had selected a chicken salad sandwich on rye bread and a tuna and cucumber sandwich on sesame seeded wholemeal. She was touched to see that he had also complemented their alfresco lunch with some kale crisps, an apple and a choice of melon and pineapple fruit juice. He had obviously tried to please her with his choice of healthy options. He had even bought a rhubarb chocolate cake for them to sample.

"I'll have the chicken salad if you don't mind".

"Go for it. Or we can share and have half of each".

"Yeah, let's do that".

"My brother and I are going up to Scotland this weekend".

"Oh, for your mom's birthday?".

He nodded with no more enthusiasm than he had expressed when they last had this discussion.

It had been no surprise to her to see that he had baulked at his mother's commitment to her new partner which gave more than a hint to her that he may well be harbouring commitment issues himself. His reaction to her perceived haste only confirmed her thoughts. She leaned back on one elbow and shielded her eyes from the sun with her free hand, listening intently to him as he began to open up about his family which she found incredibly touching.

"She's been single for quite some time before that to be fair, so I suppose it's totally understandable, but then again, that's all the more reason that I'd prefer she took her time, get to know him a bit more first".

"Does she seem happy?". She could tell by his expression that he didn't appreciate her line of questioning.

His response was a heavy shrug. It was like watching a child as his mother departed to go out for a social evening, whilst he sulked resentfully at having been left with the child minder. She wondered what emotions this scenario was triggering for him.

"What does your brother think?".

"I don't know yet, the plan is to have a chat about things before we go".

Mixed in with the reticence, she noted a familiar glimpse. "Aaaah, are you being the overprotective son?". Cayenne could just imagine Diego having similar reservations although for the most part, he would place her happiness above his own caution.

"Funnily enough, my dad is on the verge of ending his current relationship as well. The writing appears to be on the wall, which we are all secretly delighted about".

"Why? What is it you don't you like about this one?".

"She's after what she can get, namely, our family home".

She deduced that it must have been his mother that had left the family whilst the father raised the children, which perhaps explained the bias in his differing emotions towards them and the possible reticence to the parent he perhaps harboured resentment for, forming relationships.

Cayenne chuckled to herself. He seemed to be displaying the characteristics of someone whose parents had separated later in life. The children in such cases, in her experience, seemed to take the blow harder than those who could scarcely remember their parents being together.

She felt a little privileged that he was entrusting her to these nuggets of family life and history, especially as he appeared to be a fairly guarded person.

He glanced at his phone. He still had the dated looking black one. Not the sharp top of the range one that would be expected of a top accountant.

"God, I've got to go back soon". He pulled her closer to him and explored her mouth, hungrily, desperately.

"Are you gonna walk back with me?".

Cayenne leaned back on her folded hands and gazed up into the clear sky.

"No, I think I'll stay here for a while and enjoy the sunshine".

He smiled in response. Although he would have liked her to accompany him back to the island, he also relished the thought of her lying here with her midriff exposed, glistening in the afternoon sun like a true splendour in the grass.

He made sure to relay the pleasing thoughts that buoyed his return to the office. "I love going back to the office with the smell of your chocolate cunt titillating my senses. Jealous I couldn't stay at the park for longer".

Cayenne reached for her bleeping phone and turned over on her stomach and typed in her response.

"I am slowly coming down from the high of your touch. Cunt memory is loathe to let go of the sensation. Missing the feel of your generous cock in my hands.

I so want to be the dipping pool for your hard on".

"I'm so arrogantly hard right now".

"I'm absolutely longing to be plunged deeply, ferociously... with no mercy... pummelled into any hard surface that I land on or am levelled against.

Wish you could have pulled me into the bushes, away from prying eyes and bent me over the hawthorn and given me a prickly poking from behind.

You only got a mere slither of the streams threatening to soak my entire gym garment. I wanted to ride your face, straddling your tongue with my pussy".

"It was torturous leaving that. The smell of you. The feel of being inside.

Fuck!.... it remains delicious.

I want to be immersed in the drenching. A devoted subservient whore to your majestic cunt".

"Torturous for me to have such brutal withdrawal, just as I was enjoying the delicious invasion.

The majestic cunt is ripe for needy subservience… you must kneel and bow before it. Succumb to it's sovereignty … and hungrily await the regal offering".

Lost in time for much of the remaining afternoon, Cayenne finally made her way back.

"Finally home… what a gloriously satisfying afternoon…."

" A pleasure. Rubbish being back at my desk after that.

An utterly regrettable anti-climax".

CHAPTER 27

"Contemplating a rather unappetising Club Sandwich in my office. Much preferred my lunch time feed yesterday, especially with wet cunt juice direct from your chocolate fingers".

"Yes I can well imagine your deep sense of withdrawal. I've just finished a boxing session to rid myself of pent up sexual frustration... a release of sorts...

Reminiscing on the delicious but brief finger fuck... resting on a prickly lawn with your fingers inside me.."

"Felt so good being in, with your gorgeous gym clad ass gyrating ".

"Simply adored the sensation of cock lengthening in my hands...stroking it until I had edged my way towards the delicious mushroom atop. That's when I began to salivate."

"See how it rose immediately to you"

"Yes. I'm imagining bouncing and gyrating on that cock in wild abandon, daring you to try and stop my pent up fuck frenzy. There is an intense dribbling sensation between my legs… my poor pussy is being tortured by my imagination".

"Drench my face you delicious goddess".

"Chance would be dandy… you wouldn't have a hope of breathing as I grip your cheeks in my pussy vice… forcing you to pulse your tongue in my vag… be fervent in your pursuit of my caramel…. Add to my frustration at your PERIL.

I will be brutal in my demands… anger rises even now having to wait for the next tongue invasion… this procrastination is horrid.

What a glutton for absolute punishment you are you wretched soul…

What per chance do you hope to achieve by causing my puss juice to build up and bubble like a cauldron…

My pussy thrusts may yet decapitate you, such is the force of my wanting."

"I'm hardening at the thought of being used.

I'm having an arrogant adrenaline rush that I'm a toy to such a delicious regal body. Savouring the memory of the smell of your

271

cunt lingering on me yesterday. Such caramel intoxication. How does one stop needing it?".

"Perhaps an intense feeding session would put paid to your addiction... A lengthy and erotic overdose until you can take no more. Perhaps if I ignore your inevitable pleas for me to stop... pay no attention to your begging for air under the Niagara cunt falls that will drip into your open mouth.... Take no heed to your surrender. Then you will be able to leave this pussy splendour behind you and disappear into suburbia... a contented man."

"I'm worried that I will need my continuous superior regal black cunt feed."

"...Admittedly the Royal Standard will surely be at half-mast at the White Knight's retreat".

CHAPTER 28

"Hey you... looking at either Thursday 6th or Wednesday 12th for a proper high-end catch up. Wanted to check what works. 12th may be better for me actually".

Cayenne was strolling to work and texting at the same time, furtively trying to avoid walking into a lamppost.

"Well hello there. 12th suits the Queen. Are we talking panoramic high end? Oh you have brightened up my day".

"I have a feeling the 6th would be better. Actually 13th also possible."

"The Queen must not be agonised by such minutiae".

"Pardon me your Honour. We are definitely on though. Will be fun. We can meet at the park to discuss exactly what's happening. I'll bring evidence of the booking. That'll really make you juice."

CHAPTER 29

Cayenne busied herself retracing the frenzied early morning steps and sorting through the debris of a hectic pre-school itinerary.

She eventually flicked on the kettle and retrieved her phone from it's charger so that she could book the next few gym classes on line. Space was limited in the gym studios and so a first come first served operation existed via the online booking app. A message from the executive distracted her momentarily.

"Lady of leisure – you've been quiet. Enjoying the sunshine?".

"Have I?

Yes loving the rays… how are you?".

"All good. Fancy that park return later in the week to discuss rain check birthday treat?".

"My hectic schedule on Royal Box duty at Wimbledon may prove fraught…".

"Sexy stuff. Watching Murray?".

"Yes, against the Rastafarian player (Brown).

Gonna be a tough one for Murray… but then all his games are tough.

Tennis fan?".

"Yes. Should be fun…. Don't think Brown as good as he was two years ago when he beat Rafa".

Cayenne felt a tinge of excitement that they had discovered something else they had in common seeing as he had succeeded in pacifying her particularly thunderous urges.

"Do you play by any chance?".

"I agree… That was a great match. Good to see Rafa back closer to his best.

In my house in Torquay, we had a tennis net set up in the back garden as a matter of fact which the children and I thoroughly enjoyed. I particularly relished channelling the spirit of Serena. Don't know whether you have noticed, we have the same ominous glare. Devastating our opponents alike. Though I'm perhaps not as good as I like to think I am".

"We should definitely play".

"Provided you can handle being thrashed by the World Number 1…

I'm assuming you must be quite a competent player to challenge me….".

"Always had a Serena crush…. Entertaining match".

Cayenne glanced at the current score on her screen, pleased to see that Murray was regaining ground against the charismatic Rasta and finding it hard to believe that this middle class white boy from suburbia who was frightened of his own corporate shadow, had really harboured a desire for the reigning Tennis Queen.

"It's brilliant. I bet Andy isn't enjoying the antics though.

Really…. You like Serena?.

You don't look too dissimilar to her fiancé come to mention it". She smiled trying to imagine his response as he compared himself to the tall dark haired Armenian entrepreneur that had captured the athlete's heart. If he wasn't familiar with him, she didn't doubt he would immediately hit his google app and run his fingers through his hair as he sized himself up with the media image.

"Brown just too inconsistent – Murray will get this in straight sets I suspect".

"Yes, probably right. Tim Henman (brilliant commentary) stated that he (Brown) seems unable to sustain his dynamism for three sets…

I am distraught when Murray loses but no doubt he'll roll into the 2nd week with relative ease".

"Semi finals at the very least".

"Oh ye of little faith

Last I checked, he held the title".

"I did say 'at least'... I'm actually a big fan of Murray but think it could be Federer's year".

"Is he playing? Havent' seen a match of his yet this tournament".

"Yes his opponent retired in the first round so not much of a test. He's back playing tomorrow".

"Oh yes I did hear about a couple of retirements. You cannot bet against the charming Swiss".

"Great stuff from Murray now".

"There's a quiet confidence as he calmly outplays this cute upstart".

"Too easy. I doubt Rafa's match will be close either unfortunately...

Next week will be better".

"Were you of the McEnroe and Bjorn era too?".

"Just a little old for me babe... McEnroe and Connors were still around but Borg was gone".

"Going gym now to perform a little dynamism of my own...".

"Picturing you in Tennis whites, bending over to retrieve a stray ball, whilst my own harden with delight at the sight of you. The slightest glimpse of what could possibly lay underneath causing my sweatbands to become soaked at the other end of the court. Imagining throwing any competitiveness aside, allowing the Queen to dominate and Her Royal Caramelness rewarding my modesty by allowing me a delicious lick at the net as she stretches post match. The white of her mini skirt forming a discreet umbrella over my head as I disappear in search of her royal box. Furtively diving beneath the folds, hungry for the humid exotic taste of her".

"Mmmm, my hands would be in your hair, applying pressure with my fingertips and aiding your tongue as it volleys against my clit. Directing your search as my head rolls back in ecstasy as I relish my opponent's surrender".

Cayenne awoke the next morning, buzzing with anticipation.

"Does 12 o clock work for you? Crossharbour?. What would the Queen like to eat?".

"Good morning. 12 is perfect. A salad and juice would suffice".

"See you then. Cannot wait for the visual enjoyment."

Visual euphoria is precisely what his eyes reflected as she came into his view as he headed down the Pepper Street slope towards their usual meeting point at the bottom of the stairs at Crossharbour Station.

She had chosen this occasion to showcase her two piece hooded midriff exposing suit with it's green, red and gold stripes and gold metallic interlinked circles similar to the Olympic logo across the front and etched onto the side of the leggings which were tight and stretchy and clung to her rounded glutes. The top had short enough sleeves to show off her firm biceps and clung to her chest, cutting off just below the breast area to expose the hint of an emerging six pack.

She wore the hood up with her highlighted hair framing her face. Her eyes were heavily clouded with red tones up towards the eyebrows, her lips stood out with mat bright green lipstick and the speckles of gold highlighter made her cheek bones stand to attention.

"Wow" he muttered under his breath, so taken aback that it was barely audible. His eyes finished the sentence as they travelled from head to toe, admiring the black high top converse trainers where the leggings were tucked in securely. As she spun to proceed towards their usual picnic spot, he continued the intense surveillance all the way to the park.

He hadn't seen anything like it. He certainly had never had the pleasure to accompany anything close to this enchanting sight. If his colleagues could only see him now, they would never guess that the boring straight laced Senior Accountant Team Leader, could possibly hold the interest of this exotic vision before him. He smiled as he watched her. The head held high, the confident, dominant stride as though she somehow owned the very ground on which she walked. As though she had access to special privileges that were bestowed upon an elect few. He resisted the strong temptation to cup her iron rounded glutes as she climbed the stairs towards the farm end of the park. Striding with purpose as though she knew exactly where she wanted him, where she was leading. Not glancing back once. Knowing he was following dutifully. Like a delirious lamb to his most coveted slaughter. Helpless in the inevitability of what lay ahead. He suspected today was not about him. This was about her. He would need to fulfil her needs. Help relieve her tension. Put a satisfying smile on her face. He really ought to be nervous considering the Queen's wrath was brutal and relentless. His very position, teetering on the perimeter wall of the palace, was treacherous, not least in moments like this when his fear of exile was most apparent.

But as she lay under the swaying trees surrounded by long strands of wild Pumila Pampas grass that had escaped the shearer's blade, all fear dissipated. Untying the gold strings that held the leggings tightly to her petite waist. Pulling the elastic lower and lower and slipping his hands beneath the gold satin thong and running his fingers through the strands of her own Pumila landing strip, he grazed amorously in her soft sweet pasture, deeply inhaling the silky sensation in it's midst.

All thoughts of inferiority disappeared as he apprehended her climb. Delving his tongue into her mouth as his fingers strummed sensual harmonies. Needing to be closer to feel the full force of her ascension. Not daring to postpone the moment, to savour it some more, lest her need be too great. All he could do was let her fly and gasp at the beauty as she glided, watching in awe as she soared.

CHAPTER 29

Cayenne could tell when she opened her emails the following morning that her white suitor was feeling immensely pleased with himself. He had clearly nailed the directive. Expertly commandeering the controls at the helm of her fanny flight path. Cruising above the torrents until the air was smooth and without interruption and then gliding back to earth and delivering a relaxed and happy Queen, restored and rejuvenated, to her terrain.

"Arrogance is back".

"Mmmmm good. Looking forward to an arrogant fuck".

"So corrupted. I need your juice".

"Fill up my parched cunt 'til my clit runneth over.

Indeed you do need my juice as my unique caramel cunt blend is pertinent to your very survival...

As vital as oxygen to the lungs.

As essential as water to the kidney. As rest rejuvenates the mind".

"I am aware yesterday was about you, your highness, though I so wish you would have crawled all over me too as I eventually laid back with exhaustion from my efforts. I was desperate for you to fuck my face".

"Perhaps had I worn a skirt and adorned my crotch-less panties.... I could certainly have garnished your Caesar salad and seasoned your pesto pasta with my own spice pepper marinade...

How my pussy would have delighted to serve you a Caribbean aperitif.

Reminiscing .... The scrumptious sensation of your fingers delving into my pussy... being lubricated with my own chocolate jelly...

I adored the progressive finger placement... gingerly touching the opening of my hidden jewel... and finally piercing the tightness and foraging into the succulence beyond in preparation for a merciless pussy plunging… deep and orgasmic".

"I absolutely adore being in.

Feeling the juice

Hearing you moan

Wanting to properly indulge".

"Hide not your flesh from the regal succulence… plunge into the depths unaided with wild abandon…. Experience fully the warmth, indeed the heat of my pussy scotch".

"I was desperate to rub my cock up and down that toned ass as you gorgeously stared out over the rural farmland over which you surveyed".

"Yes, I too was mourning the opportunity of an outdoor animalistic mauling…

Oh to be flat out in the long straw grass again, legs in the air, opened wide as you graze.

Looking hazily upward into the skies as my pussy experiences it's own heavenly awakening.

How tantalising is your delicious rock like cock. I longed to propel it out of it's cupping. Wishing to feel it's force. Willing you to throb and pulse and deliver every last drop".

" I felt like an animal whore toy – I wanted your caramel hands on my hard on, releasing me all over you.

I'm struggling to focus right now".

"I too am so fucking hungry. It's so unlawful of you to put me through this cycle of tantalisation and brut desertion. Who in possession of their faculties... fails to feed a hungry pussy?. Worrying William. That's who". Cayenne could feel her mood beginning to change and could sense the shift from the willowy memory lane over to the dark and ominous creek.

I am utterly fed up of this tiresome SAFE texting...

Whilst tortured by my cactus clit which is being starved of vital nutrients...

So pissed off with your failure to fuck me to satisfaction".

"I was wondering how long it would take for the evil Queen to resurface.

I want you nasty in the Shard".

"For fuck's sake… you act as though certain of another life awaiting you after this one…

An alternate world where you actually pursue your passionate urges with determined grit and take full enjoyment of regal eroticism when the rare opportunity arises.

May you hasten to this world where you actually have a back bone to pursue your real passions in life, where you do away with conventional wisdom and be true to yourself and finally live unhindered from mental demons… what a pitiful sod you are".

"I need to be fucking spanked. I am feeling very arrogant that you need it right now".

"If your desire is to be spanked, leaving my pussy to be agonisingly parched is not the way to go about it.

What the fuck do you care what I need… I would stand more chance of getting lucky with the grazing mammals in Mudchute farm… even they seemed more attune to the fact that I was clearly on heat. Yet Mindless Mike remained oblivious.

The preoccupied Wild Boar at the farm instinctively knew that I was in season… but the tense executive?…. clueless.

I was tempted to return to the farm to seek some attention… my tight pert arse was largely ignored yesterday, granted the sight must be grossly unfamiliar to a man raised in the flat square bottomed Suburban Shires…

Utterly ridiculous".

"Keep it coming nasty bitch. I don't remember any complaints when we parted".

"If only you would take your own advice Hesitant Henry".

"Listen, I enjoyed it very much too. I only wish I had ravaged you fully".

"Do you expect me to believe this drivel…. Reticent Richard?".

"I was in your mouth for most of the time that you were with me".

"…rather moorish it was too….

Being manhandled dominantly makes me wet".

"I am learning. I wanted to be in charge… I wanted to get it".

"I certainly hope you are as masterful when you thrust my legs akimbo and impose upon my desperate pussy with ownership…

Rather put out that you chose a later date".

"If things open up next week, I will move the reservation".

"My urgency is at the mercy of your executive schedule… my pussy is beginning to clench in disgust…

Where's the spontaneity…

Fuck me now…I need your cock this very wet moment.

Increasingly pissed off with your whore toy delusion.

You are no more my effective white whore than you are a movie star or politician…

You must add me to the wannabe list of your life".

"Such a bitch!. Some of us are having to work here Missus lol".

"For someone who claims to work, you certainly seem to have sufficient hours to pretend to be a prolific whore who delivers.

The alternate YOU, the one in the alternative universe, (let's call him K) … is right this moment, straddling an acting career with a venture into politics whilst enjoying tantric sex and wild eroticism within and beyond his jurisdiction. When he removes his glasses, there is sheer contentment in his eyes as opposed to abject fear and self doubt…

Why the hell didn't K proposition me in the Canary Caverns?. He'd have surely upped the anti by now, ferrying me across continents and ensuring a continuous caramel cunt flow".

"I do like the way you write. Damn that precocious 15 year old at Pebble Mill".

Cayenne's eyes glistened and she could feel her lower lip begin to tremble. She rested her head back and recalled one of their early conversations. Was it Bar One or Goucho?... she couldn't be sure. He was listening intently to her talking about her passion for writing and how she regretted not pursuing the opportunity that arose when she was just fifteen years old and harbouring tentative desires to be a journalist. Her conscientious approach to her work as a weekend assistant in a European hairdressing salon where she was unconsciously determined to add value by working hard from the moment she arrived to the moment they had to tear her away from her task, had caught the attention of a well dressed business woman who admired the thorough attention a young Cayenne was paying to her scalp rinsing during a perm treatment.

The lady had asked whether Cayenne wanted to pursue a career in hairdressing. Cayenne had informed her that she wanted to be a journalist, to which the well heeled lady had clapped her hands with excitement and promptly promised to introduce Cayenne to her daughter who was Head of journalism at Pebble Mill Studios. Cayenne knew very well that Pebble Mill was a broadcasting corporation in Birmingham from which the local news was filmed along with a daily magazine programme and interior shots from various television series. She immediately pictured the aerial views of the studio that emerged when the news came on, circling the large glass buildings and finally drifting through the open glass doors, navigating through some open offices full of news correspondents, assistants and researchers until finally the viewer was face to face with the newsreader announcing the 1.0 clock news.

Cayenne could barely contain herself when she went home and told her mother what had happened and counted the days until she was scheduled to meet the lady's daughter who had arranged to pick Cayenne up from New Street Station in Birmingham City Centre. Cayenne had taken to Elaine immediately. She was a pretty, smartly dressed, slim lady with an immaculate hair cut not dissimilar to a brunette lady Diana. Cayenne noted Elaine's quality red woollen pencil skirt and the red and white blouse that complemented it perfectly along with the shiny red pointed stilettos. She couldn't quite believe that this was happening to her. It seemed almost fairytale like. That a lady whose hair she happened to be washing, would be so impressed with her attitude and work ethic that she would actually tell her daughter, who just so happened to be a journalist and that that daughter, purely by word of mouth would even consider taking the time out and give up a portion of her busy day to show her around the studio.

The memory of that whole afternoon, the vastness of the studio, seeing the whole production in operation had stayed with her heretofore. It all seemed so plush and otherworldly to this little girl living in the ghettos of the Midlands, who rarely did anything out of the ordinary and had lived a relatively reclusive life under low expectation tutelage compared to the average teenager. Cayenne could still recall the actor's faces as she stood on an elevated platform looking down below as an episode of Howard's Way was being filmed. The television series hadn't held much interest for her when sitting at home, but seeing the actors in person in the mock up living room, going over their lines with intermittent orders being barked by the floor manager, had ensured that she never missed another episode, biting her lip to prevent telling her family for the umpteenth time, that she had actually witnessed an episode being filmed.

By far the overall take away from the experience, though at the time, the huge club sandwich and Pineapple juice that Elaine had treated her to would come a close second, was the fact that Elaine had thanked her for coming, shook her hand and treated her as though she were a trusted colleague. They had sat down together and Elaine had wanted to know what Cayenne had made of the afternoon. Then she had retrieved a pen and lined paper pad from her desk and written down an assignment that she wanted Cayenne to complete. She was requesting that she watch a selection of television programmes that were scheduled to be broadcast over the next few weeks and write a review on each one. Cayenne hadn't known whether to be excited or daunted by the assignment but she was immensely flattered that as far as Elaine was concerned, that this was well within her capabilities and that it was clearly not the end of their association.

She had totally expected to be dropped off in Elaine's polished red convertible and be waved off never to be seen again.

Cayenne could only scratch her head now and ponder why she did in fact never lay eyes on Elaine again. Why hadn't she completed the assignment. She had meant to and could vaguely remember making several attempts to start. She could only surmise that the self-doubt that plagued her teenage years had proved insurmountable and that the weeks had turned into months and that eventually she no longer felt she deserved the opportunity.

Kenneth had smiled admiringly as he listened to her recount the story and she was certain she could detect a look of empathy that she hadn't in fact seen it through.

The fact that he had even remembered the conversation almost a year later, made her throat feel as though it had developed an obstruction. It took several hard swallows to remove it. Perhaps they weren't so different after all.

Once she regained her composure, she was in no mood to let him know that his recollection had moved her.

"K would never let a regal damson go hungry... nor would he allow several weeks to lapse into months without so much as a paddle in my chocolate pussy pool.

What an utterly horrendous whore. I despair. I'm so fucking angry right now".

"Okay okay, let's not do the lunches anymore... fuck sake. It's not supposed to anger you!!!".

"You do anger me.

What kind of moron actively pursues a woman for months in the face of blunt rejection.... Only to leave her dissatisfied with his vain attempts to add value within the confines of an executive lunch hour?.

Not K that's for sure".

"I'm going to try to be more K like... points noted".

CHAPTER 30

After the hectic school run, a quick dash to the Supermarket and a frenzied attempt to restore the apartment to it's former order, Cayenne relaxed into her newly pumped up bronze cushions and set her steaming cup of rum tea to cool on the self-assembled two tier hallway table, that wouldn't actually fit in the hallway, flicking on the television to catch up with the latest Wimbledon results.

Less than a mile away in the Business district, an errant Senior accountant was keeping up with the results on his lap top in the office.

"This has the making of a more interesting match".

"Yes, this guy is also going to struggle to stay with him. Does he even know he's at Wimbledon? Surely this is just a practice run for Murray.

Shame Heather Watson didn't go through… she was close at times…

A visit to Wimbledon for my birthday next year would be fitting. Although I cannot promise you a spot accompanying me in the Royal box.

Whoop Murray did it again".

"Yes, he was pretty clinical at the end. Missing your touch. How about Tuesday lunch to torment each other once more before proper indulgence?. Climb all over me this time, immerse me. Fucking have me.

I hope you are out there showing off that honed black ass of yours".

"Started my day with a five mile run, followed by boxing and then synergy.

I want every toned muscle to be worshipped. I fully intend to feast off your white meat. Wear you down to your suburban bones. My biceps will force you into submission... you will be at my mercy".

"Full submission to the Black Queen. Fuck I want it.

Gives me an utter thrill and an arrogantly large hard on".

There was an image underneath his text. When Cayenne inspected it more closely, she could see that it was a chess board with the Black Queen standing proudly in the centre of the board whilst the white pawn lay slain in front of her.

" I remain your suburban whore bitch.

Force feed me your black cunt juice – whilst I'm clamped in... own me you bitch".

"The force of my thighs will pin you to the panoramic sack....

Dominating my Crown Land.

I will feed you caramel cunt juice, drop by delicious drop...".

"I will be desperate for your mocha cunt juice feed... I haven't been right since my last taste. Get your hands on my cock on our next discreet country walk".

"Don't worry, can barely wait to rectify your malnutrition....to quench your dehydration.... Top up your chocolate reserves...

season your suburban palate with sophisticated coconut cunt cuisine".

"I need my mistress… desperate thirst needs fucking quenching. I'm ready for using".

"I cannot resist the salutation in your trousers as your dick rises to acknowledge the royal presence… positively itching to thrust my hands unceremoniously inside… delving… searching… feeling… anticipating, tasting it's British content.

Your mistress is ready to serve… to feed… to nurture… to totally arrest…".

"See how it rises to you?... corrupted and indulgent.

Evil delight at what gorgeous exotic fruits your offer.

Own me. I'm a slave to the Queen's majesty".

"I am indeed High level fruit. I fully embrace your submission to Black divinity. You shall give me all that I long for, need and desire…

You will satisfy my longing… yet my abject hunger for you".

"Desperately hungry – you may need to release me in our discreet rural wanderings".

"I will consume your generous genitalia. Your release will be my absolute cure, your cum, the ultimate antidote to all that torments me… from morning… way into the early hours.

Your cock the very remedy for my dripping, pulsating fanny".

"I want us entwined in an interracial fuck fest… the Queen and her selfish corporate toy. I will gladly kneel on weather beaten foliage … come panty-less… so I can feed like a hungry elusive fox amongst the trees".

"Entangle me like a suburban prisoner desperate for a foray into the thriving city heat…

Take full advantage and embrace my exotic ambience like an explorer in undiscovered tropical terrain…. Knowing he may seldom experience these rare scenes before him… fearing his eyes will never again behold such unique beauty at such close quarters.

As I arch my back along the bark beneath the shade of a hidden tree, be the resourceful explorer, foraging for essential nutrients, the sustenance for the venture ahead, teasing my clit to delightful distraction. Tickle and delve alternately whilst I release an exotic tirade of Caribbean coolie. Just this very conversation has rendered me saturated in my own cinnamon Jus ".

"Mmmm I'm on an adrenaline rush already… A caramelised face fuck in a cool forest…

How I did I get to be such a lucky suburban white toy fuck, to grace such majestic enjoyment…

I must show my gratitude to the Black Queen in every effort I make with my hands, tongue and cock… she will be duly satisfied that every chance of a touch was taken.

Visualising you feeding me.   I am experiencing my own pre cum dribbling.

God knows what the neighbours behind netted windows would make of me discreetly stroking as I write on the terrace".

"What good fortune they would happen upon to behold your discreet weaponry.

I am indeed a fortunate Queen to have ownership of such white whore artillery.

When my legs are open wide on the panoramic floor of the capital's iconic skyscraper, be sure to unload your executive arsenal at full force".

"I want in…

Desperate yearning now to take charge of you and give it hard, deep and fast…

Rampant interracial indulgence… the right and only way to properly fuck.

Black me again. Allow me to devour your regal deluxe punani."

"Fully succumb to the exotic succulence..

Experience fully the hidden crevices of my fanny... smother your cock in my jungle pussy extract. Hear the squelching as your huge cock permeates the tightness of my hungry hymen, forcing the marinade to spill out as we cling to one another in helpless surrender. Maximise the expanse of my open thighs and reward my generous crotch hospitality...fuck me until the setting of the sun and if you could be so generous, fuck me again and again".

"Suburbia holds no magnetism for this white boy now... I have tasted something much more sublime... I want to be an inner city whore. I want your hungry black fucking chocolate cunt on me. I want to trade the country shires for a mystical black forest.

Perhaps suburbia should watch the majesty of you owning me.

If you could only see and feel how rock hard I am right now...you would juice on sight".

"Please refrain from subduing my carnal screams during our countryside frolic... for such unfulfilled longing cannot be contained...

Let me groan in wretched ecstasy.... As I will already be lamenting the inevitability ... that my enjoyment is reaching it's end as your departure heralds the beginning of yet more cunt hibernation.

300

Torture me with thoughts of your hardened cock...my pussy is damp with excitement.... My tongue salivating... longing to kneel before you for a dairy feed of my own".

Cayenne's eyes flickered momentarily towards the grass tournament battle on screen.

"How I would simply adore watching the Wimbledon final virtually upside down as my head hangs over the edge of the bed as you bang me in symmetry with the champion's forehand.

Suck me with the finesse of a Federer lob, grind me with unparalleled Rafa intensity and then turn me over and pummel me from behind with the force of a Murray slice as we face the final shots together and as we await our erotic deuce and your cock delivers an explosive Ace, giving my fanny a decidedly juicy advantage.

Your lashings of cum bringing healing to abandoned vaginal walls...

Revitalising my pussy ruins back to full vitality".

"Images of you are thought porn... I have an incessant need to taste you, to run my hands over your mahogany rump and cover you in cum.

I want to give the Queen a nice salty feed to harmonise with the sweetness of your lady syrup".

"I long for you to fully appreciate the glute results of multiple, relentless weighted squatting…

Examine… feel … touch…. Bury your face deep into the creek of my derriere…

I need to feel your appreciation of honed blackness. I yearn to be regarded like a rare oil painting… treasured like vintage wine. Savoured like the rarest saffron".

"Your Royal Black highness will be given 100% attention… I'm a whore to your physical dedication and effort. Such a tantalising specimen of delicious chocolate indulgence. You make Suburbia so weak in comparison".

"Add my Nubian Nutrients to your diet…prioritise it as a vital component of your daily sustenance".

"Give me a daily feeding routine… I will flock to you like a ravenous farmyard animal. I need to cum, need to shoot… not sure it's wise right now as I have the cleaner here".

"Oh do not deny the cleaner the vision of your ejaculation glory… for it is an absolute joy to behold… jealous though I may be… though I am safe in the knowledge that your mental target is more than likely, the golden slither at the tip of my uterus".

"She's rattling around in the next room… I like the jealousy…. Should I stop my discreet touching on regal orders?.

My hard-on is utterly obvious in the tracksuit bottoms if I do wander through the house".

"Venom is threatening to engulf my resolve to maintain a Queenly decorum...

I shall withdraw your vital pussy nutrients should my whore exclusivity be compromised".

"Don't worry. Whore behaviour will cease immediately.

The Queen had nothing to fear – this cock only rises to hot black chocolate majesty, not tepid Eastern European subordinates".

"Had I a courtier within reach, I would be tempted to discharge a priceless donation of my Champagne juice royalties. How would you like that? Disloyal whore...".

"This was to be a discreet release in response to the Queen's musings, not a chance for her whore to play peacock... The Queen shall inspect the next release directly. It is solely for her pleasure now.

Whore loyalty is not in question".

CHAPTER 31

Cayenne could tell as soon as she approached the holistic area of the gym and peered through the long floor to ceiling window panel next to the heavy entrance to the Yoga studio, that Josephine would not be taking the scheduled Yoga class today, even though the Facebook notification that the gym posted rather irregularly, seemed to suggest otherwise.

The room was customarily lit by the neon purple strip lights strategically set up around the skirting, creating a serene and calm ambience. The other thing that was brightening up the room was a pair of long skinny psychedelically clad legs that were poised in full lotus position, a posture that Cayenne knew she could never hope to achieve with her own resistant hips. The owner of these stretchy legs that Cayenne envied on sight, was a young looking man with equally thin torso and upper body, with a fresh crew cut and a thin concentrated face which hardened his soft features.

Robert had his eyes closed with his hands resting on his knees with the palms facing upwards. Detecting that someone had encroached upon his zen filled space, he cracked open an eye and when his suspicions were confirmed by the sight of Cayenne lowering herself tentatively onto a mat on the far side of the room, he opened his other eye and his face broke out into the most welcoming smile.

"Hi I'm Robert".

"Hello" Cayenne chimed, marvelling that he was able to maintain the impossible pose and converse at the same time. "Looks painful". She nodded towards his elastically entangled psychedelic legs with their purple and orange wavy stripes which seemed to coordinate perfectly with the purple hues and bright neon beams.

Robert smiled again but didn't respond to her comment. "I'm covering for Jo today". Cayenne deduced that Robert and Josephine were well acquainted by the way that he shortened her name. "She's in the Bahamas".

Josephine seemed to spend as much time on holiday as she did at the gym, so Cayenne was hardly surprised by the announcement.

The heavy fire door slammed behind them as other people began to arrive for the class, depositing their things in the corner of the room and selecting one of the perfectly aligned purple rubber mats on the floor. It seemed Robert and Josephine shared the need for an orderly yoga mat arrangement.

Robert repeated his opening welcome, introducing himself and explaining Josephine's absence.

If the class had been expecting this session to be similar to Josephine's gentle rhythmic flowy routine, they were soon to get a rude awakening.

Josephine's class inevitably began with a restful soothing Savasana, where they were encouraged to lie back on their mat whilst Josephine's eclectically clipped east end voice would typically invite them to arrive on their mat and coasted them through the usual routine of ensuring they could get as much of their back on the mat as possible by flattening their lower back and tilting their chin towards the chest to elongate the spine. Cayenne could almost hear Josephine's haunting voice preparing her class for the next hour of balance and flexibility challenged poses. "Just liiiiiiiie back in Savasana whenever you're ready and prepaaaaaare yourself to come to the mat", she would chide with a tone that urged them to be ready to oblige immediately. "ooooopen your legs wiiiiiiiiiideer than the mat and move your aaaarms awaaaaaay from the body with your paaaaaaaalms facing towards the ceiling and the backs of your fingers gently pressin' dooooowwwwn into the mat. Cloooooooose your eyes and focus on your breavin'. Feeeeeeeel the belly riiiiiiiiiise as your breave in allowin' yourself to feel niiiiice and full. Then breeeeeeavin' out niiiiiice and slooooowly until all the breaf has left your body and allowin' yourself to fee'w empty and spacious".

Cayenne rather enjoyed the soothing prelude to the class and was amongst the first to position herself in the restful posture knowing that she, more than most would need to summon as much energy as possible for the feat ahead.

Robert, however had his own approach and stirred the dozing clan by encouraging them to find a comfortable seating position.

Robert began his class with some intense breathwork which Cayenne had become familiar with from Charlotte's Yin classes. After some indepth breathing, Robert took them through a series of progressive salutations, starting with the downward facing dog, into three legged dog and then on to a succession of warrior poses but breaking them up so that after each one, they would return to the plank, followed by an energy sapping Chaturanga, back to down dog, where they would repeat the exercise progressing further into extended warrior poses each time. The speed with which Robert navigated his class was clearly unfamiliar, as she along with many others struggled to keep up. It began to feel like some sort of Olympic styled yoga with each movement hurtling swiftly into the next before you could utter a plea of OM.

Robert, at the helm of the class, demonstrated each pose to his diverse playlist which ranged from john Lennon, Prince and some other creole sounding concoctions. By the end of the assault course, a simple downward dog felt like a restorative child's pose compared to the Brands Hatch sequences that seemed to be to Robert's taste, although she rather suspected that this was the designed method behind the high speed madness. By the time they arrived at the Savasana home stretch, Cayenne could almost hear a collective sigh of utter relief as the thoroughly humbled warriors collapsed in a heap around her.

CHAPTER 32

"Lunch Thursday or Friday. Can't do before then as I've got to earn the platinum unfortunately".

"My Masterful Executive...

Thinking of you at the helm of the boardroom is such a turn on..."

"I won't dispel the illusion of imperious dominance.

Wednesday may also work – any days not an option for you?".

"Provided it is after my afternoon gym session, I am fairly flexible".

"Keep that gorgeous black ass fully toned. How is the tight specimen that I want to caress?".

Cayenne turned her back to the full length mirror in her silver and grey bedroom and glanced over her shoulder to take in the view that he was asking her to survey. Ignoring the stubborn dimples that consistent weighted squats seemed unable to remove, she clenched her buttocks one by one so that each glute rose up and down like piano keys. "So curved... perfectly rounded.

The 'tight specimen' regularly invites understandable glares of resentment. Particularly from jealous caucs' who haven't a hope of replicating my derriere perfection by virtue of genetics. They have my total empathy".

"Arrogance... a turn on... gorgeous racist bitch".

"It amazes me to consider the modern contrast of growing up in the 1970's when one's skin was considered too dark, one's lips, too big and luscious, one's bottom, huge and irreverently unaligned.

Now... every God forsaken Caucasian covets these very features... pitifully forced to attempt imitation by artificial means...

As I gaze at my exotic reflection, bursting with curvature... and smile wryly to myself, basking in the knowledge... that I was superior all along....".

"Imagine being one of those God forsaken Caucasian wretches - terrible.

See the Nadal match?".

"Over four and a half hours of play... nail biting to the very end. Tremendous effort. By the end, I couldn't be disappointed. Muller deserves his win.

I couldn't help but note that Nadal, about whom I have always harboured the suspicion that he is a secret love child of Bob Marley, owing to the protruding cheek bones and sullen expression, though inwardly distraught.... Shook the Umpire's hand, walked around to Muller's side to congratulate his opponent and then STILL took time to sign autographs and memorabilia for waiting fans.

What a guy!. ONE LOVE!!!

Now I sincerely hope that Muller is bloody exhausted and Murray, should they meet, can thrash him. Couldn't possibly sit through another marathon of Scottish angst".

Cayenne stretched her body out onto her unmade bed reaching her arms and legs towards opposite ends of the large bedroom. Her hands returned to her lower stomach and then wandered slowly towards the fluttering taking place below.

"If only a wandering pair of Caucasian hands was nearby... ".

"Fuck! The need for filth weighs upon me heavily today... you have turned me into a seasoned whore. I want my white hands all over your chocolate delights".

"My caramelised Brulée could certainly relish a pre-lunch cracking".

"If only I were kneeling in front of you now, delving tongue first in search of succulent brown sugar".

"I'm virtually feeling the sensation of my pussy lips between your teeth and the fluttering of your foraging tongue".

"Meet me now…. Let me feed in that discreet forest".

"I have not long applied the top coat to my manicure… could we give it an hour?.

We would certainly need to retreat away from the beaten track".

"Yes okay, my madness has calmed slightly, what time?. I want my tongue in your mouth. I want your caramel hands on my hard on.

I want my fingers delving into your wet chocolate cunt. I want you moaning in my ear as I pummel the pum pum".

There was something almost altruistic about lying on a bed of well worn grass, gazing skyward in a discreet gap in a bushy hedge, listening to the hungry slurps of a highly stressed executive, feeding desperately as though his existence depended on it, licking every last ounce of cream from the Cannoli of her pelvis.

She clasped his head in her hand and pressed him closer to her, enjoying the warm invasion of his plunging tongue. His hands cupped her buttocks with a succession of squeezes and prods at his attempts to disappear inside her. She hadn't meant to climax just for her own pleasure. This afternoon was intended to be purely benevolent. An answer to his plea. However, she soon found herself climbing nearer to the clouds, and to this hungry executive's utter delight, he found himself immersed in a second helping".

CHAPTER 33

Cayenne was still smarting when she awoke the next morning to find several emails that had gone unnoticed in the early hours. Grovelling messages from the executive who almost on cue, had managed to piss her off on the way home from the forest forage.

It was amazing how he managed to take her from euphoric heights to the depths of underbelly annoyance in a heartbeat.

He had told her that he had confirmed the booking for their penultimate Shard experience and in her excitement, she had let slip that she had discussed the fact that she was being treated to the Shard, with her son.

The atmosphere had instantly grown cold as any semblance of colour drained from his face.

"You told your son about it?". he had unsuccessfully tried to conceal the horror in his voice.

Cayenne paused momentarily, taking deep breaths and stifling the urge to roll her eyes.

"Well of course. I have to explain why I am spending the night away".

"You're staying overnight?".

Now she couldn't help but roll her eyes skyward and stopped short of kissing her teeth in true Jamaican styley.

"So you're prepared to pay hundreds of pounds for just a few hours. Of course I'm staying overnight. Bloodclaadt!! What the fuck is wrong with you?".

He shook his head as though to bring himself back to his right mind. "Yes of course you can stay". He was comforting himself running his fingers through his hair. "I'm sorry, I just assumed you'd need to get back home to the children. What did you tell your son?".

"Don't worry he doesn't know who you are. So what does it matter?". Cayenne could feel the tolerance draining from her. He had ruined the moment. The excitement had been replaced by reproach.

"Cayenne. Cay'....".

She could hear him. She knew he was standing there staring after her, crawling behind like some kind of stray desolate pussy. She knew without even looking back.

CHAPTER 34

Dripping with sweat, Cayenne descended the metal stairwell in the gym following thirty minutes of relentless grit cardio exertion. It was one of the hardest classes on the itinerary.

She hurried towards the cool down area to stretch for a few minutes before the yoga class began. It was a new yoga class with an instructor that had previously been used as a stand-in for Charlotte during one of her extensive travels but had recently been inducted with a regular weekly slot of her own. One of the fascinating things about Yoga, was that every instructor brought their own individual flavour to the experience.

From the moment she clapped eyes on Philippa Müller, with her frizzy mass of curls, ruck sack and worn grey plimsoles and heard her whispery Kate Bush voice, she knew she was in for an experience. Philippa certainly had a bohemian air about her and Cayenne could just imagine her seated at the foot of a mountain in Southern Asia learning Indus-Sarasvati first hand from an ancient yoga guru. Similar to some of the other Yogini's, Philippa was somewhat of a juxtaposition between a refreshing gush of healing wind and a force of tumultuous angst, her forehead often clouding over in a heavy frown as though life between yoga sessions, when the belief system demons were free to roam, was somehow incredibly painful. As soon as the session began to the strains of the Eastern music emanating from the sound system, she seemed to come alive. Her flowy Ashtanga was certainly different and it was evident instantly that she had adapted her own unorthodox approach to the discipline, where nothing was particularly structured. A style which simply wouldn't compute with Céléste's military modus or Robert's blistering turbo vein but would certainly complement Claudine and Charlotte's more soothing and tranquil take on the practice. There was no right or wrong posture. She encouraged her charges to do whatever their bodies would suggest and in their own time. Her routines gave permission for them to form whatever shape that came naturally until somehow, assisted by a succession of universal breaths, she had managed to deliver them safely into a recognisable posture.

Cayenne had always loved to observe characters ever since she was a child whiling away hours in her bedroom alone as her older brother took full advantage of the freedom afforded the older male child of that era. Phillipa was an especially curious subject to note. She seemed to be defined by blissful melancholia, as though she were carrying a weight of disturbance but that it had been her mindful choice to do so and to actively collect these clouds in her journey through life, as though this were her divine mission. Her shoulders slumped slightly when she walked and her smile which was absent but for human interaction, never quite reached her eyes, reflecting some kind of permanent migraine of the subconscious mind which prevented her from experiencing the alien fullness of joy.

She was incredibly self-deprecating and her classes were peppered with apologetic expressions and grimaces for the occasional yet customary faux pas or mispronounced words and little in-jokes between herself and the ever present assemblage of disembodied voices that travelled with her. An undiscerned gathering of spiritual guides and latent whispers from her psyche.

On the surface it would appear that Phillipa was indeed as dainty as she first appeared, as though she would go out of her way to see a distressed butterfly rescued from an entangled branch or a tadpole delivered safely back to it's lily pad. But every now and again, Cayenne couldn't help but wonder whether there was underlying tension or subdued and elective unresolved anger bubbling away beneath the surface that she had believed her smile or enforced warmth would conceal.

Cayenne was certain that Philippa didn't at all mean to offend and that she would be mortified if Cayenne ever pointed out to her how some of the things she said that could easily be misconstrued. In particular, Philippa's delivery very much appealed to the racist humour that she and Diego relished. Frequently she would say something that would cause Cayenne to have to bite her lip to stop herself from giggling and making a mental note to remember what she had heard so that she could rush home to share it with her son. The very first time that Phillipa had urged, in little more than a whisper that they were to lie flat on their mat whilst keeping their hips on one side and reaching their arms and legs on the opposite side forming a banana shape. Cayenne could have sworn that Philippa had put extra emphasis on the word BANANA and that her eyes had flickered in a nano second in her direction. Though when she glanced at her through the slit of her semi closed eye, Philippa looked as innocent as the day was young.

Cayenne tried to settle her mind to tune into Philippa's breathing directory.

"Sometimes it can be difficult to switch off and really give your mind some space to just ...BE". Philippa was wandering around now gesticulating compassionately with her hands to add more potency to her words, even though most eyes were closed skyward.

"It's in moments like this that you can.......". There were often long pauses as Philippa spoke, as she rooted through her crowded mind for just the right words to transport them from their world to hers. "... give yourself permission to switch off the MONKEY CHATTER going on in our heads and silence the noise". Cayenne bit her lip again. She could just imagine Diego's reaction when she told him this one.

Philippa tended to go off on little tangents that gave the class a tiny insight into the magical otherworldly place which was her habitat of choice. Her face would scrunch up and her forehead would wrinkle as though her zen thoughts were causing her physical discomfort. "I was watching a video this morning about CHIMPANZEES". There was a hint of a chuckle in her voice and even though Cayenne's eyes were closed, she could trace the location of the voice to somewhere directly above her head. "They were running around, so carefree.... ". Philippa's eyes roamed the room in search of but with not necessarily any regard for, a willing audience. "...so uninhibited. I made a vow to myself that one day I'm going to invent CHIMP YOGA, where we are all allowing ourselves to just...... do what comes naturally". Philippa and her disembodied entourage dissolved into a fit of giggles. "I won't be happy until we are all jumping around barely clothed with our fists under our armpits and GRUNTING at each other".

Cayenne's tongue was positively sore having been bitten to shreds to keep from laughing out loud and she was sorely tempted to sit up onto her elbows defiantly and look Philippa square in the eye as if to state …'really'.

Phillipa's yoga sequences were akin to tying oneself up into a physically tangled knot before beginning the process of unravelling again, through a succession of unusual postures, one blending into another, carried along on one continuous unstoppable flow. She herself was like a human elastic band, seemingly able to achieve positions that defied any natural albeit yoga honed ability. Cayenne certainly did not fit into the bendy Wendy category and she would often receive curious glances from slender yogis, unaccustomed to seeing someone with a more muscular physique working their way through a Chaturanga.

Following a brief silence after assuring herself that her band of chimps were thoroughly rested and restored, Philippa's voice pierced the air in her best primary school teacherlike dulcet tones…. " take a deep breath in. Begin to bring yourself back to awareness, wriggling your fingers and toes and ankles and wrists. Give yourself a big stretch and pull your knees in towards your chest and give yourself the world's biggest hug. Because you deserve it.

Turn onto whichever side you prefer and curl yourself up into your own little co-COON". Cayenne rolled her eyeballs beneath closed lids and held her breath to stifle yet another giggle, imagining the hysteria today's recollection would cause when she got home. "Close your eyes for a moment and know ....that you are totally supported by the earth...because you are. Gradually...slowly and gently bring yourself into a comfortable sitting position and bring your hands to your heart's space".

Phillipa's faint smile and glistening eyes seemed to confirm that she had achieved the objective of taking the class somewhere they hadn't been before. She had lead them by the hand to the very foot of an eastern mountain, filled them with a new vigour, scrubbed them of their worldly essence from head to toe before delivering them back to base, leaving them with a new sense of accomplishment. There was something endearingly wholesome about the bendy young woman, as she coaxed them out of the restorative Savasana at the end of the class, bowing her head humbly and stating in little more than a whisper, her voice breaking slightly with emotion as though the end of class signalled a return to her daily realm of spiritual suffering.

"Namaste".

After what seemed like minutes with her head bowed down, she would eventually raise her eyes to the class, her countenance beaming with momentary gratitude as she moved her hands from her heart space and pointed her adjoined fingers toward every single person in front of her as though spiritually anointing their heads. "Thank you everybody".

As the class emerged from their zen slumber and slowly dispersed around the semi darkened, violet illuminated room to retrieve their shoes and belongings and to roll up and replace their yoga mats in the designated corner storage, Cayenne could pick up on various snippets of information as cliques began to emerge as long time yogis reconnected and work colleagues and gym buddies, huddled for a greeting.

"Should be cool right?!!!"…

Philippa was sharing with a tiny young Asian girl about a revolutionary spiritual practice that she was about to embark upon and she was describing in detail, some intricate poison removal ceremony involving frogs and unicorns, which didn't surprise Cayenne in the slightest.

She couldn't be certain, but as she strode past the huddled couple on her way towards the exit, she could have sworn that she detected an antipodean style lilt to the end of Philippa's sentence.

CHAPTER 35

"Murray gone!..."

"I know… hadn't watched any tennis all day and was shocked to find 3 of the big 4 are out…

Federer's year I guess".

"Yes. Shame, I was looking forward to watching the semis on a Friday afternoon – bit less interested now".

"Mmmm. No Serena, No Murray… no excitement".

"Roll on Monday".

Cayenne was wondering when the executive would eventually brave the subject of their suspended Panoramic tryst. She could almost sense him holding his breath for her reaction.

"Yeah about that… I think we should perhaps follow your initial instinct and wait until you can fully enjoy it". her face crumbled with disgust even as she typed the words. His relief was palpable.

"Really? Shall we do a different venue then?"

"I'm expecting the delivery of my new iphone this afternoon…I'll forward my new email shortly thereafter"

Every now and then he showed remarkable signs of intuition. "Cheeky??? You cutting me here???".

CHAPTER 36

Cayenne had always entertained the notion that she would have loved to have become a dancer. She had attended dancing lessons on a Saturday morning at the Christina Estrada School of Dance at an early age at a small church hall with wooden unpolished floors and the musky smell of dust and rolled up carpets which lined the room. She was accompanied by her two male cousins who were more than a little reluctant to have found themselves dressed in elaborate floaty costumes for community productions and national competitions. Her own brother had refused point blank to join in much to their cousin's frustration.

Cayenne had loved it. Tap and modern dance had been her favourites and to the present day, she could still recall some of the tap routines, whereas the modern dance combinations had fallen into the mist of her distant memory. Ballet, her least favourite of the three dances, much like Yoga, often seemed just out of her reach. Her mother conceded that her love of make-up could possibly be traced back to those adventures of sparkly eye shadows and bright lipstick to coordinate with the costumes that their teacher Christina had envisioned for her young students.

Cayenne could picture herself now in a royal blue leotard with floaty bits of satin and muslin in varying shades of blue attached that created a swirling mist as they danced and twirled. Her estranged father had turned up at a national contest to see her and had taken a picture of her in one of the dark tunnels that ran around the back of the theatre.

In the pictures, she looked uncannily like her own daughter with her little urchin face and narrow eyes as she squinted towards her father who was crouched with camera poised in hand, taking in the glittery vision with her hands on her hips striking her best dancer's pose for her father who had never seen her perform. After taking the picture she remembered distinctly how he had paused to stare at her as if taking her in. In her impatience to return to the excitement of the competition, she had wanted her father to go. It had been nice to see him as his visits became alarmingly more sporadic as the years went by but why now?, on competition day when there was so much going on that she hadn't wanted to miss. After what seemed like an eternity, he had beaconed her towards him for a big hug. She couldn't remember turning around to look back. She had been too eager to return to the main hall and the next exciting instalment of the itinerary.

Had she known then that that would be the last time she would see her father, things may have been different.

Similarly, it turned out to be a thirty plus year gap before dance re-entered her life.

325

Salsa seemed to be the talk of the gym. Suddenly everybody seemed to be proficient in the South American dance and there was even a gym group that congregated every Thursday at Bar Salsa Temple, one of Europe's most popular Salsa clubs.

Cayenne having never danced Salsa before, hadn't wanted to embarrass herself in front of the gym crowd but she also wanted to broaden her horizons and branch out and socialise with a new set of people. When she heard about the gym congregation going out dancing together, headed by Baz who seemed intent on getting everyone to join him in his passion, Cayenne had considered how the need to be comfortable had infiltrated society. God forbid that Baz should waltz his way into the capital by himself and open himself up to a new crowd. She suspected, led by his need to feel safe, he had simply opted to transfer his work crowd over to his social activities.

One of the things Cayenne was most proud of was the fact that she had developed enough emotional scar tissue, to be able to walk unaided into any situation. The scarier the better. The idea of embarking on a new adventure alone didn't phase her in the slightest. So she had decided to find a beginner's class. Her google search had uncovered several classes of various types of Salsa disciplines and various African dance practices.

Feeling adventurous, she decided to book two different classes. One Salsa class in Tottenham and a Kizomba class in Croydon. Both locations were a good distance from home, at least an hour each way, but as far as she was concerned this could be a positive thing. She could feel as though she was challenging herself in a new environment that was unfamiliar. She had never even heard of Kizomba before the gym talk had began. When she had researched the derivative of Angolan Semba which was performed to music of a more sensual romantic flow, she couldn't resist.

As it turned out, both classes could not have been more different.

The salsa class was a small group lead by Alfonso, a Portuguese instructor who taught Cuban Salsa, his passion, in his spare time. An intimate group which had started with around twenty people and had slowly dwindled down to twelve by the time Cayenne had arrived for her first class on a Thursday evening at the old Social club which had clearly not been renovated since it's heyday in the 1960's. It smelt and looked as though the 60's was the last time that it had been cleaned.

The old faithful's that held up the bar had clearly been doing so for a very long time and were now blending in with the tired furniture.

Cayenne had been surprised to see that even though the group had begun their classes several weeks prior, most of them were clearly still struggling with the basic steps. Cayenne, with her natural rhythm and coordination seemed to take to the dance very quickly which delighted her.

Alfonso was an unusual looking man. His slender physique complemented his tiny frame and his tight jeans clung to his narrow hips. His white tee- shirt proudly boasted Salsa Instructor on the back and he wore white laced up dance shoes which reminded Cayenne of her early dancing days. His jet black thinning hair was swept to one side in an attempt to detract from the hairline that was tangoing its way towards the back of his head. The top of his scalp glistened under the old ballroom lights. His accent was thick and his nose was much too large to be in harmony with his other features, to the point that it almost appeared prosthetic when he stood in profile, reminding her of the image of a typical villainous character one would come across in a classic children's story. Cayenne couldn't help but think that if she had seen Alfonso out on the street, she would have thought him rather peculiar. She might even have crossed the street but for his slightly subservient demeanour which gave him just enough humility to be not considered ominous. The moment he began to dance however, seemed to bring him to life. Any oddness disappeared at the sound of the Cuban Mambo and he would be instantly transformed into a magnetic maestro. Full of suave sophistication and grace when he commanded the dance with polished savoir faire as he whisked the various student partners around the ballroom.

The small group had already paired up by the time Cayenne had arrived, slightly late owing to the underground carriages being packed to capacity at peak time.

It didn't take long to surmise that she was not in the presence of World Championship level Salsa alumni, which had put her in an immediate state of ease. Not that situations like this unnerved Cayenne anyway. She rather relished opportunities to arrive on a new stage and the challenges that it entailed, to be around new people and be open to experiences. She went as far as to enjoy to some degree, walking into a room full of people knowing that she would likely be met with intense curiosity and mild suspicion. She had grown accustomed to it over the years. As far back as she could remember she could recall similar experiences. It began growing up around her mother's hair salon. It might be pertinent to state that this was a Jamaican hair salon. Important to note as these tended to focus on chatter and gossip rather than perfecting the art of hair design and establishing a viable enterprise.

The stories that she would encounter whilst listening to the long held customers, many of whom, now demanding to be referred to as Aunty, owing to the years of loyalty to the family run business, were typically tales of sickness and whoa, gossip that tended to centre around the misfortune of others and the utter delight that it was happening to somebody else.

Her relationship with her mother had always been fraught with misjudgement and misunderstanding. Cayenne wasn't sure whether it had to do with the fact that her maternal grandmother had died in childbirth and so her own mother had lacked the maternal nurturing that she so seldom expressed. Cayenne often felt that her mother attributed everything negative that happened in her life to her

difficult daughter, just has her father's generation had nurtured the tradition of blaming the younger generation for their own woes. Often as a teenager, she would walk into the hair salon and immediately pick up on the hushed atmosphere, heavy with guilt and surprise at her unannounced arrival. Somewhere around that time she began to construct the strength in mentality that would see her through many a treacherous emotional terrain. An ability to withstand harsh criticism and suspicion. An ability to hang with a tense ambience without the usual self-inflicting disapproval that situations like this would usually garner.

Alfonso nodded his acknowledgement of her arrival and she watched as he embraced his dance partner, a middle aged woman with fading red hair that was succumbing to grey rooted dominance and demonstrated the basic salsa steps for the couples positioned to his left. Cayenne observed them closely. Even those that managed to follow his instructions, lacked the Latin flair of accomplished dancers that the music was trying desperately to inspire. The couples to Alfonso's right were clearly the real newcomers, the group with which she would be placed. An amalgamation of left footed learners with limited grasp of coordination, stepping heavily backwards and forwards as though rediscovering mobility following a prolonged debilitating injury, with others looking strangely like they were stomping on ants with intent to maim.

Cayenne let her gaze wander around the room, taking in the large open plan dated auditorium which made up half of the Social club ground level. The parquet floors were well worn now, bearing scuffs and scrapes from the Paso Dobles and Charlestons of old. The wallpaper cladding the double storeyed room was tired and dreary and darkened by layers of generational dust. The clouded windows held memories of post war soirées and victorious military celebration nights. The shadows of dances past, hung in the mist, weaving around the ornate lanterns and intricate vintage fittings that once shone and gleamed in the evening light but now hung, forlorn and abandoned.

Alfonso was walking towards her now to introduce himself, looking like an Eastern European Rumpelstiltskin. Somewhere behind the distorted dwarf like image, she could detect an endearing soul. When he smiled it readily reached his eyes and his cheekbones filled out his bony face. The mop of hair on top of his head was thinning under the weight of the over processed dyeing and only served to emphasize the lines on his ageing face.

"Hello, I am Alfonso". He nodded profusely as he spoke, and if Cayenne wasn't careful, she could easily find herself mirroring him and following suit.

Cayenne reached out her hand to shake his in response which seemed to catch him unaware as he was already preparing to lead her on to the dance floor

"Hello I'm Cayenne". He looked at her outstretched hand and shook it appreciatively.

"Have you danced Salsa before?".

"No never".

He led her to the end of the line of the left footed paraplegic crew and she followed willingly although she knew she could easily position herself amongst the wannabe Fred and Gingers pacing the far end of the floor and instantly be identified as destined for the level titled 'cut above'.

Before long Cayenne was competently performing the basic steps as though she were born to do it, her lack of self conscious trepidation encouraging suspicious glances from her new classmates which made her feel even more at home.

"Okay get your partners, get your partners". Alfonso was bellowing for them to partner up. Cayenne found herself opposite a big broad mixed-race man who judging by his coordination or the lack thereof and the stomping un-salsa-like movements she had witnessed, he had clearly led a solely Caucasian infused existence and she suspected any black contribution to his upbringing, was glaringly negligible.

His big broad feet that had begun to distort the original shape and style of the Nike design patent, were threatening to leave their imprint in the historic parquet flooring, altering it's geometric outline. Cayenne couldn't help but imagine that the way in which a man danced was probably reflective in some way of how they would seduce or make love to a woman. A sudden wave of empathy threatened to engulf her, toward any woman her new partner may have at home.

It didn't take long for her to realise that she was having a great time and thoroughly enjoying the experience. The thrill of learning something new, something that was complex and challenging but also exciting and exotic, even if the exoticism was somewhat elusive in this run down old working men's club which had seen better days. The very essence of the dance filled the room making it feel as though generations of old were joining in.

At the end of the lesson, it seemed Alfonso liked to close the class with a freestyle group dance, incorporating some traditional Cuban party moves which Cayenne used her natural sense of rhythm to grasp very quickly. It was at this point that another group of people began filing into the hall, one by one, disrobing and taking their coats off and placing their bags aside. There seemed to be a distinct air of accomplishment about them as they peered down their noses at the assortment of beginners. It transpired they belonged to the advanced group whose class began immediately after.

She paid Alfonso for the class and walked back to her table to retrieve her coat and bag. Just as she slipped out of the wooden double doors she glanced back over her shoulder as the so called advanced set were limbering up on the dance floor.

She was about to wonder quite how long it would take for her to be classed as advanced, when she caught sight of a middle-aged gentleman, stepping gingerly backwards and forwards with convex bowed legs. He seemed to be giving free reign to any impulse his gangly body suggested, exhibiting none of the frame and posture that Alfonso alluded to, which gave her an immediate surge of certainty that her ascension may not be too long after all.

CHAPTER 37

"Hey"

Being in no mood to entertain the fickle executive, Cayenne declined to respond.

She almost sprinted toward the Cubitt Town Tennis Courts, nestled in the far corner of St Edwards Park. A serene enclosed double court surrounded by trees and benches and pathways leading to the main park and basketball court and back out towards the hustle and bustle of this more exclusive side of Tower Hamlets.

This was arguably her favourite hour of the week, where she gathered with a group of women who would doubtless have anything else in common other than the fact that they all had children who were busy in their various classrooms whilst their mothers stole an hour to learn this new discipline.

The Coordinator from Sugar's school, Jill Jopley who worked tirelessly to organise and obtain funding for all sorts of parental activities, was already on the court chatting to the Cardio Tennis instructor Frida about the difficulties she was having securing funds for the upcoming term whilst simultaneously fiddling with the speaker box on wheels that she had brought along to literally amp up the atmosphere whilst the ladies were playing. Not that this was entirely necessary as before long they would be creating their own musical entertainment with whoops and cheers of delight at their own progress whilst rallying or gasps of annoyance at a missed opportunity, not to mention the squeals of enjoyment at beating the opposing team.

Cayenne barely paid attention to these monetary conversations, which was just as well, as she might have deduced that the protests were becoming louder by the week.

Frida began taking the women through a warm up routine incorporating bending and stretching with movement followed by running single file around the perimeter of the court followed by high knees and squat jumps.

Once she was satisfied that the women were sufficiently warm, she began to explain the first exercise of the day which turned out to be Cayenne's favourite.

"Okay get into two lines please", Frida barked, her Eastern European accent barely discernible as she mentally counted the women whilst making calculations in her head. "There are fourteen of you so seven on each side". She used the tennis racquet in her hand to point to either end of the court.

"This side is for the forehand", her personalised racquet pointed towards the right hand side of the court. "and the other side is for the back hand".

Frida was demonstrating what she was expecting of her charges and whilst some of the other women were continuing their conversations and chatting animatedly amongst themselves, the unintelligible banter punctuated with cultural squeals, Cayenne was paying strict attention, both out of respect and because she really didn't want to miss anything. She was sure that once into the swing of the exercise, many fingers would be raised asking for a reminder of what was expected of them, which Frida would address, resisting the temptation to roll her eyes in frustration.

Frida pointed to the line to her left, "This line will do the forehand standing on the red dot". Her finger pointed in the direction of a red rubber floor marker that she had placed on the baseline. "Once you hit the forehand, run towards the other dot,". Frida had spun on her heel after simulating the perfect forehand and was running now towards the other strategically placed dot in the middle of the left hand court. In the absence of Jeffrey, the other instructor who had began the course but had since become increasingly obscure, Frida was having to do the job of two people. "Then do a forehand volley, that means NO BOUNCE, then touch the net with your racquet, run around the net, make sure you don't run in front of me or you may get hit with the balls, collect two balls, put them in the bucket then run around to the other side". Frida fixated her gaze towards the right hand side of the court, where half of the assembled crew were dutifully lining up. "Those of you in this line, you will do the backhand". Frida was now positioned on the other red dot placed parallel to the left hand side. " I will throw the ball, you do the backhand, then run to this spot and do a backhand volley, NO BOUNCE". Frida accompanied this instruction with a stern glance over her shoulder, commanding the attention of the few women who were still too engrossed in conversation to have heard their instructions and would typically soon be wailing that they hadn't understood the rules as they ran in the wrong direction causing unnecessary mayhem. "After the backhand volley, touch the net, run around the court, pick up two balls and then rejoin the OPPOSITE line. I cannot emphasize enough, do not run across the court, it can be dangerous okay?". A succession of deaf ears draped in muslin wraps, nodded repetitively.

With that, the exercise began in earnest and it wasn't long before Frida was repeating herself with increasing levels of exasperation. "DO NOT CROSS THE COURT. NO BOUNCE. Join the

OPPOSITE line", accompanied by the skyward glance of her piercing eyes which were soon pleading silent prayers.

The sound of balls being wielded towards the far corners of the enclosed court were interspersed with Jill's East End Cockney drone, as she shared every unfiltered nuance, thought or idea that passed through her mind with a raucous delivery that her Pearly King and Queen ancestors would be proud of.

"Ooooh I missed that one", Jill was chuckling to herself as she headed around the court, scampering after errant tennis balls. " I went to 'it it, and I missed the baw di'n I". She cackled to anyone who was listening. More hearty chuckles followed as she hustled towards the opposing line up repeating the misdemeanour for those unfortunate enough to have misheard the first time. Cayenne observed with some affection, the way in which Jill had cultivated a strong rapport with these women, many of whom were Pakistani or Bangladeshi who with English as their second language, tended to only associate with their own and form their own comfortable cliques in the playground. In this obscure environment however, those barriers seemed to instantly disappear and one region of the far east, seamlessly blended with another, merging with various representatives of the East end of London in one harmonious mixture. Jill, in an extension of her coordinator role in the school and in the wider community, seemed to have become a kind of surrogate mother figure to many of the women who were not, it seemed averse to hugging and cuddling this middle aged white woman in a way that was uncustomary in their own communities.

338

Even the quietest among them with the smallest grasp of Western culture, seemed to understand cockney slang with ease as they giggled along at the continuous flow of Jill's audible thought pattern. "D'you know what I fink it is?.... it's the we'ver innit?. It's made the ground a bit slippery, so I was gonnu 'it it and I missed it di'n I?", came the repetitious cycle followed by more raucous cackling.

Cayenne threw herself wholeheartedly into this exercise and adopted the poise of a professional circuit player as she crouched low, transferring her weight from one foot to the other whilst adjusting the grip of the racquet in her hands and briefly checking the strings in her racquet as though it were common practice, her eyes fixated on the slightest movement of Frida's hand as she awaited the simulated serve.

"Nice shot", Frida called out as Cayenne whisked the ball over the net with a double handed backhand, landing the ball just shy of the line in the opposing service box. Cayenne smiled inwardly as she touched the net and ran towards a discarded array of balls in the corner of the court. She balanced as many as she could on her flat racquet and tipped them into the bucket, before racing around to the other side to attempt the forehand. As she hopped and skipped her way around the court, she couldn't resist narrowing her eyes in feigned concentration as though she really were Serena, limbering up for the inevitable devastation about to be unleashed on the group of unsuspecting opponents.

CHAPTER 38

Several days passed which Cayenne made sure were full on with extra curricular activities, taking in extra classes at the gym, ensuring regular attendance at her two new dance classes, outings with the children for meals and cinema dates, sparing little room for executive shenanigans.

Not that this had ever stopped him before.

Monday

"Hey!"

Tuesday

"You gone???"

Wednesday

"Just drove past the Westbury….. good times (memories)".

Thursday

"Come Back"

Friday

"Working late tonight... No choice now as suspected, but I so wish I hadn't made this decision".

Cayenne rather suspected that this message was deliberately ambiguous to perhaps prompt her in to making enquiries.

Saturday 301am

"I'm sorry"

Sunday 4:56pm

"Found someone else to play with?"

Sunday 19:47

"You are missed... sincerely".

Monday 9:20am

"Fuck! It would have been easier if I would never have tasted of such a delicious distraction like you".

341

Tuesday 5:30 am

"Gaucho lunch???..."

...Cayenne smoothed down the front of her wrap dress, pulling in her stomach muscles as her hand hovered above her abdomen. The ruched material forming a knot just above her hip, creating a tight fit that would not forgive any additional roundedness but would rather draw attention to it. Fortunately, the hidden waistband held her in effortlessly.

Her inner thighs kissed each other with their silky film of coconut oil, perfectly assisting her effervescent glide through the restaurant towards the suited executive that awaited her in a discreet corner of the second floor.

As usual, he was unable to disguise the effect she was having on him. The fact that she had dismissed him so cruelly had only served to fuel his hunger.

He leaned back in the booth sofa, resting his arms on the tops of the chair, his legs unconsciously widening, accommodating the almost visible pulsation taking place beneath the sharp pinstripe trousers. She allowed herself an indiscreet glance at the groin movement which a slight shift of his hand had rather given away. Her gaze following the

342

outline of the hardening forming between his legs, lengthening before her eyes, her groin area receiving furtive messages of their own.

He slipped off his blazer and casually folded it and placed it on his lap, giving away his intentions with the greedy steel of his eyes. His free hand loosened his tie and scraped back his newly cropped hair as his lips let out a deep gush of breath to attempt to cool the temperature of his brow.

Cayenne sat down opposite, ensuring the chair was pulled out a little distance from the table, to facilitate the torture that she intended to inflict.

No matter how much he consumed today, she would ensure he left with a definite unsatiated hunger.

She sat down gingerly, placing her bag and coat on the seat beside her intending to wait until the waiter returned with their drinks, to cross her legs as slowly as she could. For now, she allowed her knees to fall out into diamond pose, just as they did in Yoga class when opening up the hips. Leaning back and edging her groin in his direction, allowing her short hem to ride up to her glistening thighs, stopping just short of answering his almost inevitable question. Was she wearing any panties?.

It was a question he would most certainly have taken home with him had her resolve not waned. Meanwhile no straining of his eyes would solve the mystery, though the slight tilt of her eyebrow was indication enough that his torture was certain.

He looked captivated as his eyes finally returned to her face. His brow wrinkled slightly as he tried to fathom her expression. It took moments for a light bulb to flip on in his mind just as the corners of his mouth twittered at the realisation that she was bringing herself to orgasm right there at the table.

She hadn't meant to, of course. But in response to the silk that her pussy was weaving, her hands couldn't help but obey. In the semi darkness of the empty restaurant, with a minimum complement of staff busying themselves on the fringes, her knees resting on the seats beside her, with the smallest of movements when her hand had swept from her thigh towards the carnal urging. Barely had she even stroked the tip of her taught clit, when an explosion had erupted within her. It had taken every effort of control to minimise the movement of her body and luckily only the open mouthed executive was privy to the sight of building ecstasy on her face and the shortening of her breath, the rising of her chest and eventually, the stiffening of her legs that had now uncurled and lengthened to ballerina pointed toes on either side of his legs, as her diaphragm tipped upwards to empty her of every last bit of sensual manna. Her body released and relaxed in her seat, the legs returning to a normal stance, her breathing restored until all that remained, was the sensational appetiser that she offered to his lips with her fingers, just in time for the arrival of their hors d'oeuvres.

Once their main courses had been delivered, their wine glasses topped up and the waiter surely dispensed of for some considerable time,

Cayenne edged her way around the semi circular seat towards him, leaning into his side briefly and pecking his cheek with the lightest of touches as not to leave a trace of her ultra violet lipstick.

Placing a large French fry into his mouth, her free hand simultaneously slipped under his blazer that was now dome like on his lap. He had clearly attempted to comfort himself as his zip was already undone and his hardened cock was protruding out of the gap in the front of his boxer shorts like a magnificent monument. Cayenne had an insatiable urge to mount him and gallop in homage to the former carefree life of the Aberdeen Angus that now adorned their plate. For now, she had to make do with allowing her hands to continue the mission. The high table hid the frenzy of her movements. Although anyone observing would have taken one look at the open mouthed executive and guessed that it wasn't the medium rare Sirloin causing his euphoria. Cayenne, ever poised, adopted an innocent expression on her face that belied the cardio taking place beneath the table as she conjured up a tartare to complement her own juicy cutlet.

CHAPTER 39

Cayenne could always guarantee that should she ever fail to hear the alarm on her phone in the morning, that Ocean would ensure that the slumber did not continue for too long. Every morning without fail, usually before sunrise, her middle child could be heard scampering around his room. There would be the undeniable thud as his feet hit the ground from the top bunk and just as though she were programmed to wake from whatever level of consciousness she was coasting, moments would pass when she knew that he would be resolutely spreading his bed with military precision, and bar any other distractions, he would head promptly to the other end of the long corridor to his mother's room where he would fling himself unceremoniously onto her bed.

Any delusions of a lie-in would be obliterated as the hectic morning routine began ardently.

Thankfully, he was now at an age that he could adequately take care of his own needs with minimal guidance and supervision, though if left unprompted, he would eventually get lost in his own train of colourful thought.

"Ocee', good morning. Did you have a good sleep?"

Ocean responded with his usual level of enthusiasm for small talk. "Yes".

"Kiss". Her son was clearly not in the mood for morning cuddles. Affection was something that he usually dispensed on his own terns. Not unlike his maternal guardian.

"Okay, put your pyjamas in the machine and have a shower". Ocean stood and walked towards her bedroom door, turning to look at her with one finger poised in the air, awaiting the inevitable instructions that usually followed. "eyes, nose mouth, ears, neck…." Ocean proceeded to mouth each body part as she spoke, from head to toe in complete synchronicity with her voice. She did this to emphasise to her son that he needed to pay particular attention when washing and not just go through the motions.

Walking past the bathroom, Cayenne could hear him thoroughly enjoying himself under the force of the shower. He had always enjoyed playing with water, as was common with children on the sensory division of the autistic spectrum. She could just imagine him having a field day with the selection of shower gels aligned on the multi-level shelf. Where once it was a pastime that would need to be heavily supervised, Ocean still couldn't quite believe his good fortune that he was actually allowed to indulge in both at the same time every morning at his leisure.

Cayenne squinted as she entered the dimly lit living room, dark except for the outside lights straining through the gaps in the curtains. Gaps that were an unfortunate by product of her own DIY. Two years earlier she had single handedly put up the extended curtain rail which were extra long to accommodate the huge glass doors leading out to the balcony. She had tried her best with the less than adequate drill which hadn't been up to the job and had failed to penetrate the thick wooden panel above the door. She had then had to resort using a hammer and a combination of nails and screws from an assortment abandoned in a drawer.

Apart from a few minor adjustments when one of the children had zealously yanked open the curtains, her handy work had stood the test.

Not wanting to turn the light on and disturb Sugar, who had insisted on sleeping in the living room for at least the past year, Cayenne stepped gingerly around the outline of the brightly patterned duvet that was spread out on the floor, the sofas having been discarded in favour of the thick copper rug in the centre of the room, edging her way towards the kitchen to begin preparing Ocean's cereal.

The black painted kitchen was a far contrast from the stark white room they encountered on their arrival. In fact the entire apartment was now unrecognisable from the bright but bland, typically magnolia space they inherited from the previous occupant. Cayenne knew full well that her home which had now been firmly imprinted with her own unique stamp, wouldn't be to everyone's taste. A fact that made it all the more special to her because she felt it was a real expression of her character and personality. A courageous act of daring where most people played it safe. She would have bet money that all the other apartments in the building would be practically white washed, with an additional featured wall showcasing the general trend of the season. Cayenne had taken her license of self expression to a whole new level, painting ceilings, skirtings, any surface that she could get her hands on to eradicate it of anything resembling a blank canvas. The coffee in her cup blended perfectly with the dark kitchen which was illuminated solely by the lights from the extractor fan and the in-built bulb of the kettle, with their matching tinge of blue bouncing off any reflective surface it could find.

She was reminiscing on years past, when Ocean was much more demanding and their daily lives much more of a challenge. It was easy to forget quite how far they had come from the days of outbursts in supermarkets and emotional break downs on public transport and having to deal with a frantic child whilst fending of the inevitable judgements of the ogling public.

Every moment of every day would require avid surveillance of this child who was likely to do anything unpredictable at the first sight of freedom. Her levels of anxiety and stress at the time, were often dangerously high. Thankfully she hadn't realised quite how severe it was until they had come safely through to the other side. Diego, her elder son and man of the house, had stood shoulder to shoulder with her since his early teens and made sure that she hadn't felt alone and from that memorable day to this, she really hadn't.

Cayenne often wondered to herself, quite how she had managed to raise such a rare young man. So mature for his young years, so level headed and wise, there was not so much as a flicker of uncertainty regarding the task ahead. He had a level of groundedness and a humble self assurance that was scarce. Her sister in law Katya had summed it up best when Diego had travelled to Torquay for the weekend and managed to fit in a catch up lunch with his auntie. They had always been close and Katya was enamoured with Diego from the first time she met him as a toddler. "I can't believe it" she had exclaimed when Cayenne had returned from work whilst Katya was babysitting her son many years previousy. "Whenever you used to tell me that crowds would cross the road to take a closer look at him, I secretly thought ' she must be exaggerating'. But we were coming back from the parade shops and I swear to God". Katya had begun swinging her arms in dramatic fashion as she often did when she became animated. "This groups of teenagers ran across the road. At first I though ' my God, what do they want?'. They all crowded around us and were cooing at him and saying how cute he was with his little bandana and leather boots. It was like he was famous. Unbelieveable!".

When Diego had returned from his weekend on the South Coast, Katya had texted her to recount their catchup. Cayenne had practically glowed when her sister-in-law had concluded her text by summing up " Do you know what it is?…", she had questioned herself aloud having observed her nephew effortlessly assist her with her own demanding toddler. "He has this aura as though he has no unanswered questions".

CHAPTER 40

Friday

"Thanks for being such a great lunch guest. Enjoy your weekend".

Sunday

"Just reliving the rush I felt chasing you at North Greenwich…. Not to mention getting that taste".

Monday

"Want a picnic today?

11.50 usual place.   What non Michelin starred delights would you like?".

"Just a hot chocolate… oh and a sprinkling of cinnamon".

The Glorious sunshine dictated her fashion choice for the day which she had already decided upon even before the picnic invitation.

A bright orange sheer, almost beachwear combination of baggy pants which would be worn with a bright orange bikini to cover her modesty, and a matching hooded top. There were always compliments when she wore it as   apparently, it was her colour. Cayenne loved it because she could roll the waist of the pants repeatedly so that the see through fabric hugged her butt cheeks and had no choice but to disappear into the crack made by her bikini bottoms beneath, causing the outline of two voluptuous glutes to protrude behind her as she walked. Or rather strode. The rays of the sun only served to illuminate the garment further until she was practically a glowing figurine in a sea of ordinariness.

As usual, she was the first to arrive at their spot. He could surely be forgiven after having to negotiate an appropriate lunch slot with his hectic city office, stopping en-route to attend to her lunch request. Though she had only stipulated a hot beverage, he would always ensure he brought a selection of things she might like. Usually an assortment of healthy options as he knew she would either be coming from or heading to the gym that afternoon.

When she eventually saw him striding hurriedly towards her, swinging his head from side to side as his floppy fringe following suit, he was indeed juggling a couple of small paper bags in each hand.

Cayenne turned on her converse heel and began to walk very slowly in the direction of the park. She wanted him to have a good look at her from behind. She knew that she had already made his day.

It was a while before he caught up with her. This was deliberate of course. He was taking full advantage of the neon visual before him. No doubt watching each glute rise with every step. The rise and fall causing their own tumultuous stirrings. In his mind they had reached the park already. His imagination had ploughed ahead to ensure no one else was around, and that his prey had no regard for this hindering garment and bore no objection to him ripping the trousers directly along the seam whilst bending her over into a downward facing dog hovering above the overgrown grass and burying his face deep into the crack. Wishing to insert himself as far into her anus as her tightness would allow. Smelling, licking, slurping hungrily, desperately. Angrily pushing her upper body deeper into the foliage should she show any sign of emerging and interfering with his mission. Pulling her hips back skyward and continuing to rummage in search of her aromatic pelvis.

In his wildest dreams, any fear of consequence would be incinerated into the heat of her body and turn to ash as he pulled out the loaded weapon that she had created and mounted her like a male lion. Or preferably grasping her like the toads in the African wild that cling to their chosen suitor for days on end until their desire is totally fulfilled. How he would love to be able to do that. Pump her incessantly. Disregarding any resistance. His genitals fastened to her insides like a glue stick. Unmovable. Rigidly pulsating inside her until every last drop of him was spent, again and again. The ultimate fantasy.

The beep of the traffic lights, brought his thoughts back to reality as he continued to walk just a step behind her. At best he would get a feel of her today. He'd be lucky to get more. He was constantly trying to ascertain her mood to see how much of herself she was willing to reveal. Her guardedness was partially of his own doing. So many let downs, he had to live with that. He would leave insatiably hungry. Always hungry for her. A touch would appease him slightly. His ego would feel sufficiently assuaged if he could get her to touch him too. God knows he was straddling three legs already. He had to push his fists deep into each pocket to allow room for the arrival of the additional limb.

He could barely speak. Occasional pointless drivel escaped his mouth in response to something she was wittering on about. It was all he could do to control himself. She may as well be holding his cock and leading him like a dog with a lead, such was the internal pull to stand close to her. To somehow get the tip of his cock to brush the enticing rump currently overwhelming his senses.

The Executive's busy schedule usually ensured that he was the first to leave the park. She more often than not elected to stay behind, basking in the afternoon sun and watching the various activities taking place in their designated areas. From the far corner of the park, she could just make out the gated basketball court which today was occupied by a group of teenagers rehearsing their Mamba Mentality slam dunks.

A small group of Asian men were playing a game of cricket in the centre of the field where one end was set up ready for an ICC tournament, whilst the opposite end tended to be used by rugby and football teams. On this day however, a group of primary school children, draped in oversized high visibility jackets were being escorted around the park by teachers and assistants.

If she strained her eyes, she could even see the small assortment of facilities for the younger children to play on, way on the other side, tucked under the black alder trees.

Occasionally a jogger would run past or a cyclist taking advantage of the clear skies.

As usual her phone alerted her to a message shortly after the accountant's departure.

"Hope my choices for you were ok".

They hadn't gotten around to sampling the goodies that he had bought, preferring to spend the limited time lying discreetly in the grass on the borders of the farmland and ensuring that they kept watch by looking suitably distracted by the captivating activities at either end.

That is when she wasn't lying on her stomach thoroughly enjoying his hands acting as foam rollers, massaging her bottom.

The firmness of the muscles thoroughly excited him. The roundness of the shape proved thoroughly mesmerising for a suburban white boy.

He could hardly believe his good fortune.

"Eating my sea salt and cider vinegar crisps and marvelling at your thoughtful selection".

"Glad the crisps gave you some satisfaction despite your high end food blogging.

Have a good week enjoying yoga, Planet of the Apes and Turkish Cuisine – nice".

A smile curled her lips as she realised he had remembered what she had told him over lunch at Gaucho. He had asked what she had planned for the weekend ahead as he was always curious to how she was spending her time. She had told him of plans with the children to take in the latest Planet of the Apes movie and of Diego's promise to take her out to eat.

However, she wasn't quite in the mood to show him this appreciation.

Soon after their meetings, which doubtless left them both in a more heightened state of arousal on their departure, typically, her frustration would be channelled into several terse emails by the end of the day. By now he could almost predict them.

"You showed such early promise... such spontaneity and excitement pre Zurich...

Missing lying in Mayfair airing my pussy in anticipation of an Executive arrival.

Whatever travesty has taken away the cinnamon pussy hunger ???

Will undoubtedly feel a tinge of regret to have to replace you with a more impassioned admirer with more defined athletic prowess.

Alas… thanks for the memories".

"I still want you in my face… gorgeous".

"A regal pussy needs attention".

"Cheeky, let's hope my successor can give you Mayfair.

Let's go back to Mayfair week after next".

"Likewise, I sincerely hope, Suburban Sally gives you equatorial moisture and chocolate succulence, as my hunger does not permit me to wait that long…

You have successfully procrastinated your way out of the Royal running.

Have a tofu-esque summer".

"I know I know. What a terribly poor whore".

"Detestable".

"Fuck! Not liking this… I should have owned you earlier".

"Oh don't be too hard on yourself. Your naturally cautious nature would need to evaluate any possible risk.

God forbid your future offspring inherit your inclination to see danger at every turn....

Doubtless they will excel in the corporate world, outwardly exuding excellence whilst harbouring inner torture and private hell.

Whatever happened to the underbelly Cavalier that grasped his opportunity in the face of potential failure. That brave dastardly individual that seized the moment....

Whatever have you done with Spontaneous Silvester who stopped at nothing to satiate his appetite for caramel pussy.

Damn you Zurich".

"Caramel pussy still utterly desired".

"You sound thoroughly pitiful... like a speedboat, once powerful and coveted that has since lost it's momentum and lustre. How dare Suburbia rob you of such manliness.

Now your black ass slapping memories will be hijacked by an infinitely more masculine and daring suitor....

My honed muscles will be ogled at close quarters by your successor.

My caramel clit tasted by your replacement.

Little wonder, the Canary underbelly is populated by haunted women...

They have no doubt suffered at the hands of the phantom White Whore, with his empty promises and fruitless lofty ideas promptly followed by a spaghetti junction of anxiety and personal stress deflected as executive turmoil.

"Aahh I have missed this journalistic character destruction. I have taken you too lightly.

You deserve a fucking spanking. I am now terribly distracted".

"Oh I am sorry. You'll have to excuse me. It's been several weeks without so much as a pussy lick.

I'm putting all delicious thoughts of saturating your face with succulent cunt juice right out of my mind. Thankfully I can release my pent up energy at the gym later".

"You know exactly what buttons to press".

"That's the thanks I get for simply wanting to give you a generous feed. When one's pussy is throbbing with unrelenting juice... it's very difficult to supress...

Once again......sorry".

"No don't stop... tell me how you want to drench my face.

Tell me how you will utterly quench my thirst

Tell me how you will hold me tight in position fully clamped until your full orgasm breaks through.

I want it.

I want your generous black pussy feed. So lucky to still have it offered. How fortunate I am. I want the delicious caramel cunt juice".

"and I want to clamp you between my thighs… pull back your head before plunging you face first into my climatic abyss.

Suffocate you into my aromatic scent, watching as it engulfs you.

Urging the tip of your nose to tickle my clit as your tongue pulses into my cunt simultaneously.

I won't be able to resist riding your face to speed up my release".

"I'm still your white bitch".

"I am now imagining turning you over when I can no longer take it… and throwing you on the bed and clambering onto your head.

With no thought for your comfort or breathing ability… purely overtaken by my desire to release my cunt marinade onto such a willing and hungry participant.

Let your tongue simulate a ravenous cock and poke my pussy and ease my pain".

"Give it to me. I'm totally yours to fucking USE".

"I am in total surrender mode now, giving in to the need to lie back with my legs open wide… I need your face probing my vagina…

I want to savour your tongue's journey to chocolate utopia.

My pussy is reacting... fearless to previous disappointment.... Dribbling in confident anticipation.

I'm in urgent need to satisfy this pussy hiatus...

My face riding will be unapologetically merciless. In need of a pussy tease.... My cunt strokes..... my clit rubs.... Leading to an urgent release.

I may yet decapitate you with the force of my thrusts as your face becomes further embedded into my cunt...

I need your chiselled face to relieve me. I always wondered why Caucasians have such pointed noses. What a remarkably ingenious Creator we have".

" I want to see you in full flight. Toned gorgeous and delicious, A Queen".

"Once you have assisted me to my euphoria... I need stillness.... Stillness to allow every last drop of hard won Caribbean marinade to dribble from my pussy... this must not be rushed...

Indeed, if I need a subsequent release... perhaps finger aided.... You must wait, open mouthed for your second helping.

How long must I wait to show off the newly cultivated chiselled back and sculptured shoulder muscles... how can such a specimen go so long without examination and appreciation. Rub oil over every ligament and leave a trail of kisses all over my body.

Labour over me like a resplendent meal spread before a hungry peasant.

Lick, touch and stroke as though you perceive ownership".

"Nice images.. summer lounging now an absolute must".

CHAPTER 41

"Fuck!. Unable to give a shit on this conference call. Would much rather be knee deep in cinnamon".

"If only I could curl up in your lap under the conference table and suck on you until I fall tenderly to sleep to the sensation of your free hand toying with my lady lips….

Teasing out the coconut milk threatening to dribble over your conference floor".

"Arrogantly hard for you.

Gorgeous chocolate gym bunny with such delicious tasting juice, sucking down hard to relieve my boredom and bring me back to life.

Mmmm so fucking nice imagining your head bobbing up and down whilst I take note of the European figures whilst running my fingers through your weave.

I'm slowly unravelling – noticeable that my attention is elsewhere".

"Put the call on hands free and place me face down onto the conference room floor... spread open my toned arse and taste it before dipping into my coconut milk cone and creating a dynamic cocktail.

Your distraction must be forgiven... for who can resist the urgency of our needs...

Close your eyes... picture your stealthy approach to my open cunt. My arms are braced to grasp you between my biceps before submerging you inside me.

I can barely abide missing yet another hardening.

Feels like I'm missing something... feeling left out

I must be present to touch and to lick and to suck

Almost got distracted myself... must now run to my Yin Yoga class."

"Fucking you hard whilst on hands free in our boardroom would be quite intoxicating.

Letting the grey men in suits hear you moan as we indulge".

CHAPTER 42

Cayenne had to admit that the executive certainly brought out a different side of her. Somehow, she felt sexually uninhibited around him even though they weren't actually having sex. Most of their communication had been suggestive. Virtual and imaginary. Expressing their desires openly to one another which she supposed was a kind of intimacy. She wondered whether it was actually bonding them deeper than if they were actually meeting and fucking on a regular basis. A sensual meeting of the minds.

His early dawn messages seemed desperate as though he needed her, though it was also apparent that any replication on her part would send him running for the suburban hills.

She was sure that the only reason they were still in touch was purely to ease her occasional boredom or curiosity. Had she really been concerned about the outcome, things would have come to a head by now. As it was, it almost seemed as though they were humouring each other. Him teetering on the brink of faithfulness to a phantom significant other and her, simply enjoying the fact that he helped her access a side of herself that no one else had, all whilst having an understanding that they were definitely ill-matched.

At times he would even ask "Is it bad that I'm using you".

She knew what he meant. To her mind, he was the public school boy who lacked the charm and confidence of his peers. The floppy haired studious one that probably secured friendship at school by allowing the coveted peer group to copy his work or inundating them with benevolent kindness, never feeling certain that he was enough to maintain access to the elite otherwise. Having played a chosen character for so long, Cayenne sometimes wondered whether he had forgotten to go back and retrieve himself.

Making the acquaintance of what he perceived to be an exotic, attractive virtually unattainable woman was almost like reliving those university years albeit in a more romantically successful vein. Maintaining her attention gave him a sensation of winning. Finally, though mostly by simulation, he was on the 'come up'.

She wouldn't have been at all surprised if he had even confided in some of his old friends or current colleagues about their association. Boasting of some perceived sexual know-how in capturing the attention of a stunning black Queen in a show of what must surely be evidence of his erotic magnetism.

At times when she looked at him, it was as though she were looking at that very young Kenneth trying to find his way in an adult corporate world, when inside he was still unsure and almost overwhelmed with self doubt.

The manner in which he would expound upon his team, and how he had to make frantic trips to troubleshoot at a European branch of his firm. Hints of the power he exercised in hiring and firing or needing to make conference calls to the big boss in the big apple, was a side she could scarcely imagine. The willowy, haunted chap who seemed to adopt a perpetual expression of anxiety, was barely recognisable as some sort of executive tycoon and yet in order to have reached such a status, clearly, he had hidden depths or else advancing the corporate ladder was an exercise in smoke and mirrors.

Sometimes she wished that he would bring that aspect of himself to the fore where they were concerned. Take charge more. Take the lead. Make decisions and follow through. Stop hinting at wanting to fuck her and actually take her to fucking task. Stop the school boy fantasising and actually get down to it.

She knew he got off on being a little reckless, that the naughtiness of their liaison turned him on and by 'turn on' he really meant, it redressed the insecure tipping balance constructed in his formative years. Unfortunately, he was also very quickly mortified at the actual thought of following through and facing reality.

When they had first met, there was certainly more of a swagger about him. He was full of promises of the kind of experiences they could share. High end adventures and escapism from what he perceived as her daily grind of parenting, not stopping to consider that she actually didn't require an escape from her life at all. He did. He had seemed quite prepared to lavish her with gifts and reward her for her time even if it were simply a stroll, or a light lunch or a quick catch up over a coffee in Chanel.

Slowly, gradually, this ebullience had given way to the tentative caution of his default setting and yet in moments of frustration when she would berate the fact that it had all seemed to be one big tease and threaten to withdraw, he would show immediate signs of remorse and almost beg her not to cut ties.

Weeks, sometimes months would pass without word. He would always be the first to make contact. She would never respond immediately. Sometimes not at all until such time as he managed to catch her in the right mood.

There would even be distinct times when she could feel that he had gone away. Some inexplainable energetic vibration that he wasn't available right now. Not that it altered her life in any way. Sure enough when they eventually made contact, he would mention that he had been away or that a family member was in town which had prompted a clearing of his usual schedule.

They were encroaching on one of those time now, only this time Cayenne detected a very slight sense of jealousy within herself, even though she was irked at herself for the absurdity of it all.

Whenever she felt overcome with sexual urges, she would take out her frustration on him. A routine that he had come to take pleasure in and highly anticipate. Perhaps he had interpreted it as evidence of some need for him. An acerbic rant would be typically followed by a period of vitriolic silence until he could take no more and then the inevitable grovelling would begin.

"I'm sorry – I haven't done more

Don't be too harsh – I only have nice opinions of you. It is worrying how much I think of you.

You there????"

CHAPTER 43

"Please corrupt me again with your utterly delicious cinnamon beauty.

Shit.....I'm in that mood where I want and need to be your whore... Hope you haven't gone for good....let's meet in the week".

Following month

"Hey you good?".

"You been ok?".

Following month

"Hey tried getting in touch last month.

Concerned you've gone for good… can't blame you but will miss you…. Let me know if you are at a loose end this week. I hope you can be".

Cayenne wasn't certain what made her finally respond.

"PROCEED WITH EXTREME CAUTION

Becoming perturbed by your disrespectful persistence on this old email account that I am merely keeping for filing purposes.

For the record… people with fulfilled purposeful lives, don't encounter loose ends.

However, should you know of any theatre performances or London highlights that I may enjoy, then forward a contact number and note my free times are Monday, Wednesday, Saturday and Sunday AFTER 7pm".

Cayenne knew full well that he would not provide her with his telephone number and that he certainly wasn't likely to be available in the evenings as their time together was resolutely relegated to working hours, typically lunch time.

"Failing this stipulation, kindly cease your annoying pitiful attempts at manhood and continue your counterfeit prance around suburbia pretending to be a fully fledged heterosexual that has even the slightest inkling of how to please and satisfy a woman.

Attempt contact without regard for these non negotiable clauses – at your fucking peril".

It was several days before the familiar email address resurfaced.

"Proper appropriate response coming. I have actually been re learning some brother, uncle, godfather responsibilities which have been unrequired for a few years.

372

Hope you are ok – ignoring the irritation that I provide".

So he had indeed been away attending to family events and things in his other life. His real life. Her feelings about that were complicated. Not bad or good. Just complex.

It's not as though she wished to be there. To be a part of it. She didn't fit into his world and didn't want to.

In any other context, their world's really ought not collide. He wasn't the type of person she would usually gravitate towards. She would smell his insincerity a mile away. Not insincere in a beguiling way, but she would detect almost immediately in social settings at least, that he was not being authentic with himself. She seemed to have an innate ability to detect the hidden soul behind an avatar. The smarmy grin would turn her off immediately, as would the inability to disguise his enthralled hunger. He was playing some sort of corporate role and that role defined him completely. Whereas she had always been the type of person to look beyond the façade. To see the person behind the front. To get a feel for what made a person tick. She somehow could not connect with the surface. She suspected others could see that in her, which is why she was the last person anyone with less than defined self esteem would gravitate towards.

She wondered whether he was different in his world. Would he disrobe this outward self once he was home and amongst his loved ones and family members, or did they too, buy into this image and alter ego. After all, wasn't it true that people could even be married for years and not really know each other. One could only be as honest with others as they had learned to be with themselves. People could only be as truthful as much as they had confronted the truth of who they really were.

He had confided that he hadn't shared his innermost thoughts with even his closest friends and yet in their own intimate conversations they had unearthed a side of each other that had lain dormant, at least for her.

A carnal hunger, a sordid vacancy.

CHAPTER 44

Whenever Cayenne became discouraged or disheartened by the challenges that Ocean faced with his disability or the difficulties that they endured as a family as a result of his learning difficulties, Diego was always on hand to offer support and to remind her that he had in fact come such a long way. The public meltdowns and erratic seemingly uncontrollable behaviour seemed a long way in the distance now. Diego only had to mention Asda, Newton Road and they would now dissolve into fits of laughter as they were immediately transported to a seemingly devastating episode when a six year old Ocean decided to demolish a shelf of pasta sauces. She hadn't known which was worse, the disruption that he actually caused, trying to discern what in fact had sparked this sudden outrage or the judgement she had felt by disgruntled onlookers who were clearly above raising a child that would behave in such a way.

At the time she had disappeared into a safe place inside, somewhere hidden and detached from what was going on around them. At some point later in the day she would emerge from the secret place and slowly begin to process what had occurred. It was often then that the emotional effects would surface. The shame. The ridicule. The judgement. The pain. The confusion. The sense of helplessness. A young Diego would be right there with her. Sometimes just listening as she expressed herself in pity, anger, bewilderment. Even as a young boy, he had the ability to process what she was saying and after a moment's thought, bring forth his own outlook or perspective that she couldn't yet access. This remarkable young man undoubtedly helped her heal. Helped her try to come to terms with the situation. Just observing him playing with his brother with no judgement or expectation in his eyes, was an inspiration that at times felt out of her reach. She remembered flicking through a magazine in a doctor's surgery and coming across an article written by a parent of a special needs child who went on to describe in touching detail, the realisation that the child that you were expecting, full of hope and promise, does not resemble the child that you were now responsible for and having to make the necessary adjustment. Almost like a process of mourning.

Cayenne knew that without Diego, she would not have been able to come to terms with it quite so well. To this day he inspired her in the way that he loved his brother unconditionally and saw the autism as secondary. He would often say, "I don't see him as autistic. He's just my brother. Cayenne didn't quite have the same perspective. She loved her son, but she did see the autism. It stared her in the face. Taunted her on a daily basis. Forced her to hold him to a higher standard. She resolutely refused to cater to this condition. She certainly had no intention of allowing it to limit him. So conversely, whilst she saw the condition, she refused to give it ammunition. She insisted Ocean mount that obstacle and willed him to conquer it and join them on the other side. Perhaps it was her way of coping, perhaps there were still elements of denial. But to her mind, call it what you will, she expected all her children, to become all they could be. PERIOD.

There were days that Diego's support was timely and essential. Like the days that she would collect Ocean from the bus and the driver or assistant would comment that his behaviour had been disruptive. He had banged on windows or persistently removed his seat belt on route. Or the days when she would get home and look through the home school record and the teacher had written that he had caused harm to another child or had climbed to the very top of the P E apparatus in the hall and looked longingly towards the floor as though he were Falcon in an Avengers movie and it were some kind of game, before the quick acting staff intervened. The despair that would threaten to engulf her in those moments was at times devastating. In those moments, when she couldn't find the words or the energy to explain how she felt, Diego would instinctively know, what to say or do. She would know in those moments that she wasn't alone. That they were in it together and furthermore, how lucky they were to have each other.

"Do you think that if we didn't have Ocee that we would be different people?" she had asked him one day over breakfast as they watched this ravenous, fast growing boy help himself to his third round of toast, the seemingly blistering energy inside him, preventing him from sitting in a way that remotely resembled stillness. Typically, Diego had inhaled the question first. Taken a moment to process his thoughts. Just as she were about to prompt him for an answer he replied, " Yeah… but…. but we wouldn't be as strong".

CHAPTER 45

"Miss me?, or are you being fully entertained by admirers who appreciate, 100% what they have in you?"

"Taking comfort in the fact that wisdom prevailed".

"Finally!!!!!

Morning You ..... literally got an electric pulse on receiving a message from the one true black Queen.

I'm sure you won't mind me saying, it went all the way through to my white cock.

Anyway, I want to suggest we catch up for a joint status update and do what we do best and escape for an afternoon in Mayfair".

CHAPTER 46

Choosing an outfit to wear to tennis was probably the only time that Cayenne actually paused for thought. Most of the women in the group of around 15 were from Pakistan, India or Bangladesh and arrived adorned in variations of their traditional attire. Only a handful of them wore western clothes and proceeded with an uncovered head, yet still Cayenne thought it only right that she have some regard for how a facing a fully exposed midriff could potentially put them off their serve. The entire group was made up of all shapes and sizes, various backgrounds and divergent personalities, but one thing they all had in common, was that they were falling increasingly in love with tennis. This was by no means a professional league, but rather a cardio initiative funded by the Borough of Tower Hamlets which extended not only to children but to this group of mums to come along and improve their fitness whilst incorporating some basic tennis skills.

At first Cayenne had approached the group with her usual reticence and caution, though before long, the physical trials and shared enjoyment bonded them all to some degree.

She began to sense from a few of the women, mild admiration that her game had improved. They liked her dedication and drive. Her fitness certainly helped and without the agility that her lifestyle afforded her, the slow progress would certainly have thwarted her enjoyment of the game, a fact made evident as she watched many of the women ambling hopelessly after the ball. As it was, she was able to accelerate at will and speed her way around the court and catch those loose balls that might otherwise have gone astray. It gave her an amazing sense of achievement even if her swing still required some attention.

Nothing gave Cayenne the thrill of playing quite like the forehand/backhand drill. She loved the running forward, the positioning, moving back if the return was long or running toward the net for a volley if it was short. Deciding in a split second, which response would be to her advantage, even though there was no opponent as such, as the instructor was on the other side feeding the balls, but Cayenne always created one in her head. She was sure there were some who scorned her inwardly or considered that she approached the exercise far too seriously. The crouch, the twisting of the racquet, the Williams' sisters' glare. She had it all. She supposed that even the Serena-esque outfits tested their nerve.

"Okay let's play Queens". Frida shouted as the group erupted into a chorus of approval. This was one of the many enjoyable games that they had come to know where a Queen was selected for each court who would position themselves at the far end, whilst the other women queued up to challenge her. Whoever won the point would either retain their title or be denounced and have to return to the back of the queue as the new Queen took her place.

As usual, the time flew past in a whirl as the women regaled in the excitement of the competitive spirit.

Just moments before the whistle to signal the end of the game, Cayenne did her usual saunter around the court to collect the balls. It was something she enjoyed doing and rarely needed prompting.

"Cayenne, you won the point. You're Queen". Indira shouted as she dismounted the throne to make way for her successor.

Cayenne waved her hand to signal for the current Queen to proceed.

"Are you sure?" Indira enquired, gleefully repositioning herself for the next challenger.

Cayenne and the instructor's eyes met and Frida's face creased with a naughtily humorous smirk.

She began assisting Cayenne in gathering the balls whilst confessing...

"I am reminded of a programme I watch back home where you have the real Queen and then there's all the fake queens".

They both collapsed into a fit of conspiratorial laughter, whilst the other women unwittingly continued their futile pursuit for the crown.

CHAPTER 47

"I seem to have lost my work swipe card, having to retrace my steps, so if you bump in to me, this isn't me stalking….. very irritating".

Cayenne smiled at the message but placed her phone back onto the arm of the chair whilst she continued with the arduous job of repainting her nails. She wasn't entirely happy until she had managed to execute her French manicure to a nigh on professional standard. Even it if took several attempts. Just as she had mastered perfection, she would repeat the whole process at a moment's notice if needs be, because she knew that even the slightest kink would only serve to distract her. Many times she had been faced down in the middle of a set of burpees or mountain climbers or attempting to hold her downward dog in the yoga studio, only to become annoyed to discover an imperfection on a thumb nail, or a fragment of fluff beneath the transparent top coat.

It seemed the executive couldn't get enough of her right now.

They were to meet for lunch several times over the next few weeks.

"Picnic? How's that gorgeous ass?"

"Like steel"

"No doubt I'll be dribbling into my sandwich"

"I'll have a Greek Salad".

"Sorry, that last sentence wasn't particularly appealing".

"No it wasn't. Struggling to list your appealing qualities".

"What time are you free? We can work on my short comings in person".

"2.30"

"For your ass, I'll make this work. What else can I bring?"

Mentally tracing the steps from his office building through Canary Wharf, across the bridge onto the Island, Cayenne recalled that several pop-up food shacks had emerged along the route, bearing all kinds of cultural offerings that she hadn't yet been adventurous enough to attempt.

"Don't you pass some interesting street food venues on route to South Quay?

Surprise me. I am glad you will make it work, though I will bear in mind that you could be head hunted to Zurich at a moment's notice".

She wasn't quite sure when she intended to let him forget about his sudden disappearance the previous year, just as she felt that they were reaching a climax, literally. Nor could she forget the dramatic story with which he attempted to explain his disappearance. She couldn't quite bring herself to believe it.

He would have to be some kind of Clark Kent character who once at his desk, morphed heroically into a valiant leader, armed with spear and breast plate as he took the helm, ready to avert the imminent threat of disaster and steer his dependent crew back to safety.

A vision of masculinity that bore no resemblance to the hapless Harry that she encountered, who carried himself as though he were being chased by an unknown entity causing him to appear permanently flustered and agitated with a daunting and ominous glaze in his eyes indicating the certainty of doom.

"Ok Queen, let's see what I can find. Will it be gym gear?"

As the gym was mere paces from her apartment block, he had grown accustomed to seeing her strut around in her various coordinated lycra outfits.

"Not sure. I've timed it to allow for a nip home for a quick change if necessary".

"I worry I might be too attentive to your features. You may have to put me in my place".

"I can quite understand that my features are extraordinarily intoxicating and alluring for you.

I have become accustomed to the sharp intakes of breath as I glide seductively through the gym, knowing full well all eyes will be drawn.

Smiling inwardly because I am fully aware that I appear untouchable… unreachable".

"I harden at the breathless arrogance and appreciate my fortune of a picnic rather than a purging".

The months of avoidance that signified the start of their association seemed to haunt him and he would regularly petition her good will to stave off a time when she inevitably grew weary of him.

Cayenne revelled in his uncertainty. "Purging, as with all things, is initiated in the mind…. It can take some time for the evidence to become apparent".

"I somehow know you are smiling devilishly as you write. On my way via food stalls. Two minutes away with picnic delivery".

Cayenne paced in the afternoon sun, at the foot of the stairs leading up to the light rail station. As usual she was the first to arrive, but it wasn't long before the inimitable executive plodding could be seen amongst the lunchtime civilians, causing his floppy hair to sway from side to side in the light summer breeze.

Typically, his presence exhibited little command nor any sense of authority or slither of evidence to demonstrate his apparent corporate prowess. She could detect no ripple through the crowd that someone of significance was in their midst. Mind you, she supposed the world was different now. People didn't always mirror the aura of who they professed to be. Most make up artists that she read about, the very same magicians that created awe inspiring beauty on the faces of their clients, could easily be mistaken as some sort of cash strapped kiosk assistant judging by their own appearance. Often designers barely looked as though they could be trusted to assemble a coordinated outfit. The media image of Gym instructors had created a veneer of perfection with glistening perfectly toned limbs, which was often a far cry from the reality, few of whom, in her experience, endeavoured to maintain their own fitness. In this modern society, it was becoming increasingly difficult to even differentiate between teachers and students. From this perspective, she reluctantly supposed that the executive could indeed feasibly herald a team of advancing bankers as his title suggested, even though his demeanour would most suitably place him as some sort of mailroom intern.

His eyes lit up as they absorbed the details of her outfit. She had settled for black harem pants which had zips on the sides which she had left open to reveal a slash of bronzed, muscled thigh, matched with a black and gold crop top which perfectly complemented the sheer muslin hoodie which she had tied loosely around her waist.

His appreciation of her style could not be hidden and his cheeks betrayed the affect the sight of her was having on him, turning pinker with every stride.

He wrapped an arm around her waist pulling her to him for his usual greeting.

"You look gorgeous"

Cayenne simply smiled in acknowledgement.

"Wow, I do like the trousers".

"Thankyou".

Together they strolled along their usual route to the park and adjoining farm, stopping occasionally when there was no one else around to insert a tongue or a hand into the other's space. Shortly they sampled the dishes he had selected, none of which she recognised though they were variations of meat and rice with unusual sauces and spices.

"This one's Bulgarian. Try some". Before she could resist, his spoon was heading to her mouth.

She chewed the concoction slowly trying to decipher the flavours, desperate for a glint of recognition.

"Not sure". She picked up a napkin and blotted her mouth so as to retain as much lipstick as possible.

He hung his head in disappointment. She adored how he appeared to actually mind what she thought and felt.

The only time his mood appeared to lift was when they discovered a hidden patch of grass behind some trees on route to the farm, just off the beaten footpath, where he marvelled at the ingenuity in the design of her harem pants. The zippered slashes on her thighs were a genius invention as they provided such easy access for him to strum away inside her panties, whilst simultaneously listening to her regale about her latest gym routine. Just the sight of the oiled skin on her bronzed biceps sent him into a near frenzy. Her head rested in her arms as she lay back in the brittle grass and soon she was singing to the tune of his symphony. Groaning and writhing rhythmically to greater heights, stiffening at the peak and sighing heavily upon her descent.

He watched the now familiar sequence avidly as her chest rose and fell, her mouth fell open and her pussy dribbled it's satisfaction onto his baying hands

Reaching inside his trousers, his response was hugely evident. Long, hard and dripping, she longed to suck it's delights like a straw, guiding creamy milkshake to her mouth. But it was too late. He had held on for as long as he could but the simple touch of her hands was enough to complete the call. The spill that now seeped between them was as rich as silk.

She ran her hand around to his bottom and let her fingers trace the crack down to the area that she knew would tease further arousal. She could sense his apprehension, but he needn't have worried. She hadn't planned to explore in depth today. She simply wanted to circle and stroke and give a hint of sordid promise, subject to due diligence.

Cayenne lay back onto the grass, gazing up at the light blue sky and embraced the awesome sensations flooding her womb. It was as though it was alive and tingly. Open and receptive to the atmosphere, she suddenly became aware of an indescribable connection between her pussy and the very core of the earth.

CHAPTER 48

"Delectable"

"Thank YOU".

"Bending down in worship was very pleasurable"

"Probably just as well time was limited… my cock curiosity seemed to have got the better of me"

"It rose as expected"

"Naturally"

"No surprise".

Cayenne found herself in the unusual position of pondering the gym itinerary when considering what best to wear. Something that would adapt effortlessly from Bootcamp which followed core class but that would also be suitable for her to run down to Yoga shortly afterwards. This narrowed it down to two obvious choices consisting of an electric blue shorts set, comprising of tiny bottom enhancing shorts and a crew neck crop top or her all in one body suit which was black with white double lines running up the sides. She opted for the latter as the deeply scooped back which rested just over her bottom, strained around the glutes causing them to stand to attention, showed off her chiselled back to perfection, whilst the taught lycra material clung to her waist and abs, though it was fairly unforgiving and so a large breakfast was certainly out as the subsequent bulge in her abdomen would destroy the devastating effect this outfit was undeniably designed to cause. The fact that it was black also left her with more options makeup wise. She decided to go with red matte lipstick which doubled up as eyeliner, which she then proceeded to smudge with a powder brush adding some delicate dabs to the tops of her cheek bones.

Staring at her image in the main studio of the gym, she confirmed that she had made the right choice. In the generous light her taught stomach muscles pierced the front of the body suit and the brilliant red on her face popped like an illuminous light against the bronzed backdrop of her complexion.

The studio was almost full to capacity when the instructor, a young university graduate called Paul finally emerged with seconds to spare. Cayenne glanced at the clock on the wall to her left and then followed Paul with her eyes as he stomped moodily towards the sound system and made the necessary adjustments to connect it to his phone until the heavy beat of rap music blared aggressively across the room. Observing the young man who it appeared had other places he would much rather be and who seemed to think that listening to Gangsta rap, somehow altered his genetic makeup, Cayenne couldn't help but think that he was no more suited to rap music than he was to a Vivaldi Concerto.

She couldn't resist her tendency to observe how unprofessional it seemed when instructors failed to introduce themselves or position themselves in front of the class to address them formally. Few of them did. Diego would roll his eyes at her observations, chastising her for taking things far too seriously. But to her mind, surely it was common courtesy at the very basic level. Although when Paul did eventually speak, minus any concept of apologising for his lateness, on hearing the prattle that seemed to tumble out of his mouth, she almost immediately rued the onslaught on her ears. For one he appeared perpetually bored as though he really had something far more important to attend to but as circumstances would have it, he would reluctantly fit this class in first. He took no effort at all to formulate each word into something remotely discernible to the English language and tended to sound much like someone who was just about to drift off to sleep and so the words became more and more slurred as his untrained tongue succumbed to cultural norms. He clearly considered utilising his facial muscles profoundly offensive and it was evident that it would consume far too much energy to have to navigate his mouth to ensure clarity for his audience and so whilst he spoke, his face barely moved as the words appeared to cascade into one another.

She glanced around at the other faces to see if she could detect a communal struggle. Affirmative.

Paul seemed to at least pick up on the blank faces staring back at him though one got the sense he hadn't reached the conclusion that he was the one at fault and rather returned their gazes with acute disdain.

"My name's Pau' and I'm your instructor for today. Does anyone 'ave any injuries that I don't already know about?". Cayenne was quite certain that had anyone been harbouring a sore back or any other overworked limbs, that Paul's lack of genuine concern and enthusiasm would cause them to keep it to themselves as his emotionless delivery exposed the possibility that the question was simply a line that they had been taught in training and that must be asked simply as a formality.

Paul did become slightly more expressive throughout the class and elements of the existence of a personality flickered intermittently, although he still sounded rehearsed as though everything he said was what an instructor ought to say at a particular juncture.

"Ok peopuw' let's warm up, start runnin' on the spot". Paul demonstrated what he had asked and also began jogging on the spot and his voice took on a military sergeant major drill tone. " Now take your knees to your chest. Come on, high knees". After thirty seconds there was another command. " Now kick your legs back, try and touch your bum with your feet. Move your arms as well. Burpees. Come on. Burpees". This was Cayenne's least favourite exercise as it seemed to drain her energy immediately but it was also one which she approached with competitive venom, refusing to let them beat her, even if it meant going at an altogether slower pace than most.

By the time the group repeated the whole entire sequence twice, they were well and truly warmed up and several women reached for their water bottle as others hung their heads towards the floor to catch their breath.

As it turned out, Paul's class was extremely well constructed, consisting of three rounds of each cycle which concentrated on various body parts one at a time, incorporating dumbbells and barbells, moving on to some body weight exercises and cardio with an abs routine to finish.

After a miniscule cool down, the class was dismissed and many of the women congratulated each other with high fives and shoulder slaps for having survived not only the gruelling routine, but that they had managed to decode Paul's garbled delivery, mostly by lip reading amidst the explosive resounding beats of the South Central chant 'Fuck the Po'lice'.

Moments later, Cayenne found herself semi conscious in the dimly lit yoga studio in the basement below listening to the light strains of the unusual but intoxicating sound tracks that Josephine selected for her classes. Music that she had never heard anywhere else and couldn't begin to recognise or even identify the genre of. Catchy tunes with eclectic rhythms and whimsical lyrics that seemed anointed to assist in helping the mind escape from it's sore limbed confines. Cayenne adored these moments before and after class where they could just lie there without expectation, eyes closed, completely relaxed with only the purple strobe light for illumination, creating a calming hub of tranquillity.

Josephine would occasionally chime in with her own subtle hum to compliment the tune, largely unsuccessfully. To Cayenne's discerning ear, she was almost always off key and an acute sufferer of tone deafness. And then there were the intermittent jagged movements that seemed to be an attempt at a dance but which were hindered by the fact that any coordination she possessed, was clearly limited to this eastern ancient practice.

"Start to liiiiiiiiie back in savasana, taking up as much space as possible. Let your aaaarrrms reach either side of your body, turning your paaaaaalms to the ceilin'. Open your legs as wiiiiiiiide as the mat. Start to take some deeeeep brefs. Breavin' in, fillin' the lungs with as much air as possible, takin' a moment to feew' fuw' an' energised and then breavin' out fully until the lungs are completely empty and allowin' yourself to feew empty and spacious".

Cayenne's mouth flickered at the corners as she stifled a giggle at the familiar sound of Josephine's clipped dialogue juxtaposed with her exaggerated elongation.

As usual the mats were perfectly aligned, which Cayenne also appreciated, whereas most instructors allowed the class to assemble their own practice space usually with varying degrees of success.

Josephine's class began with some extensive breath work, which Cayenne loved as she saw it as a form of meditation, where she could really connect with the vibrations outside of herself on a deeper level as well as an opportunity to breathe fully, which life's hectic routine often distracted her from doing.

As usual the gym manager's class was challenging and progressive, an attribute which clearly set her apart from most of the holistic line up which had a tendency to be repetitive. There was always a new advanced pose to practice which she would demonstrate at each intricate stage so that the class could decide what level they felt ready to attempt. There would be a scheduled slot just for practising a particular movement which today happened to be the crow pose and a choice of either a jump back straight into a Chaturanga or a crow straight into a head stand with either bent or for the particularly advanced, straight legs up towards the ceiling.

Josephine would walk around at this stage assisting and adjusting or encouraging people to go past their limitations and comfort zones. Cayenne executed the crow to the jump back quite impressively in her own opinion but when attempting the head stand, it seemed yet out of her reach. But then so had the crow when she first began to practice, so she had proven at least to herself that the headstand was possible too once she had practiced enough for the body to make the necessary adjustment.

Cayenne's muscular frame certainly felt challenged to it's limit in this realm of flexible elastic yoga limbs, but that made her all the more determined to master it although Josephine's reminder as she coaxed them out of their Savasana slumber was timely. "Bow your heads and thank your lovely, able body for taking the tiiiiime to practise today, rememberin' that this is a yoga practise not a yoga perfect. Namaste".

CHAPTER 49

"Good weekend?"

"Yes thank you".

"Were you a good girl?.   Such a stupid question, sorry".

"Driven and disciplined as usual".

"I could so do with some tuition, you should coach".

"Yes I'm a natural"

"I do need to worship. I wanted to suck those hardened nipples on Friday afternoon, so badly".

" I detected the longing".

"Flipping them with my tongue would be so good right now. I'm in my office... wanting to see your black ass. Want a walk in the rain today or lunch tomorrow?"

"Yoga has been cancelled last minute today so a brisk walk would do me good. I deserve lunch tomorrow too".

"You do. Just fucked off some white hags by moving their inconvenient meeting to 1.15. Want me to bring anything?".

"Be careful... you're destined to spend your retirement with an old white hag such as those you speak of"

"Remember to keep lipstick to a minimum and need I remind you, you know exactly what I need a taste of.

Now hard".

"I'll have a hot chocolate please"

"Makes perfect sense".

Cayenne could just detect the intermittent drone of moderate traffic, even from the other side of the park. She sampled the now tepid and far too milky for her liking, cup of chocolate from the plastic carton and screwed up her face in disgust at the flavourless substance in her hands. The executive failed to notice her displeasure and from beneath her dress, she could hear his ravenous slurps as he ferreted furtively between her legs thoroughly immersed in the pursuit of his own hot chocolate. Had anyone strolled past the field, along the dirt track, beyond the row of acorn trees, she would have made for a peculiar sight standing rigid in the centre of the field with a cup in her hand. Only an ambitious roving eye would have detected a corporate crouching tiger amongst the tall wild weeds, guzzling at a rate of knots like a hidden dragon preparing for hibernation. She couldn't even say she derived any pleasure from it. In fact she almost felt peeved that he was clearly enjoying his afternoon aperitif leaving her to make do with an unacceptable beverage and feeling decidedly bored.

What a hopeless executive whore. Was it really so difficult to lick a pussy with a little more strategic emphasis. At the very least, making an attempt to inflict some excitement on her clitoris. He portrayed himself like a greedy child, scavenging for the last lick of icecream from the tub. She recalled watching white people lick their plate after a meal. A pattern that in a Jamaican household, would be an abomination tantamount to disposing of a batch of Sinsemilla, mistaken for degenerating cabbage. What a boring lover he must be, she thought to herself. Not a hint of consideration for turning her on. Clearly her mood today would demand a more inventive foray.

She often wondered whether their fleeting flirtations during this relatively sexless period of her life was in fact having an adverse affect on her state of mind. She was likely to find that once she returned home following brief alfresco titillation, that rather suddenly she would be overcome with a bout of sore bitterness which she then proceeded to inflict upon him in verse and prose.

He seemed to have grown accustomed to this and in fact rather anticipated it with bated excitement. He seemed to get off on her vitriol. Luckily for him, whilst he had failed to arouse any genital excitement, he had succeeded in filling her with utter contempt.

"Let me put it this simply...

If you should contact me again...

I will have little option but to consider you a self serving, opportunistic, user who seeks to take advantage of women because he lacks the backbone and fortitude to confront the areas of his life that are unfulfilling.

Instead of being a man and addressing these issues, he succumbs to any distraction he can find. This type of so called man, is too effeminate and under developed to ever be a real man, though he will attempt to look like one using ill-fitting business attire and adopting a falsified corporate demeanour.

One day, sooner rather than later judging by the greying hair, both on your head and often protruding from your ears and nasal cavities, your suburban hag will once and for all take you in hand.

I often suspect that when your weedy adolescent self, enrolled at University and you immediately suspected that your peers were more worldly wise than yourself with a more developed self-image, that you quickly identified a character that possessed the qualities of someone you greatly admired and simply adopted their persona as your own.

I imagine they too had the parted curtain hairstyle and walked with their hands stuffed in their pockets to appear more confident. Perhaps they were on their way to a career in accountancy, so you subsequently opted to change course and embrace their path and purpose as well, which would explain your sheer apathy towards the institution.

I can just picture you, a pathetic figure studying the elected individual from across campus... the individual most likely unaware of your candid imitation.

Once your studies were complete and you embarked upon real life... you simply forgot to develop your own sense of self. Doubtless your peers, colleagues, associates and even family think they are relating to the real you, when unbeknownst to them, the real you, is still languishing somewhere between high school and Uni, quivering in his pubescent body, totally ill equipped by his inadequate parents, for the realities of adult life.

You can either continue this farce... hoping, praying that your real identity remains undiscovered... deliberately seeking out people that you perceive to be of low intelligence or lacking in any depth to ensure that any curious probing be kept to a minimum, or you can take a good hard look at yourself.. stripped bare... without the false embellishments.... Stop running your fingers through your hair with your mouth slightly ajar, just as your uni idol was prone to do. Stop pretending...

It will take courage that you have not yet demonstrated, but you will find it if you dare to dig deep and are prepared for the discomfort of self analysis and discovery.

Good luck".

"That will teach me for having the audacity to serve the Queen tepid hot chocolate".

At opposite ends of the wharf, two people were suddenly overtaken with fits of rapturous laughter.

CHAPTER 50

Following a four month hiatus…

"Annoyingly, I still miss it….(you)

I've smartened up and am in the running for this year's promotion process – if I get it, you must let me treat you to dinner and a good bottle of red".

"Oh my God. Hello you…

Don't say 'if' say 'when'

The subconscious mind cannot tell the difference between reality and desire and that's what controls our thoughts. So every morning say 'When I get that promotion…. '

Visualise yourself already operating in this new position. How does it feel. Embrace the feeling.

That being said... I will accept nothing less than a five star restaurant and the finest Chateau Lafite 1787".

"Goodness, so good to hear from you

Are you well? Did you seduce your instructor? Are you still gym mad? Still hot?

You are so right, positive attitude all the way.... It's so important"

"The gym is a confirmed lifestyle choice.

I am ripped and taught and firm all over.

People in the gym are now doing a double take. Girls are showing up in the classes I select. They must have deduced that success leaves clues.

People are asking what my gym routine is. I get dirty looks from women who have belonged to the gym for years and cannot hope to attain my results.

I push myself further every day because I am conscious there are those that will try to beat me. I cannot let them win".

"I want to see.

The urge to be used has not fully dissipated. How bad is that!!!"

"I did not seduce the instructor because I refuse to pursue something which is beneath my level of achievement.

Their intimidation is palpable… I deserve someone who fully believes they are worthy… you can see my dilemma".

"I've sincerely missed your prose despite the assassination essay.

Does my return allow a picture or is that a cheeky indulgent ask?"

"I can only be fully appreciated in person I'm afraid. I cannot trust the lens to capture every nuance of what pure unadulterated blood sweat and tears have crafted and cultivated".

"Fair comment I suppose, despite my purely selfish need.

So any Waterstones moments or other dating fun been happening?

Shall we catch up so I can admire your work… the white hags remain a bore".

"Do I sound as though I have time for futile pursuits?"

"Lunch this week? Don't you want the pleasure of seeing me drool knowing that you WON and that I couldn't keep away?"

"Not sure that I need such distractions in my life. I could possibly be persuaded to break from my gym itinerary for some high end haute cuisine delicacies".

"Ok. Appropriate options will be found. How long did you think I'd hold out?"

"The thought hadn't crossed my mind. No matter that I don't always hear from you, I am safe in the knowledge that your life has been forever altered by the invasion of the Queen of Sheba".

"How's the gym?".

"Men tend to think that standing in front of a mirror lifting weights and posing makes them tough. I am much more inclined to be impressed with the guys that brave the grit or body pump classes as they are designed to push you to your limit within a set time with little recovery.

I am always the winner but judging by your level of determination and persistence, I would bet that you would progress quickly.

Today I did three sessions in total. Body conditioning, very tough indeed, followed by 30 minutes of core exercises. Followed by body balance, a combination of tai chi, pilatés and yoga to music.

I daresay the wannabes that will show up to grit cardio tomorrow won't have put in three hours today, which means I am already ahead of the game. So I fully intend to retain my crown".

"I'm just imagining the results of your efforts. It's enough to harden me. You deserve a majestically noble treat. The underbelly has provided nothing in comparison".

"I'm not ashamed to say there are moments that I astound myself. Now if I could only stop drinking red wine every evening, I would look so good it would be illegal".

"Come on, show yourself so I don't have to stalk South Quay on heat".

"I'm sensing that de ja vous feeling.... I'm wiser this time around though".

"Sorry you.

In all honesty, when I do get promoted, I do genuinely want to get you dinner for being a positive influence".

"Once a stalker, always a stalker".

"Once you try black...."

"Shouldn't that be .... Once you attempt black?"

"Completely. Good to see you're as sharp as you were. I'm glad you're doing well"

"There you go again... typically you've offended me already.

I'm not one of many black women... I am exquisitely unique. Do you think you are ever likely to encounter a black woman with my mind, wit, determination, strength, body, stamina, intellect, humour, beauty.... You'd be hard pressed to find this combination in any nationality... the sun just happened to shine on you perchance one warm crisp November day".

"Cayenne, don't' be daft. No offence from me is ever intended. Of course I am utterly aware of how unique and exquisite you are. Completely and utterly aware".

"That's good. I simply cannot abide people lacking awareness".

"Don't we know it. It will be nice to grace her majesty's table again. Any classes tonight. Shame no picture."

"I have started a weekly tennis course. The coach said that I had some good shots. I had an inclination that this may be the case".

"That's really cool. Are they indoor courts?".

"I once stumbled across an imbecile who almost made me regurgitate when he said…. ' I want to share your summer, let's climb the 02, let's play tennis'

Thankfully the universe saw fit to remove such debris… the residue thankfully is superb tennis lessons.

Outdoor courts a stone throw from home. I love my life…"

"Fantastic. The offer of a game still stands".

"You really can't help yourself can you?. Let's play an international game. England against Zurich".

"Baby that would be England vs Switzerland. You do realise there was nothing in Zurich".

"Is 'nothing' Swiss for underbelly Imbecilic tarts".

"Whoever was that imbecile?"

"I really ought to have known better... there had been posters up warning women about a lewd stalker in the Wharf. Lo and behold, I found him".

"I can only imagine your tennis game is well assisted by those powerful arms of yours. They must be fucking gorgeous with all recent efforts".

"Depends. Opinions are split... some could argue that I look excessively muscular, certainly women balk when I mention muscle development as though that is the last thing that they would want... why then do they try and compete with the weight I lift?

Surely not to enhance their wrinkled bingo wings.

I personally adore the muscle definition that my image reflects. I relish in putting on a layer of moisturising cocoa butter oil on my body just prior to a class so that they stand out all the more".

"The enjoyment of being tightly clamped in you still sits with me".

"I can well imagine. I am solely responsible for decimating your cultural hymen. I shan't be forgotten. I feel honoured that the memory of my presence is providing life giving energy to an otherwise pitiful and bland existence in suburbia".

" I can see the wicked smile as you write".

"I've often thought about writing this experience into a story, but can you possibly comprehend the task before me.... To transform a quivering, excitable Caucasian who is intimidated by his own fantasies, into a daring lothario who throws aside caution and thoroughly enjoys the delights of his secret thoughts and puts them into action".

"I am smiling and laughing … you know me so well.

It's a fucking gorgeous idea".

"There are dreamers and there are visionaries… big difference. If I had a penny for the dreamers I have encountered. One such fantasist I came across seemed to be longing for the day that an angel descended from heaven to pluck him out of suburban obscurity and deliver him happily into a much longed for career in politics".

"I will think about this as I run in Hyde Park and will try to ignore the blood gushing to my loins".

CHAPTER 51

"Out?"

"No. you?"

"I was. Anything fun coming up. How are the arms?"

"The arms, back and glutes and upper abs are sizzling. Lower abs have room for improvement. So where were you that was so exciting that I emerged in your thoughts?

Or should that be – whose company was so dire that you longed for the tantalising company of old?"

"Annoyingly memorable aren't you… I don't need to feed your ego anymore now.

You know I still release…

You in a good place?"

"Always. I only wish you could experience such contentment. However, I suspect it would require a little too much self mastery"

"Fuck! I wish you were just using me right now… simply getting off on me… rubbing that gorgeous delightful pussy in my face and bringing yourself to full satisfaction.

Owning me like a bitch.   Only one agenda… getting what you want from this white whore.

What the fuck is wrong with me?"

Cayenne knew that when he spoke like this he was inadvertently revealing his fears that she might develop feelings for him which would then lead to his greatest fear.   Some kind of imagined personal and financial demise.

Of course, Cayenne was well aware that his propensity to make her feel nauseous on sight would make this inevitability highly unlikely, though she fully intended to continue if only for her own twisted amusement.

"I'm certainly long overdue an orgasm let alone a full on climax… oh to find someone who isn't likely to bail. Yep!... I need to identify someone who actually wants to fuck.

I bet you are only equipped to handle a geriatric, saggy, decrepit moistureless pussy. That's where you feel safe. Hence the fear.

Suburban peasant.

To answer your question, I believe my assassination email identified fully what was wrong with you… if memory serves… I even left you with a personal assignment".

"Very true. Fuck, that incessant need from the early hours is still sitting with me and won't dilute. Humour me for a few minutes, degrade me. Thank you for the strictest confidence as I work through this".

"I honestly thought I couldn't pity you anymore, what with the false personality, identity crisis, inability to enforce your own will over your life, the self deceit in tricking your mind into believing that you are actually happy, the delusion of what a couture pussy actually looks and feels like...

Now you have the added burden of eliminating the most honest exchange you are ever likely to have had and feign ignorance forever more..

You did secretly desire to be a movie star as I recall... as it turns out... your whole life is a charade...

If you ever do dare to fly and discover wings and soar.... And I am almost salivating at the image of the new improved you, drop me a line with an actual number, like a grown up and let's do the adult thing...

There's no mention of your promotion... I guess that's why you are even giving me the time of day. Perhaps even the corporate world can see when someone harbours conflict within and are resisting living in their truth. Some go through their entire lives avoiding self analysis. Don't let that be you."

CHAPTER 52

Title: Assassin :2:22am

"You up?"

It was hours before Cayenne discovered the message although she had now become quite accustomed to his nocturnal stirrings, no doubt when his household, whoever that consisted of, were asleep. The moment they sensed that their subject was stripped of his daily counterfeit demeanour, his nightly dementors were released to wreak havoc.

Heading towards the supermarket after the school run was when it occurred to her to check her phone just as he posed his second question of the day.

"Thinking about what you deserve for our Christmas party and your festive present. Any ideas?".

"Yaaaaay. Do Not limit yourself here…

Push the boundaries".

"Don't worry, your contribution to my year needs fully rewarding …

Are you still looking fucking awesome?"

"Not only do I look awesome… the content can totally back it up…"

"We know…. Come on send a picture whilst I get organising"

"I am almost insulted that you would think I would fall for that marlarkey again... May I remind you, I live a life of continual self improvement... therefore I am not the same person you encountered before... I daresay that minimally, you remain exactly as you were and might even have regressed substantially (Hence the constant juvenile requests).... Owing to your humdrum suburban existence".

"Ohh God... Ok ignore".

The local Asda seemed to be full of mums picking up essentials once they had dropped the children off at the neighbouring school. Many of whom Cayenne recognised but thankfully she had never quite been initiated into the school run clique. She couldn't bear to stand chatting mindlessly at the gates or pretend to find little Charlie and Sarah as adorable as their doting parents. It irked her no end when parents expected people to gush over their child in the manner that they did. Such an expectation, to her mind, should only be extended to family members at best.

To avoid the façade altogether, she usually ensured that she turned up at the very last minute although sod's law often dictated that this was the time that 4K would be the last to be dismissed.

Strolling along the meat aisle, Cayenne found herself in the usual predicament of trying to come up with an idea for dinner that didn't fill her with utter tedium. The routine was usually a rotating cycle of chicken, mince and lamb even though mince was her least favourite and so whilst the children were busy tucking into spaghetti Bolognese or Shepherd's pie, Cayenne would usually pick at a salad or soup with bread.

The executive was seemingly having a similar predicament.

"How's the diary. I am trying to decide between Zuma in Knightsbridge or Balthazar in Covent Garden".

"Sounds intriguing"

"You will love either one. Balthazar is French cuisine. Their lobster spaghetti is to die for. Zuma is Japanese so should appeal to your clean diet living. Sea bass, sushi...??".

"Oh There you are". There had been a lengthy pause following his last communication. "I'm flexible".

"You know full well I don't stray far from you".

"I would imagine it is highly improbable"

"I'm wrestling with a strong urge to display all to you as I get in the shower. I will resist".

"Spoil sport".

As she was trying out a new class titled ballet barre, Cayenne decided to christen her new yoga pants. An olive green ensemble which came to the knee where straps were attached with which to entwine her legs down to the ankle with a couture styled criss cross. She teamed this with a green crop top and decided to wear her green lipstick to complete the look. She hadn't quite known what to expect from the class as she hadn't come across it before and other than a brief introduction to ballet when she was seven years old, she had no real experience to speak of, so when it appeared on the timetable, she was quick to sign up simply to challenge herself and to add balance to her predominantly weight and strength oriented timetable.

She was the first to arrive in class which took place in the yoga studio of the gym, to find a tall spindly lady limbering up at the barre.

Her black sweaty betty leggings and matching vest top, totally complemented her slender figure. Her hair was piled on top of her head into a tight top knot and as Cayenne watched her warming up, there were glimpses of the former ballerina from a previous life. Her once plump youthful skin now bore the lines of a hectic work schedule and an arduous life on the road and the roots of her once glossy brunette mane, were now streaked with silvery strands.

There was loud 80's pop music blaring out of the sound system, which Cayenne imagined was an era that signified success and vitality to the listener, perhaps an era that she secretly longed for and was reluctant to leave as it inevitably threw her back to the height of her career when she had been at her youthful peak. The loud beats pumped the atmosphere with punchy enthusiasm but Haley McSweeney's voice pierced the air above it as she challenged the recording artist, singing the lyrics as though she had written them herself.

"Like a virgin, whoooh ,touched for the very first time... like a ...... oooooh Helloooooooo", she sang as she accompanied Madonna's iconic rendition revealing a voice to rival an operatic soprano. Her smile was bright and warm and her eyes, while secretly curious, lit up to welcome her first client. She exuded a confidence that only an extensive and revered career could cultivate, all of which shone through in her voice.

"Hello". Cayenne answered as she strolled over to the far side of the room to take off her coat and trainers.

"I'm Haley, nice to meet you. Is it your first time my love".

Haley spoke in a friendly familiar tone as though she had known you for years.

"I'm Cayenne and yes it's my first time".

"Cay-en?"

"Cayenne, like the pepper".

421

Haley laughed theatrically. "Yes I was thinking, where have I heard that name before" she placed her hands on her hips as she spoke and adopted a pose like a porcelain figurine.

Cayenne noticed that Haley's eyes flickered over her, taking in the fact that she clearly wasn't new to the gym itself.

Other women began to enter the room although this was to be a small class owing the existence of only one barre. An oversight for such a large progressive gym.

Haley began to count the heads. "There's nine of us so far and there are only supposed to be eight. But it's okay because there's room for two more over here". She strode towards the staircase on the other side of the room which lead up to the main studio above and pointed to the handle bars at either side, demonstrating how they could use the handlebars in much the same way as the actual barre.

"But if there's any more than ten, then we may come unstuck". Haley's giggle was never too far from the surface and the bright smile rarely left her thin face, although it didn't always disguise hints of a strict disciplinarian.

Haley guided them through a warm up consisting of a variation of pliés and a ballet inspired cardio sequence which she punctuated with sudden outbursts of song to the blaring Kylie Minogue albeit with her intrinsic operatic tone. Her personality certainly helped them through the pain of the unusual exercises, which targeted muscles that usually remained dormant during other traditional classes, most of which required them to maintain first position with their feet turned outwards, stimulating the inner thighs and firing up the buttocks.

Haley had no intention of going easy on them in this pilot class and pushed them beyond their limits in a routine of poses that felt totally unnatural to all bar the few that had a ballet background. They were easily spotted, as they took every opportunity to kick higher than everyone else, despite Haley's insistence that keeping the hips square was infinitely more important.

"Can you feel that?. Yeeeeeees". The sight of the gruesome winces on their faces, seemed to delight Haley. "This one is getting right into those quads and the muscles inside the glute".

If Cayenne wasn't mistaken, Haley seemed to revel in singling out a member of the class that hadn't quite mastered the concise technique that ballet required and wouldn't hesitate to interrupt her flow and walk over to the individual concerned, spelling out where they were going wrong in an arguably loud voice and repeating herself in a barely detectable critical tone all wrapped up neatly with a patronising chuckle. To Cayenne's mind, she marginally stopped short of looking at the rest of the more pleasing students and rolling her eyes.

There were funny moments too, as Haley seemed to enjoy throwing in the occasional Elvis thrust complete with the Presley 'uh-huh', entailing the uninhibited swirl of their hips as they were strongly encouraged to dip further and further towards the floor until they were all shook up, to a running commentary on the virtues of strengthening the glute.

423

Whilst informative, the guided tour of the inner workings of their behinds did nothing to ease the pain.

Another cardio routine followed which saw them performing jumping squats in first position to the sound of Human League, followed by a cool down and some abdominal work, where Haley's flexibility and age defying agility was on full display.

"Stand to your feet, raise your arms in the air and leading with your head, drop down into a forward fold. Shake your booty in the air and then come back up slowly, making sure your head is the last to come up. Hands in the air. Shake your booty one last time. Yaaaaaay. Well done ladies". Haley was applauding them enthusiastically genuinely impressed that they had pushed through a difficult first routine. She was a thirty plus year veteran of ballet and pilates and knew exactly how to challenge them with the slightest of movements. It soon became clear that she was more concerned with technique than flair and often encouraged them to keep the movement small and to concentrate on keeping their hips parallel or square to the front to ensure they were working the exact muscle that she intended to focus on and ensuring that they weren't utilising other muscles to compensate, as a result it didn't take long for the pain to kick in.

She was keen to find out what the women thought of the class. Her bright smile doing it's best to disguise desperately probing eyes. "What did you think of your first time ladies?". The few that were able to speak, nodded agreeably though clearly in as much pain as the others. Haley nodded her approval. "Yeah yeah. Good isn't it", she affirmed, her gleaming eyes sending sparks around the room as she embraced the accomplished feedback. She was clearly very passionate and delighted in her craft which was refreshing to see. Suddenly, with a raised hand and an elegant swirl of her wrist, Haley spiralled up the staircase, singing a soprano farewell at the top of her voice.

CHAPTER 53

"Luckily made the tube this morning, as the desire to expose to you was scarily strong.

I'm thinking Christmas catch up next week and that her majesty might fancy a central pad to assist with her preparation for the festivities".

"Ooooh The Queen approves her courtier's thinking...

Apply this brain power to the selection of personal gifts, exuding all the appreciation and gratitude that you expressed last week".

"I've got something special up my sleeve but I'm looking to confirm tomorrow at Green Park once I get a sense of when my holidays can truly start".

"I've been a terribly good monarch having graced the school nativity play with my presence followed by Body Balance. Plan away white knight.... So excited for my platinum exec worthy gifts and Mayfair treats".

"The perfect good girl too... annoyingly a toxic combo".

"Toxic? Moi?"

"Sorry. The wrong implied meaning".

"Didn't sound very festive".

"What are you offering good festive girl?"

"The Queen's generosity is highly dependent on your ability to deliver and how appreciative you are of my contribution to your year.

Can't believe I'm still falling for this BS".

"Come on, this BS isn't all bad…but your contribution certainly needs to be fully rewarded. What are you doing up so late?"

Cayenne glanced at the top of her screen and realised that it was well past one in the morning. "Reading. So where have you gone shopping for my elusive gifts. Harrods I expect… Tiffany's have beautiful watches and necklaces I'm told. I can just picture them encased within a Michael Kors handbag with personalised stitching". Cayenne had never been much of a jewellery person and didn't really care about Harrods and Tiffany's but was thoroughly enjoying toying with her eager pursuant".

"Funnily enough I did see something in Michael Kors that made me think about your elegantly honed body".

"Really made you think huh? Interesting. I have total faith that you will demonstrate exquisite taste this week, even with no prior evidence. Everyone deserves a second chance. Or third".

"Where's nativity Cayenne gone? Kind to the end aren't you?

Gift exchange Thursday or Friday if convenient"

"Thursday would be dandy. However, having had time to reflect… I am having misgivings about said 'gift exchange'.

Firstly, I seem to recall you referring to my birthday present in order to get my attention, which never actually materialised.

Secondly, do I really want to spend my time with the kind of marginal personality that would show me a reservation for the Shard and then back out of it?

Who ignores my insistence on weekends and evenings and who skulks away for a while under the guise of executive turmoil and then slithers back months later with no further grasp of integrity.

I once heard the wise words: 'don't make someone a priority who considers you an option.'

Bearing in mind I have my own contented routine, I have to ask myself, based on previous experience, which do I value more?

I'm afraid the honest answer leaves you well and truly left out in the suburban Basel-esque cold...

Merry Christmas".

"Your odium is totally understandable considering your experience of my over promising and under delivery in 2017... and wise words too. BUT I would urge you to bear in mind, considering we are extremely busy at this time of year, surely my insistence that I'd like to at least see you before the big day is a nice gesture.

Ignore 'present exchange' I was obviously only hoping for a smile and a laugh from you".

"So you are admitting that you are a compulsive liar and a fraud as well as a marginal human being... you really ought to be ashamed of yourself.

Who do you think you are? When I say marginal, you do realise that I am merely referring to your character as judging by your last appearance, I certainly wouldn't be referring to your frame. Clearly you have been having a few too many pancakes and corporate lunches. If I were you, I would recommit to running around Hyde Park but make it more of a daily occurrence. At the wrong side of forty, ones metabolism tends to slow down. It is apparent that yours, much like your libido, has practically regressed to a standstill.

Don't eat too much over the festive season will you. Perhaps convert to the spirit of goodwill and share your culinary intake with those less fortunate. What on earth are you 'extremely busy' doing anyway? Cancel all arrangements that you deem so important and join a gym immediately with the determined intent to make use of your membership... otherwise I fear that your increasingly expansive frame and decidedly unchiselled necks (plural) will be too wide to climb your fucking corporate ladder any further.

Ps… wondering what your present was going to be were you? At least I actually bought one.

The big reveal……

LISTERINE motherfucker

Now get lost".

"Hey, what's up? I have presents for you and want to meet up. What is the matter? Why the need to be so nasty".

"I think that you are one of the nastiest people I have had the displeasure to come across… just because you are a passive assailant… doesn't mean that you are a good person. You are sly, deceptive and dishonest. So I ask you the same question… why so nasty?"

" I never wanted to upset you and it's simple why I wanted to see you before Christmas.

I'm sorry".

CHAPTER 54

Cayenne couldn't quite believe that she was packing for New York for the weekend. He had surprised her with the trip when they had met up to supposedly exchange gifts.

She had gone to great lengths to arrange for delivery of a traditional Fortnum & Mason Christmas Hamper, which he had mentioned receiving as a treat once as a child, as well as a biography of Winston Churchill which she knew he would appreciate from their previous conversations about politics and a book about addiction by Russell brand, which she knew would amuse him, as it was a nod to their in-joke about their shared fetishes. She had inscribed the foreword page with the message … 'in the hope that you can heal yourself'.

She would always remember the look of shock on his face that she had even bothered to get him a gift at all and the glistening in his eyes when he saw what trouble she had gone to.

He had taken her post Christmas acerbic attack with good grace, probably because she had hit on numerous home truths.

After their meal at Zuma and cocktails at a swanky bar, he had presented her with a black smooth leather, Michael Kors satchel tote which contained a sealed envelope. When she had opened it up, it had taken a few moments to take in the contents as it was the last thing she would have expected.

Although it was a work trip for him, organised so that his team could meet the big boss in the Big Apple, he had arranged to leave before the group so that they could travel together in business class. He had explained that he really wouldn't have an awful lot of time to relax, owing to his schedule, but that they could at least spend a couple of afternoons taking in the sights. She had always wanted to go to Central Park, ever since she was child and learned that Bob Marley, for whom she had developed a fascination, would jog there before a concert.

He had clearly remembered this from their previous conversations which was touching. The whole thing was touching. What was she to make of it?. Had his execution caused him to rethink what this was. She hadn't come to terms with what it was herself. Whilst mildly entertaining and occasionally endearing, she found him to be marginally bearable most of the time and with intuitive timing, he could also be a source of acute nauseous irritation.

He had waxed lyrical about the hotel, the Renaissance in midtown east, close to the Chrysler and Empire State Building and stated that he rather hoped that they would be able to fit in a quick shopping tryst to 5th avenue. At times he touched her hand and looked at her strangely and deeply as though running questions through his mind.

On the days leading up to the trip he had maintained regular contact. She saw none of the ghostly disappearing acts he was prone to. She had been softened too by his concern that the arrangements for the children were going well. She had assured him that Diego would be at hand and that between them they would be more than capable of looking after themselves for the weekend. She would only be away for two nights at any rate.

He had cautioned her not to overpack, stating that they could always pick up any essentials in New York if need be.

Diego had been pleased for her, happy to see her being given such special treatment. He didn't ever enquire too much about the stranger. Not wanting or needing to know any more than was necessary, trusting her discerning judgement.

Kenneth had also presented her with a spa treatment at the Mayfair hotel, a bottle of Moet champagne, an elegantly boxed iced cake for the children and a Michael Kors dress. It was a lace dress in deep red, almost burgundy with a sheer flesh coloured underlay. He had chosen this colour because of all the outfits he had seen her wear, the deep red velvet cut out dress had made the biggest impression and he thought it had most complemented her complexion.

She immediately thought of her burgundy thigh high boots that would go perfectly with it. She had held it up to herself in the restaurant and spun round to look at her reflection in the mirrored wall. She knew that it would fit her and suit her, though it wasn't a style that she would have picked out herself, which somehow made it all the more special.

She hadn't even minded that their flight had been delayed due to severe weather and eventually cancelled and rescheduled for first thing the following morning.

They had been transferred to the nearby Sofitel airport hotel and she recalled thinking how unusual it was that they were at opposite ends of the hotel suite, making the necessary phone calls to update whoever needed to be made aware of the impromptu change in travel plans. Diego had assured her that everything was under control and encouraged her to have the best time.

If the executive had been thrown by the unexpected change of plan, he kept it well concealed, which she was grateful for. He probably hadn't wanted to spoil the weekend with his usual fretful concerns.

She couldn't resist trying on the Michael Kors dress which he had insisted she pack for the trip. She hadn't even tried it on at home. It fit her well albeit ever so slightly tight on the arms, owing to the bulging biceps that he so loved. Seeing how much she liked and appreciated her couture frock and how well he appeared to have chosen, lying back on the hotel bed gazing at her in the dress of his choosing seemed to have an astonishing effect on him.

He looked directly into her eyes, holding them there as he climbed off the bed and strode towards her with a white fluffy towel still wrapped around his waist. His hair was still damp from the shower and his skin slightly moist as he grabbed her and placed her delicately on the edge of the bed.

All she could see as she lay back facing the light grey ceiling dotted with sunken spotlights, were her thigh high burgundy boots suspended in mid-air, wide apart and the top of his scalp bobbing up and down in between as though he were playing the party game when the objective was to grasp an apple from a bowl using only the mouth with restricted hands. From the deep throaty sounds coming from below, she could tell he had hit upon the desired toffee apple he so sought.

That night, it wasn't just a fuck. It was different. Slow and intense, deep and intentional. Eyes locked. No words. He couldn't possibly have gone deeper, though he tried with every determined thrust. Changing his positioning frequently to attempt a greater vantage point towards the heavenly core. He held her tightly in place whilst he eclipsed. They simultaneously held their breath as though witnessing a profound exchange. The flow was so plentiful it almost filled the rubber sheath to capacity which he removed and discarded of before laying beside her and falling asleep.

Her last thought before joining him was whether he had remembered to set his alarm for their early flight. She recalled him asking reception to give them a courtesy wake up call, she was certain.

She wasn't quite sure what had woken her up but her eyes flickered open with a start to a darkened room with only the light from the bathroom piercing the darkness.

The semi conscious state must have lasted for a few moments more before the realisation that they had an early flight to catch slowly began to sink in.

Her eyes widened further this time, before squinting again to try to focus more clearly.

The other side of the bed was empty and still crumpled from where the warm body she remembered from the previous night had lain. She listened attentively for the sound of the shower faucet or a tap or the hint of a flush. There was no sound at all. She reached for her phone which was lifeless from a dead battery which she must have forgotten to charge. The passion of the night before seemed to have eradicated all of her usual pre-bedtime routines. Shaking her head violently to rid herself

of any more sleepiness, she flicked on the lamp on the bedside cabinet nearest to her and waited for her eyes to adjust to the light.

The wardrobe was pulled open where a white robe hung in solitude.

She was still wearing the Michael Kors dress and tutted at herself thinking briefly that she would now have to get it dry cleaned in haste in New York if she planned to wear it again.

Sitting upright, her feet fell upon the crumpled velvet boots at the foot of the bed.

As her mind awakened, she saw her travel bag just as she had left it on the main desk next to her handbag. Her loungewear which thankfully didn't require much ironing remained thrown over the desk chair. Her eyes scanned the room afresh as though waking up for the second time, flickering as information began to register signals to her brain... He had gone.

How long ago, she couldn't possibly know, why, she couldn't bring herself to care. It must have been quite some time that she sat there, numbly looking at herself almost from outside herself. Just observing, remarkably without judgement. Just observing. Taking it all in with an unfathomably calm acceptance.

This was no time to berate herself, or question what she couldn't answer.

She remained in this state in the taxi home and if there was ever a time that she was thankful that she had somehow created the most remarkable children in the world, it was now. The kind of children that didn't feel the need to ask questions or demand answers. That knew when to hug silently and knowingly and then retreat as though nothing was untoward.

The award winning Sofitel Heathrow Hotel was renowned for it's luxurious comfort and prestige. It's seasonal decorations attracting clientele from all over the world. This Christmas the guest's experience had been furnished with an exceptionally distinct embellishment on top of the huge elaborately decorated fir tree which dominated the glittering lobby.

As never before had they seen a Michael Kors runway ensemble, draped across

it's branches like the most exquisite festive mannequin.

THE END

Printed in Great Britain
by Amazon

79268748R10254